DARK GRAPHIC NOVELS

FRANKENSTEIN BY MARY SHELLEY

A DARK GRAPHIC NOVEL

ADAPTATION
SERGIO A. SIERRA

ILLUSTRATIONS
MERITXELL RIBAS

Enslow Publishers, Inc.
40 Industrial Road
Box 398
Berkeley Heights, NJ 07922
USA

http://www.enslow.com

Translated from the Spanish edition by Stacey Juana Pontoriero. Edited and produced by Enslow Publishers, Inc.

Library of Congress Cataloging-in-Publication Data

Sierra, Sergio A.
[Frankenstein. English.]
Frankenstein by Mary Shelley : a Dark graphic novel / adaptation Sergio A. Sierra ; illustration Meritxell Ribas.
p. cm. — (Dark graphic novels)
Includes bibliographical references.
Summary: A graphic novel adaptation of Mary Shelley's classic tale of a monster, assembled by a scientist from parts of dead bodies, who develops a mind of his own as he learns to loathe himself and hate his creator.
ISBN 978-0-7660-4084-7
1. Graphic novels. [1. Graphic novels. 2. Monsters—Fiction. 3. Horror stories.] I. Ribas, Meritxell, ill. II. Shelley, Mary Wollstonecraft, 1797-1851. Frankenstein. III. Title.
PZ7.7.S483Fr 2013
741.5'973—dc23

2011035826

Future edition:
Paperback ISBN 978-1-4644-0104-6

Originally published in Spanish under the title *Frankenstein*.

Published by Parramón Paidotribo, S.L., Badalona, Spain.
Production: Sagrafic, S.L.
Text adapted by: Sergio A. Sierra
Illustrator: Meritxell Ribas

Printed in Spain

012013 EGEDSA, Barcelona, Spain

10 9 8 7 6 5 4 3 2

To Our Readers: We have done our best to make sure all Internet Addresses in this book were active and appropriate when we went to press. However, the author and the publishers have no control over and assume no liability for the material available on those Internet sites or on other Web sites they may link to. Any comments or suggestions can be sent by e-mail to comments@enslow.com or to the address on the back cover.

FRANKENSTEIN
BY MARY SHELLEY
A DARK GRAPHIC NOVEL

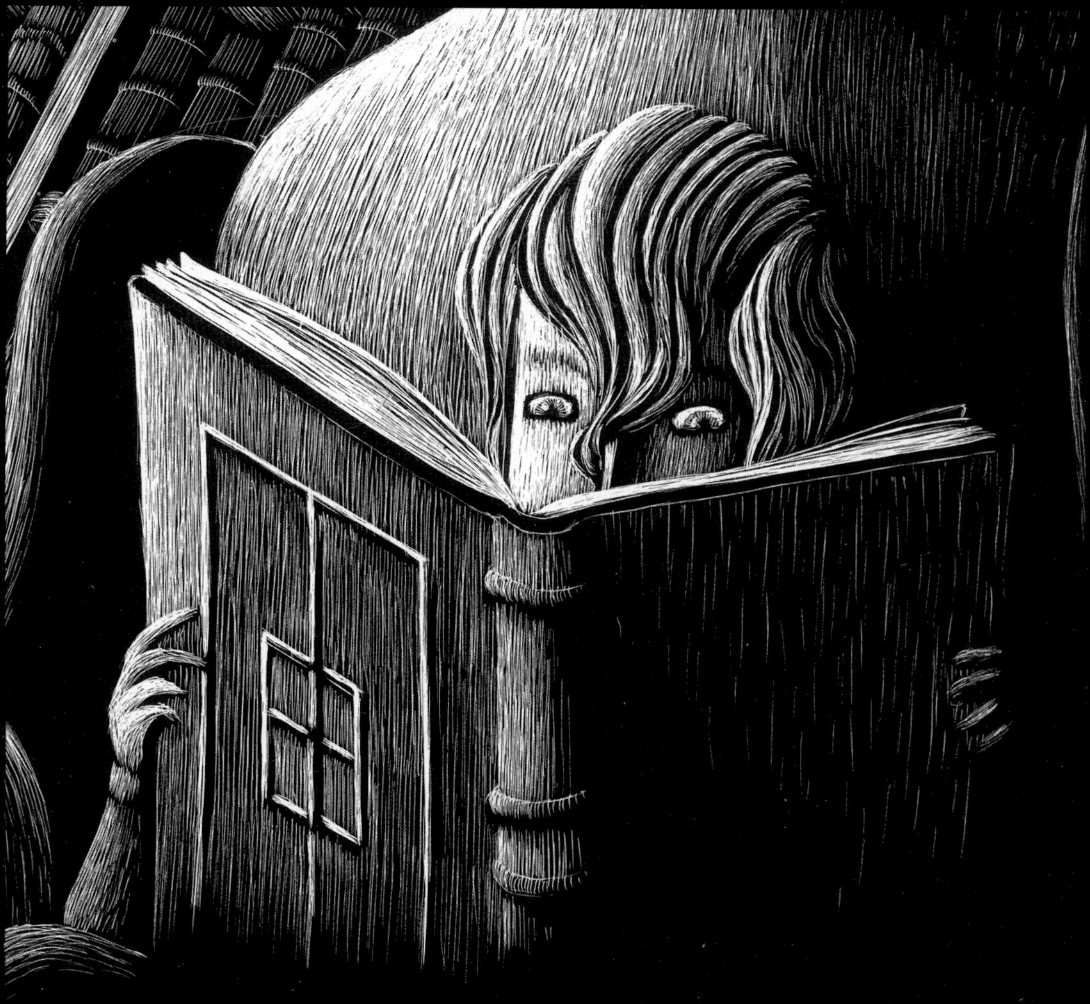

Did I request thee, Maker, from my clay to mould me man?
Did I solicit thee from darkness to promote me?

– J. MILTON, *Paradise Lost.*

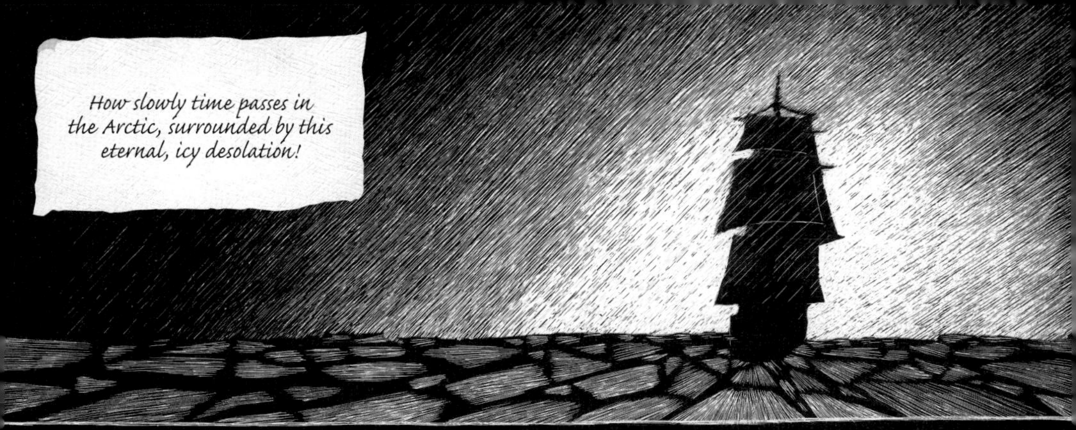
How slowly time passes in the Arctic, surrounded by this eternal, icy desolation!

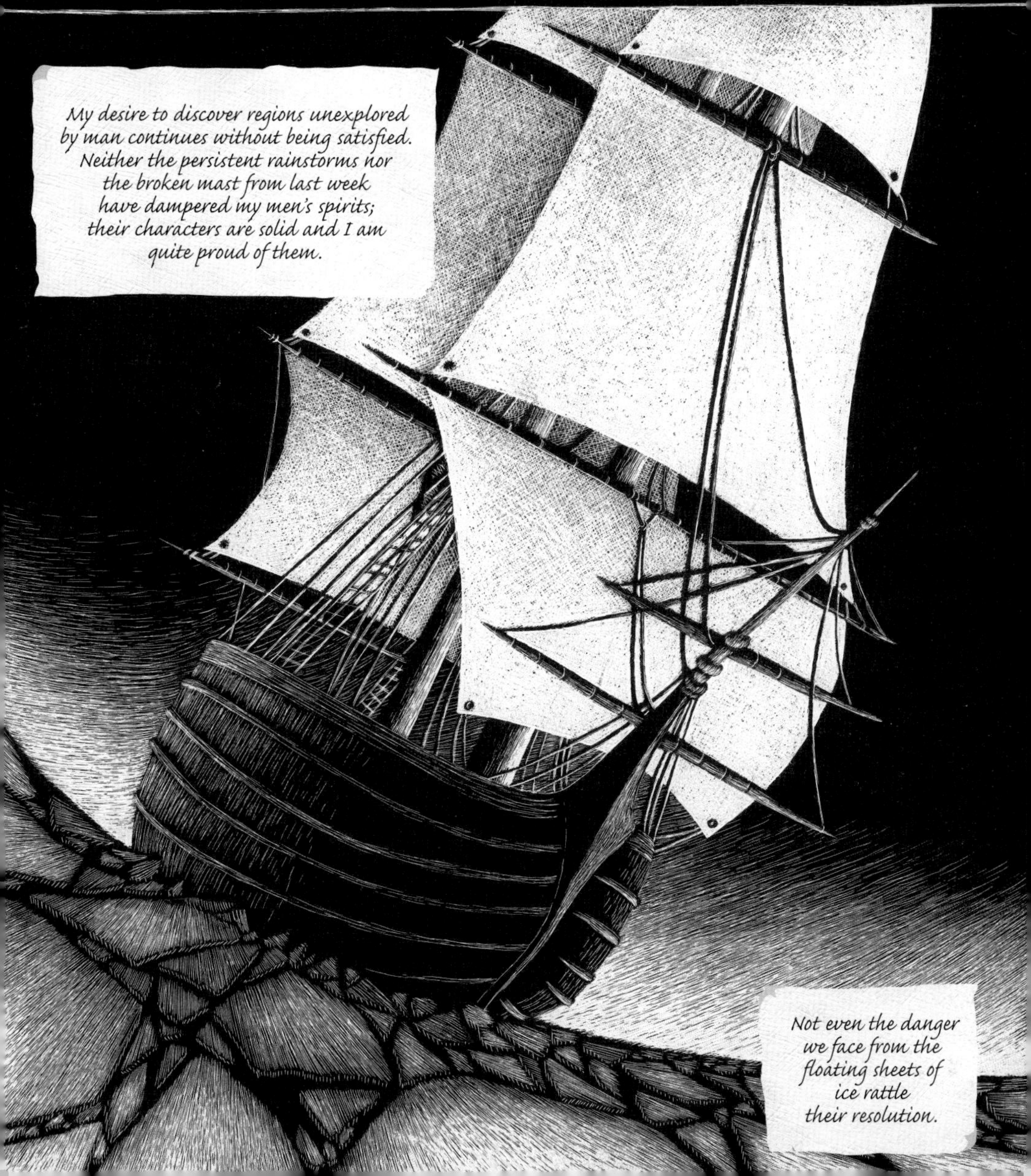
My desire to discover regions unexplored by man continues without being satisfied. Neither the persistent rainstorms nor the broken mast from last week have dampered my men's spirits; their characters are solid and I am quite proud of them.
Not even the danger we face from the floating sheets of ice rattle their resolution.

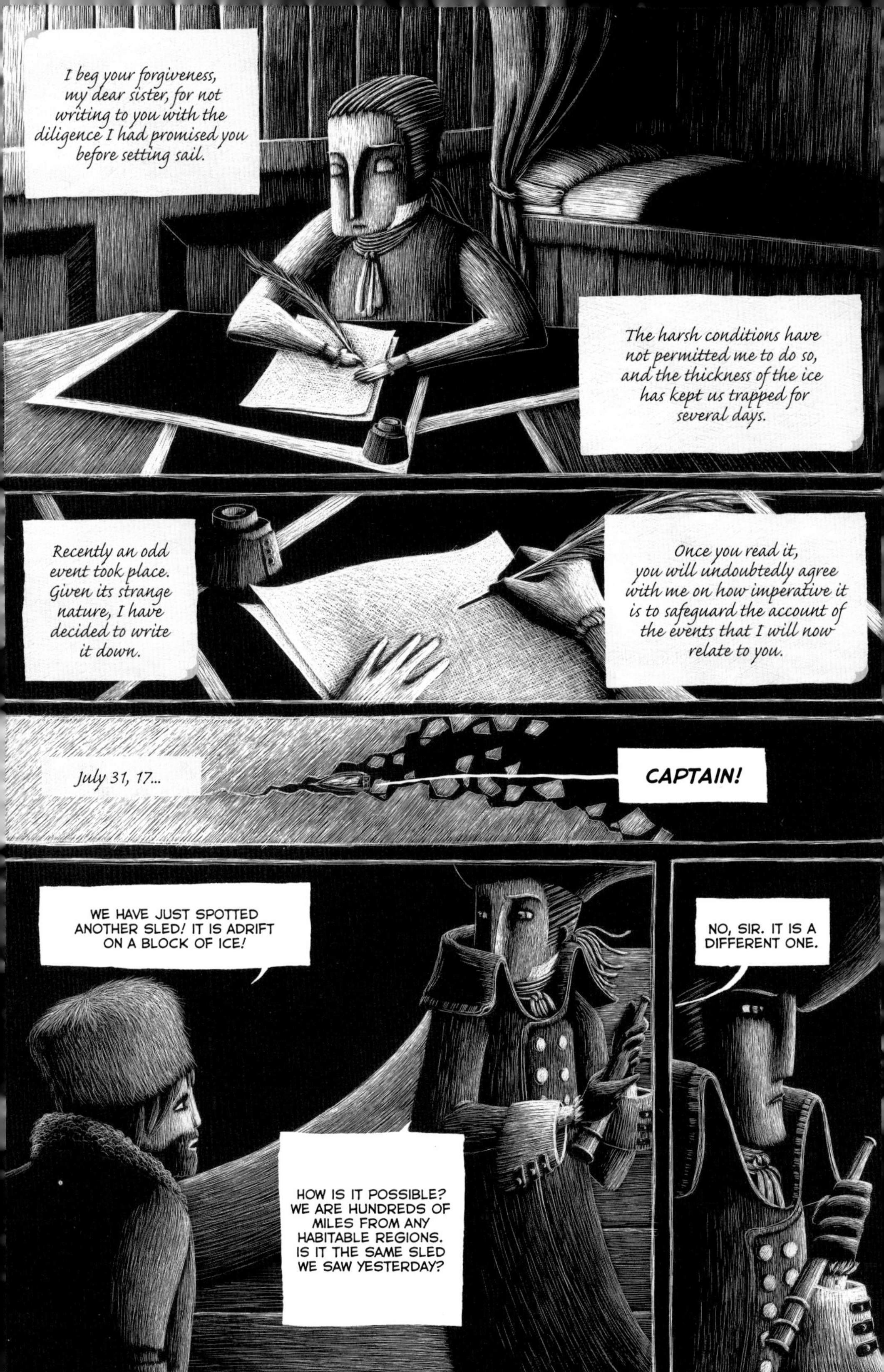
I beg your forgiveness, my dear sister, for not writing to you with the diligence I had promised you before setting sail.
The harsh conditions have not permitted me to do so, and the thickness of the ice has kept us trapped for several days.
Recently an odd event took place. Given its strange nature, I have decided to write it down.
Once you read it, you will undoubtedly agree with me on how imperative it is to safeguard the account of the events that I will now relate to you.
July 31, 17...
CAPTAIN!
WE HAVE JUST SPOTTED ANOTHER SLED! IT IS ADRIFT ON A BLOCK OF ICE!
HOW IS IT POSSIBLE? WE ARE HUNDREDS OF MILES FROM ANY HABITABLE REGIONS. IS IT THE SAME SLED WE SAW YESTERDAY?
NO, SIR. IT IS A DIFFERENT ONE.

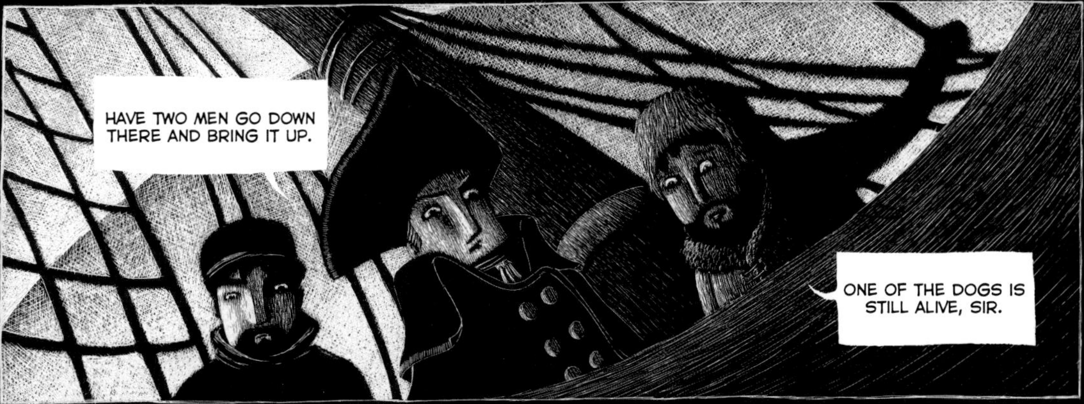
HAVE TWO MEN GO DOWN THERE AND BRING IT UP.
ONE OF THE DOGS IS STILL ALIVE, SIR.

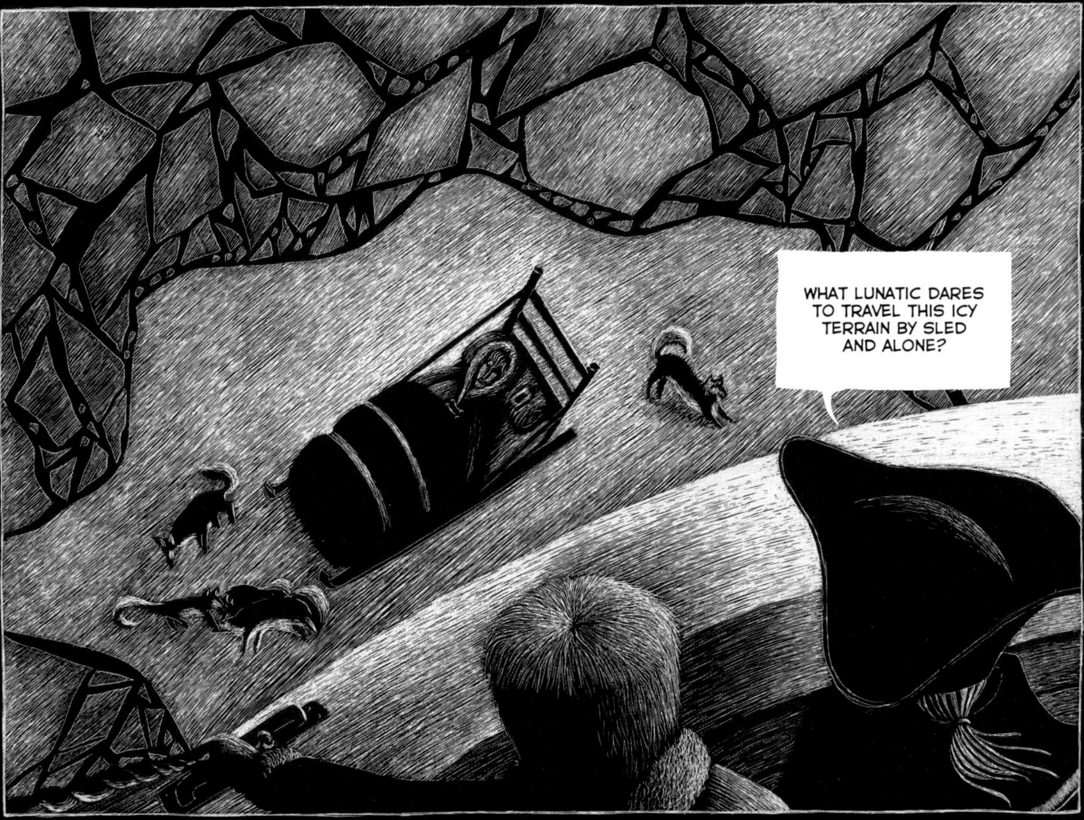
WHAT LUNATIC DARES TO TRAVEL THIS ICY TERRAIN BY SLED AND ALONE?

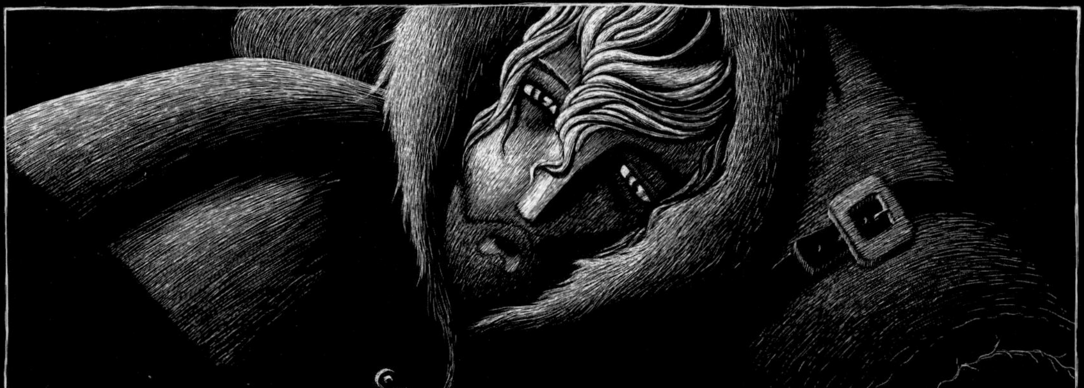

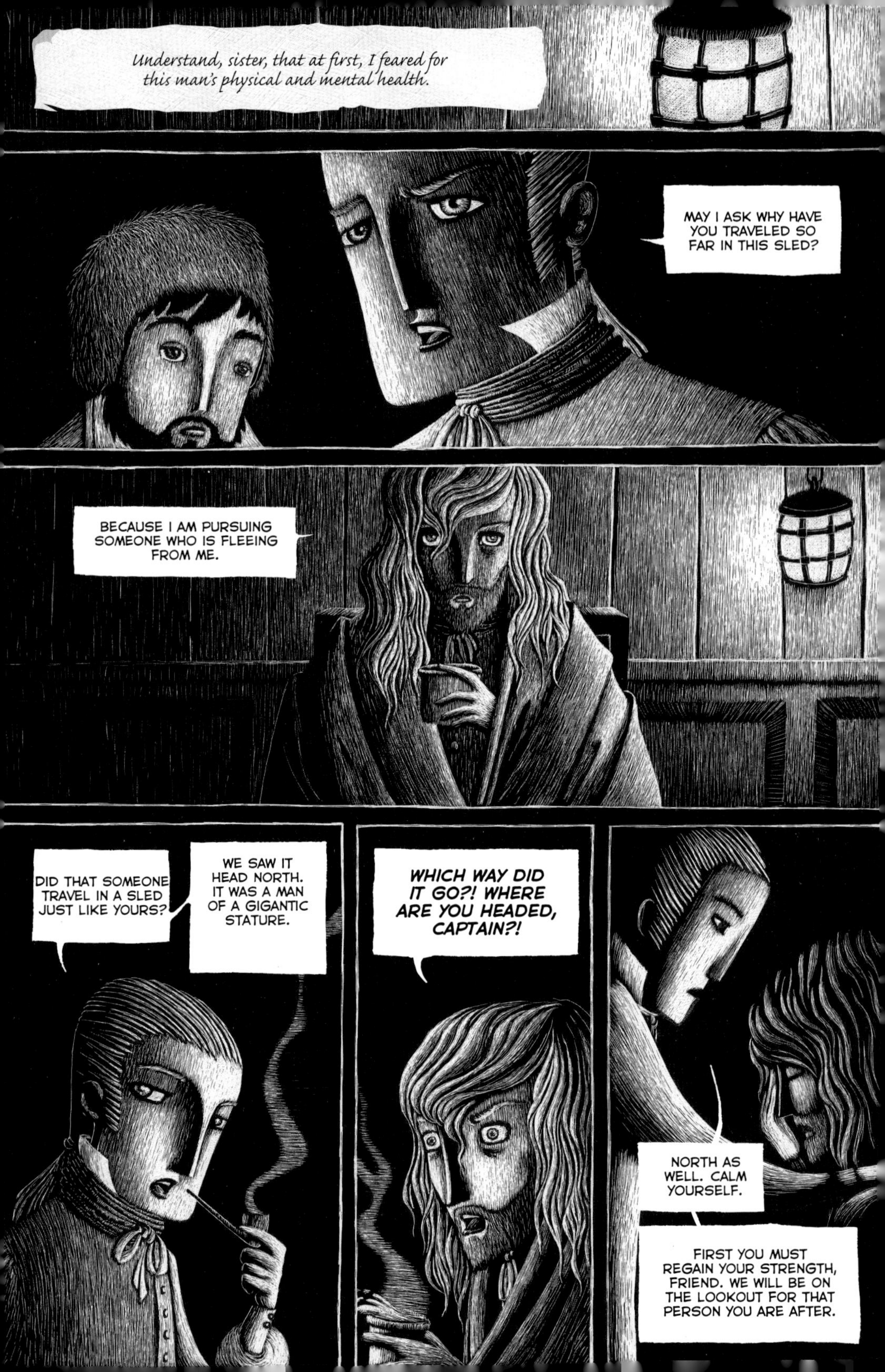
Understand, sister, that at first, I feared for this man's physical and mental health.
MAY I ASK WHY HAVE YOU TRAVELED SO FAR IN THIS SLED?
BECAUSE I AM PURSUING SOMEONE WHO IS FLEEING FROM ME.
DID THAT SOMEONE TRAVEL IN A SLED JUST LIKE YOURS?
WE SAW IT HEAD NORTH. IT WAS A MAN OF A GIGANTIC STATURE.
WHICH WAY DID IT GO?! WHERE ARE YOU HEADED, CAPTAIN?!
NORTH AS WELL. CALM YOURSELF.
FIRST YOU MUST REGAIN YOUR STRENGTH, FRIEND. WE WILL BE ON THE LOOKOUT FOR THAT PERSON YOU ARE AFTER.

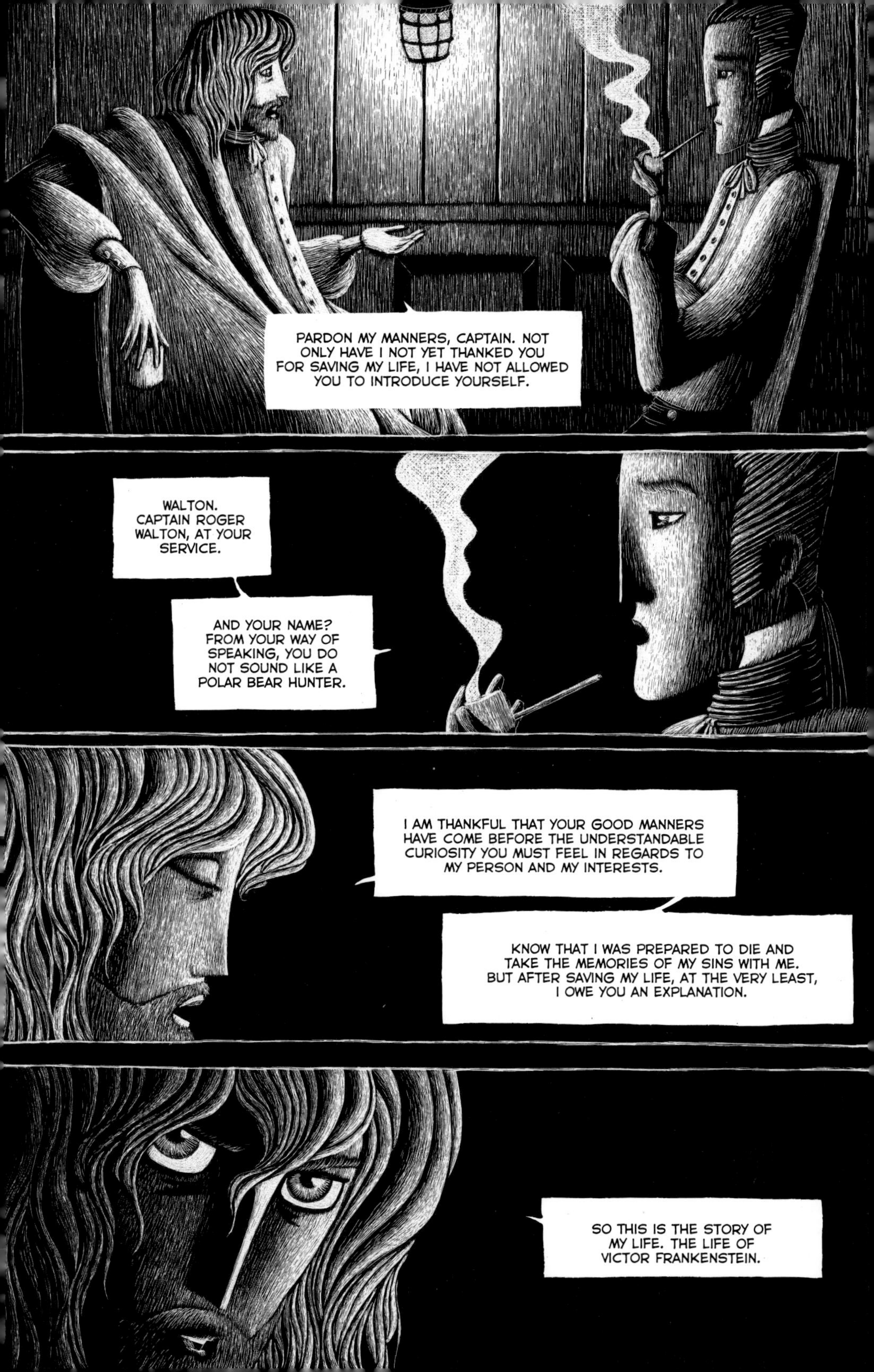
PARDON MY MANNERS, CAPTAIN. NOT ONLY HAVE I NOT YET THANKED YOU FOR SAVING MY LIFE, I HAVE NOT ALLOWED YOU TO INTRODUCE YOURSELF.
WALTON. CAPTAIN ROGER WALTON, AT YOUR SERVICE.
AND YOUR NAME? FROM YOUR WAY OF SPEAKING, YOU DO NOT SOUND LIKE A POLAR BEAR HUNTER.
I AM THANKFUL THAT YOUR GOOD MANNERS HAVE COME BEFORE THE UNDERSTANDABLE CURIOSITY YOU MUST FEEL IN REGARDS TO MY PERSON AND MY INTERESTS.
KNOW THAT I WAS PREPARED TO DIE AND TAKE THE MEMORIES OF MY SINS WITH ME. BUT AFTER SAVING MY LIFE, AT THE VERY LEAST, I OWE YOU AN EXPLANATION.
SO THIS IS THE STORY OF MY LIFE. THE LIFE OF VICTOR FRANKENSTEIN.

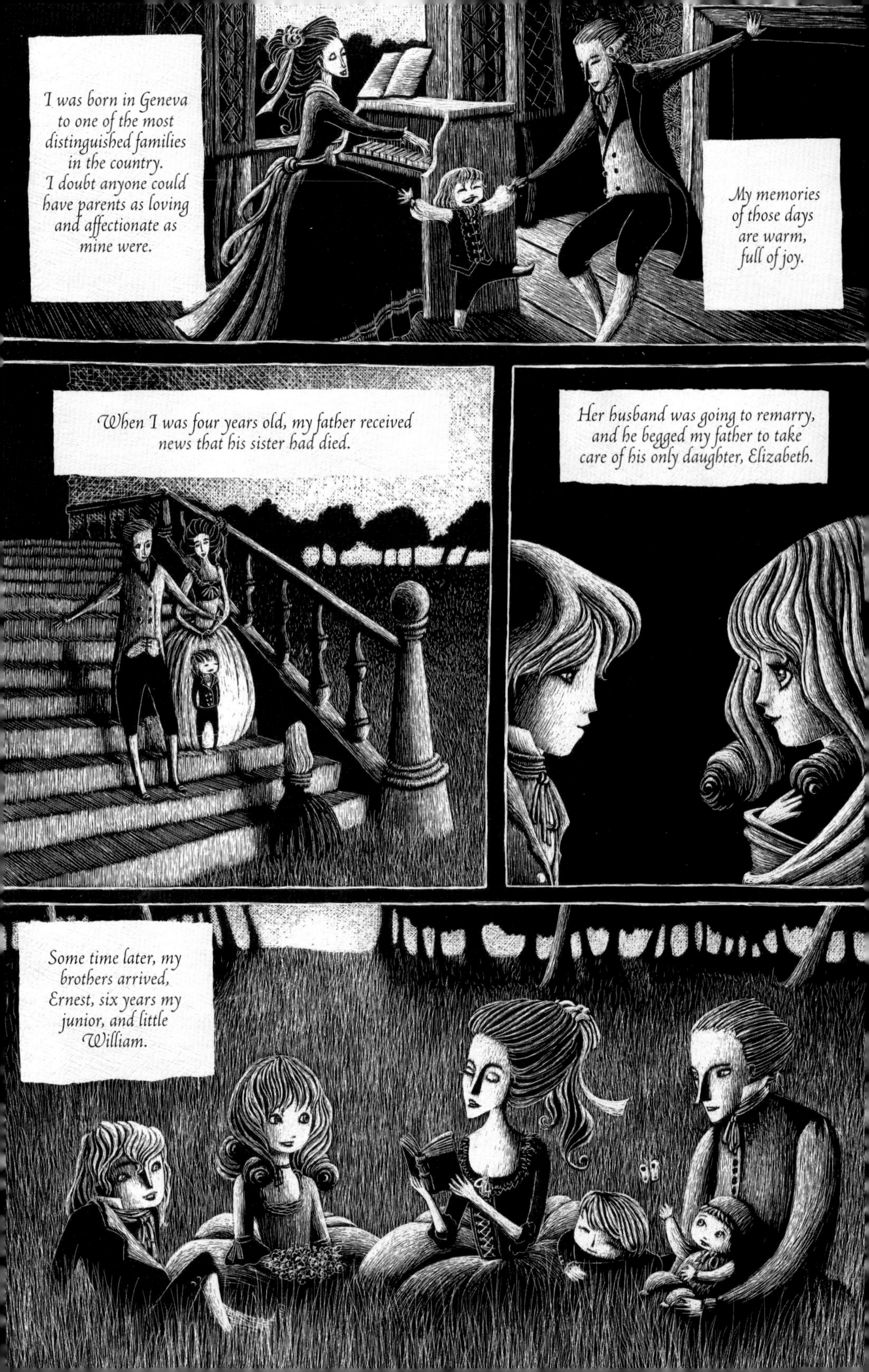
I was born in Geneva to one of the most distinguished families in the country.
I doubt anyone could have parents as loving and affectionate as mine were.
My memories of those days are warm, full of joy.
When I was four years old, my father received news that his sister had died.
Her husband was going to remarry, and he begged my father to take care of his only daughter, Elizabeth.
Some time later, my brothers arrived, Ernest, six years my junior, and little William.

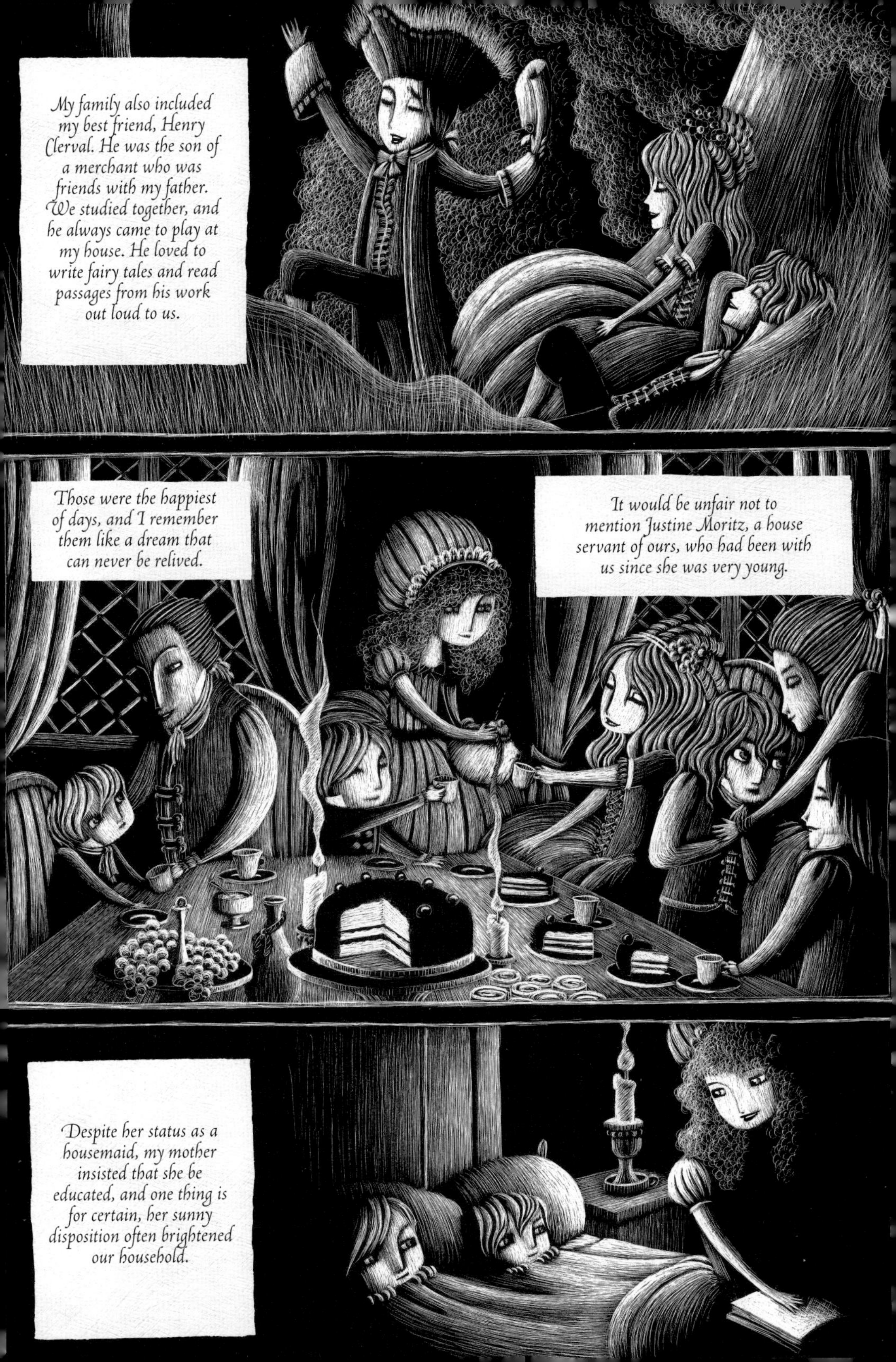
My family also included my best friend, Henry Clerval. He was the son of a merchant who was friends with my father. We studied together, and he always came to play at my house. He loved to write fairy tales and read passages from his work out loud to us.
Those were the happiest of days, and I remember them like a dream that can never be relived.
It would be unfair not to mention Justine Moritz, a house servant of ours, who had been with us since she was very young.
Despite her status as a housemaid, my mother insisted that she be educated, and one thing is for certain, her sunny disposition often brightened our household.

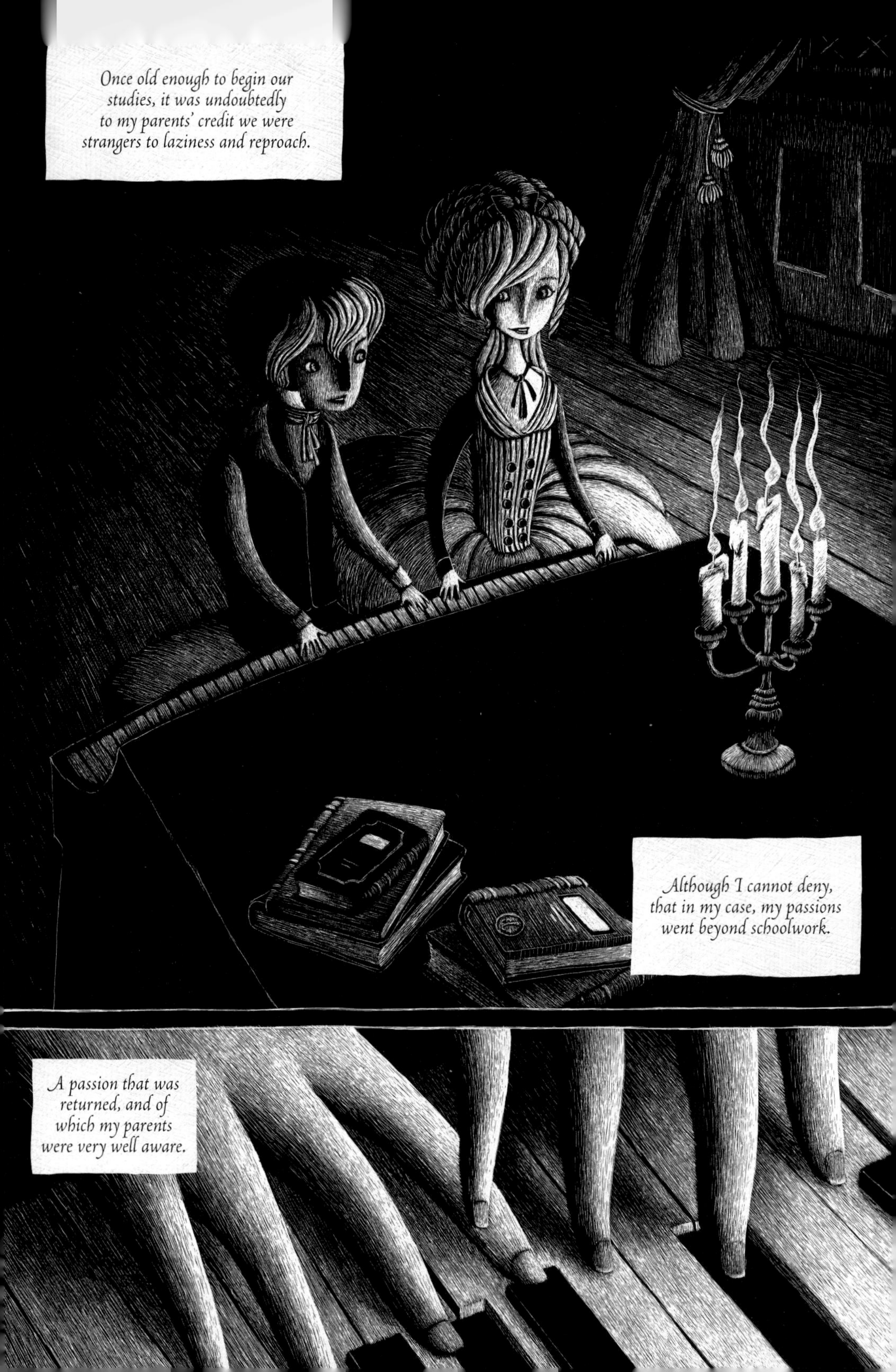
Once old enough to begin our studies, it was undoubtedly to my parents' credit we were strangers to laziness and reproach.
Although I cannot deny, that in my case, my passions went beyond schoolwork.
A passion that was returned, and of which my parents were very well aware.

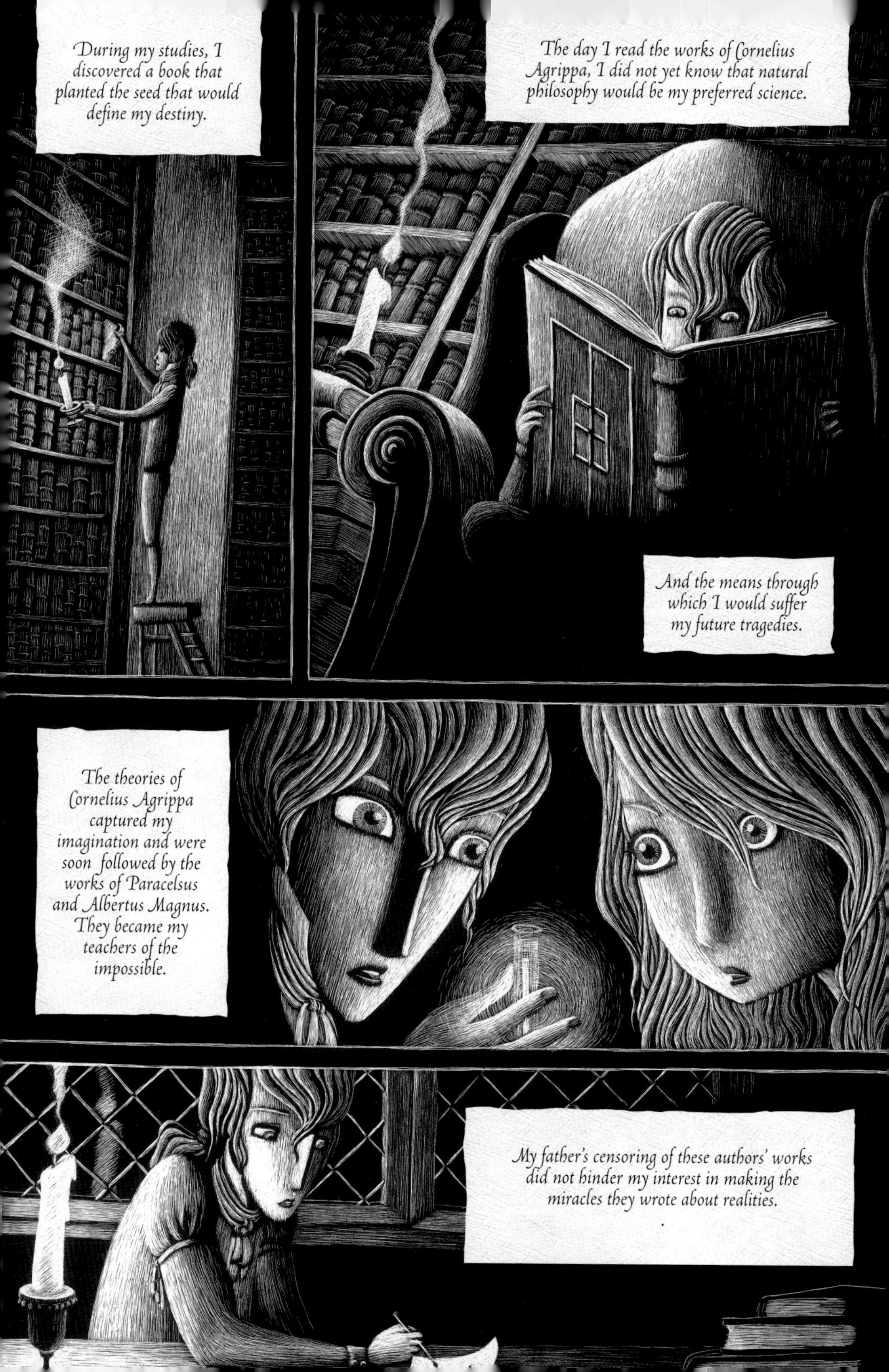
During my studies, I discovered a book that planted the seed that would define my destiny.
The day I read the works of Cornelius Agrippa, I did not yet know that natural philosophy would be my preferred science.
And the means through which I would suffer my future tragedies.
The theories of Cornelius Agrippa captured my imagination and were soon followed by the works of Paracelsus and Albertus Magnus. They became my teachers of the impossible.
My father's censoring of these authors' works did not hinder my interest in making the miracles they wrote about realities.

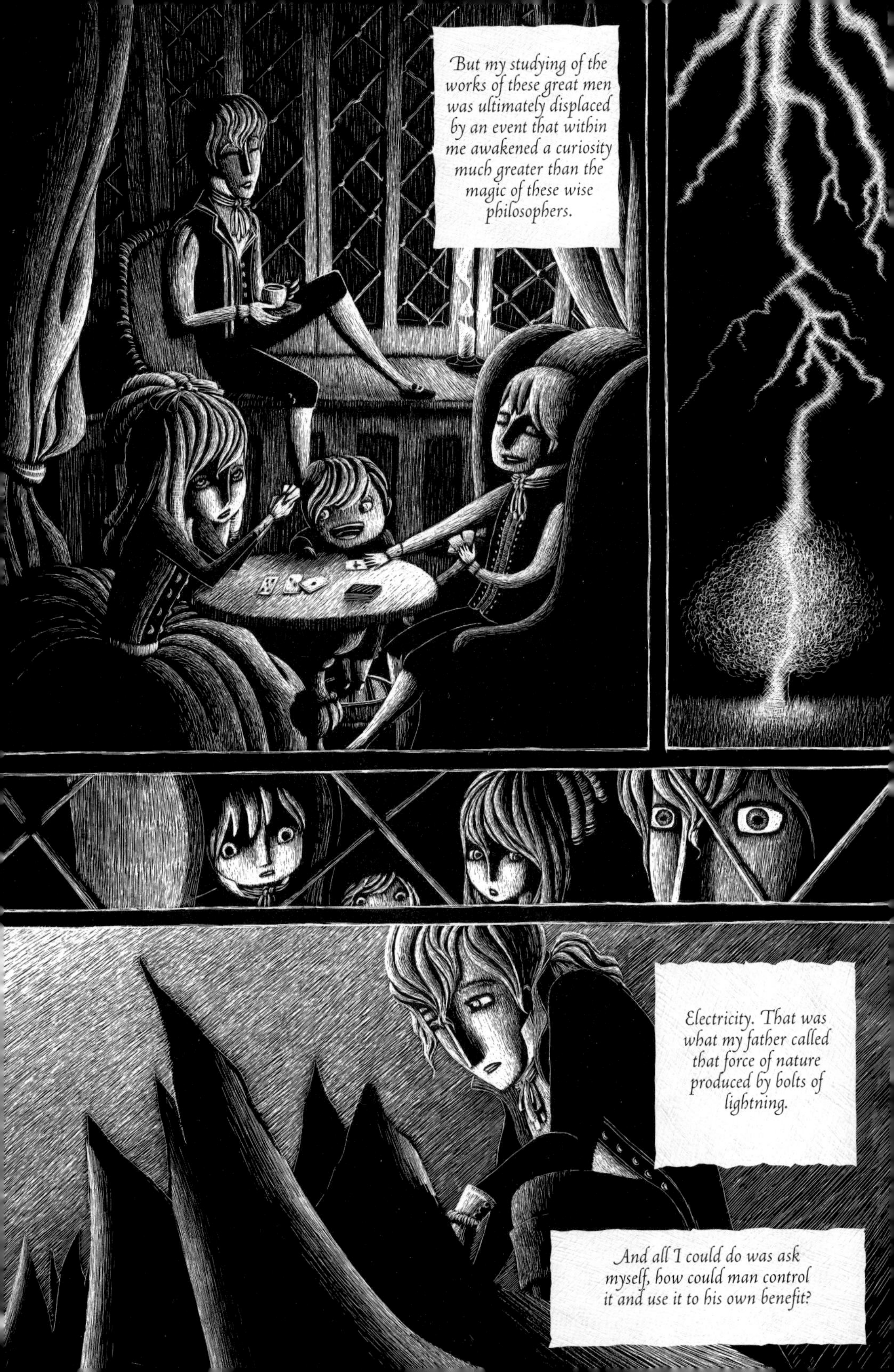
But my studying of the works of these great men was ultimately displaced by an event that within me awakened a curiosity much greater than the magic of these wise philosophers.
Electricity. That was what my father called that force of nature produced by bolts of lightning.
And all I could do was ask myself, how could man control it and use it to his own benefit?

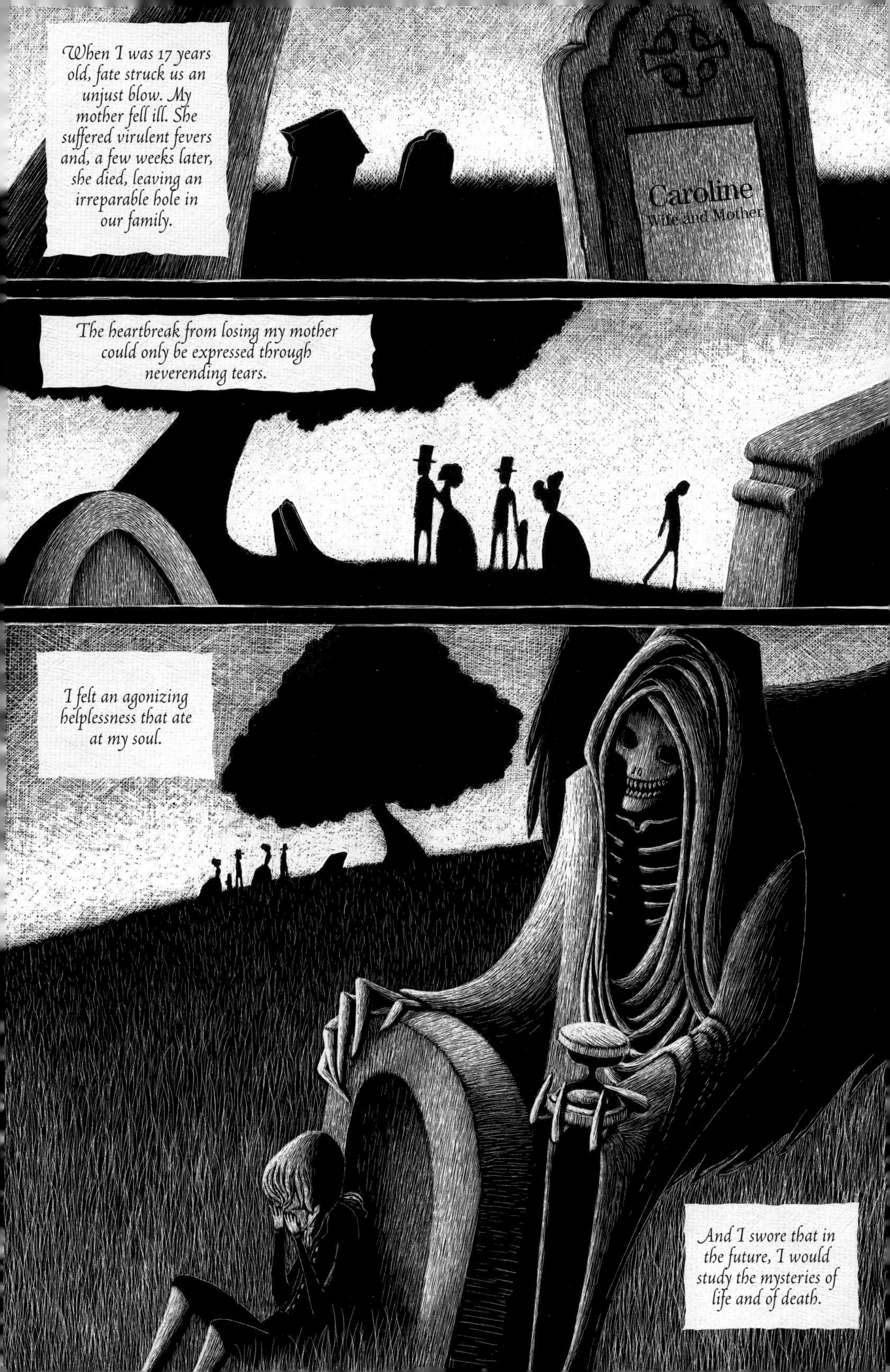
When I was 17 years old, fate struck us an unjust blow. My mother fell ill. She suffered virulent fevers and, a few weeks later, she died, leaving an irreparable hole in our family.
Caroline
Wife and Mother
The heartbreak from losing my mother could only be expressed through neverending tears.
I felt an agonizing helplessness that ate at my soul.
And I swore that in the future, I would study the mysteries of life and of death.

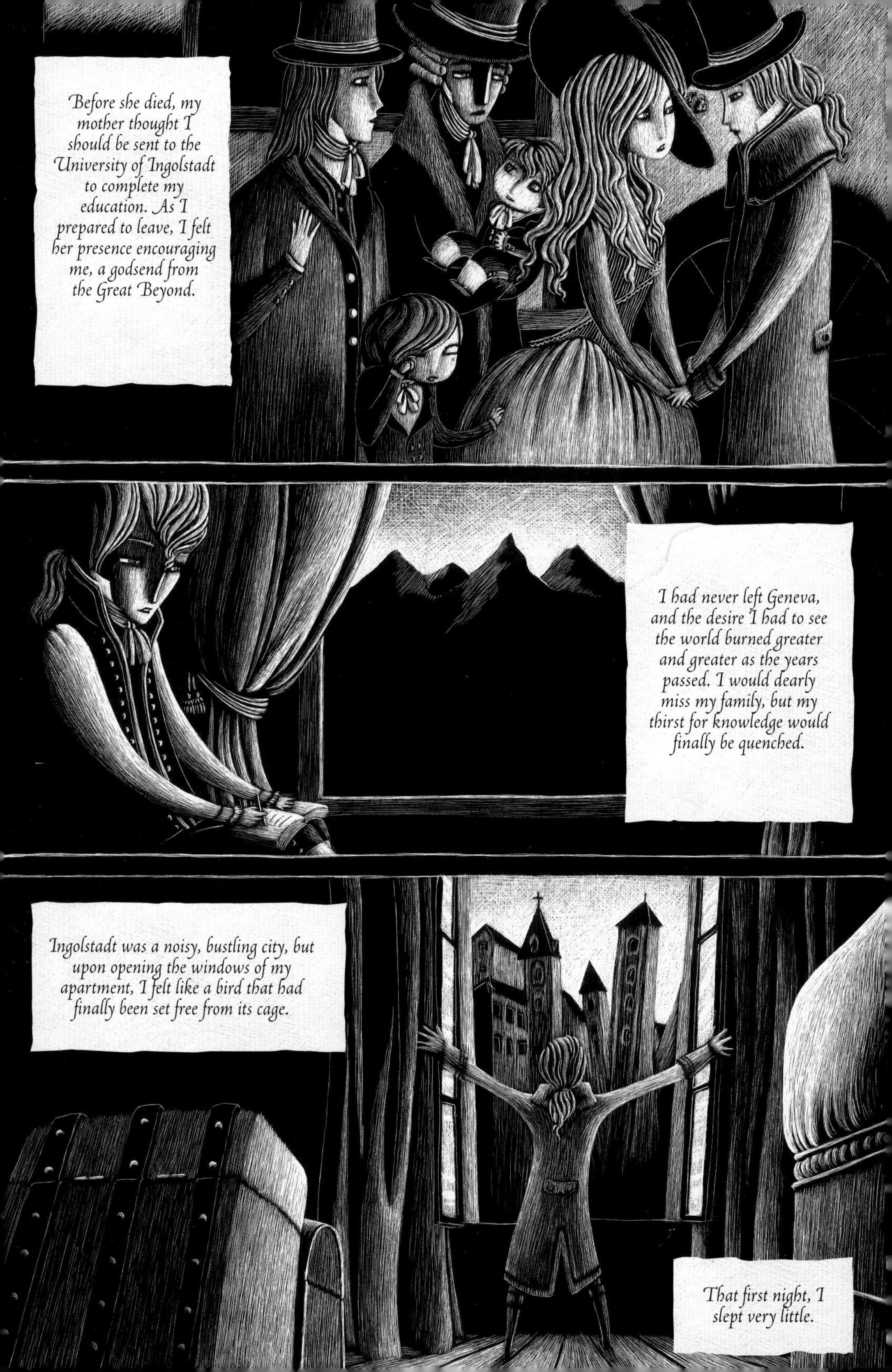
Before she died, my mother thought I should be sent to the University of Ingolstadt to complete my education. As I prepared to leave, I felt her presence encouraging me, a godsend from the Great Beyond.
I had never left Geneva, and the desire I had to see the world burned greater and greater as the years passed. I would dearly miss my family, but my thirst for knowledge would finally be quenched.
Ingolstadt was a noisy, bustling city, but upon opening the windows of my apartment, I felt like a bird that had finally been set free from its cage.
That first night, I slept very little.

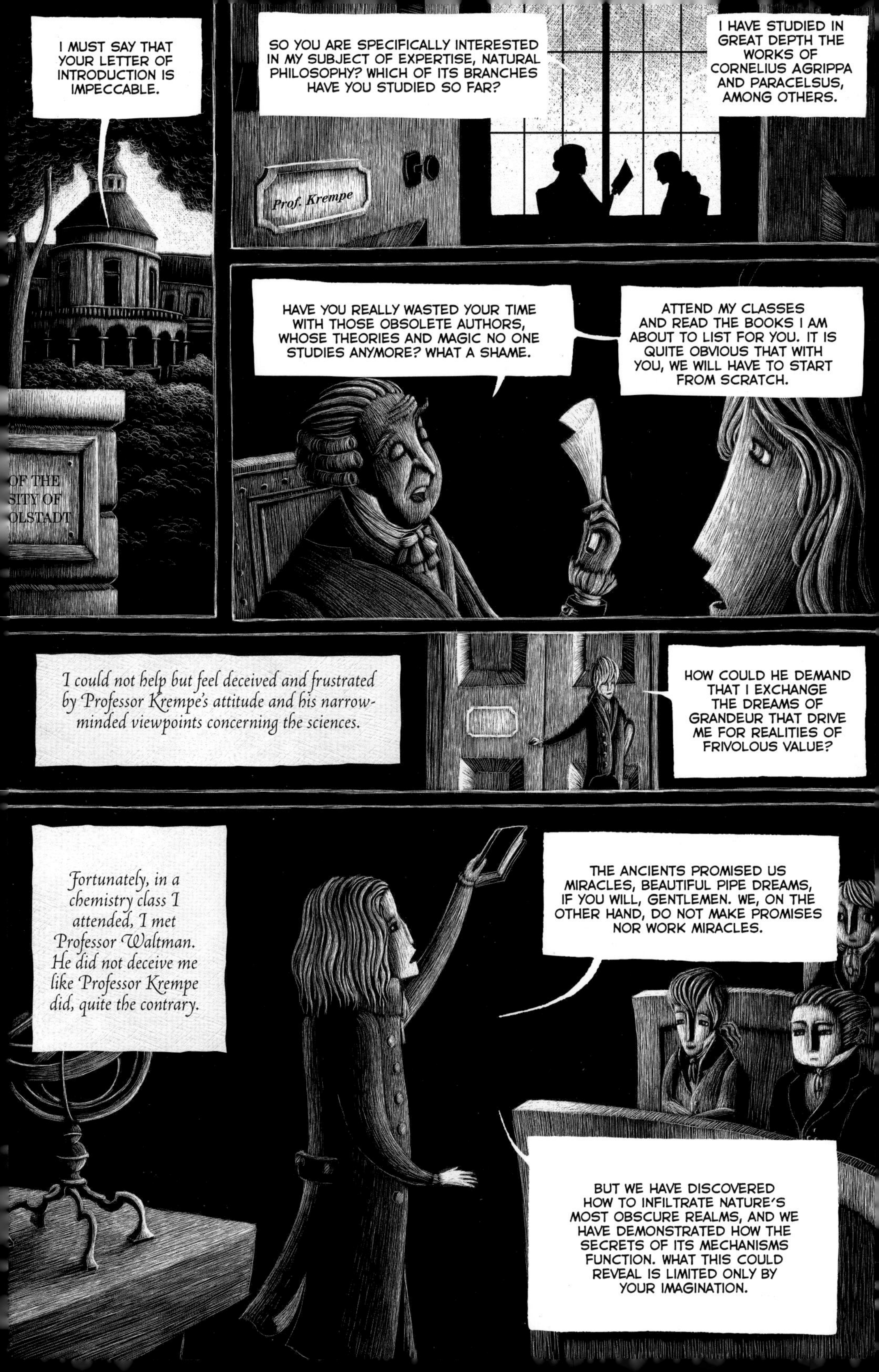
I MUST SAY THAT YOUR LETTER OF INTRODUCTION IS IMPECCABLE.
OF THE
SITY OF
OLSTADT
Prof. Krempe
SO YOU ARE SPECIFICALLY INTERESTED IN MY SUBJECT OF EXPERTISE, NATURAL PHILOSOPHY? WHICH OF ITS BRANCHES HAVE YOU STUDIED SO FAR?
I HAVE STUDIED IN GREAT DEPTH THE WORKS OF CORNELIUS AGRIPPA AND PARACELSUS, AMONG OTHERS.
HAVE YOU REALLY WASTED YOUR TIME WITH THOSE OBSOLETE AUTHORS, WHOSE THEORIES AND MAGIC NO ONE STUDIES ANYMORE? WHAT A SHAME.
ATTEND MY CLASSES AND READ THE BOOKS I AM ABOUT TO LIST FOR YOU. IT IS QUITE OBVIOUS THAT WITH YOU, WE WILL HAVE TO START FROM SCRATCH.
I could not help but feel deceived and frustrated by Professor Krempe's attitude and his narrow-minded viewpoints concerning the sciences.
HOW COULD HE DEMAND THAT I EXCHANGE THE DREAMS OF GRANDEUR THAT DRIVE ME FOR REALITIES OF FRIVOLOUS VALUE?
Fortunately, in a chemistry class I attended, I met Professor Waltman. He did not deceive me like Professor Krempe did, quite the contrary.
THE ANCIENTS PROMISED US MIRACLES, BEAUTIFUL PIPE DREAMS, IF YOU WILL, GENTLEMEN. WE, ON THE OTHER HAND, DO NOT MAKE PROMISES NOR WORK MIRACLES.
BUT WE HAVE DISCOVERED HOW TO INFILTRATE NATURE'S MOST OBSCURE REALMS, AND WE HAVE DEMONSTRATED HOW THE SECRETS OF ITS MECHANISMS FUNCTION. WHAT THIS COULD REVEAL IS LIMITED ONLY BY YOUR IMAGINATION.

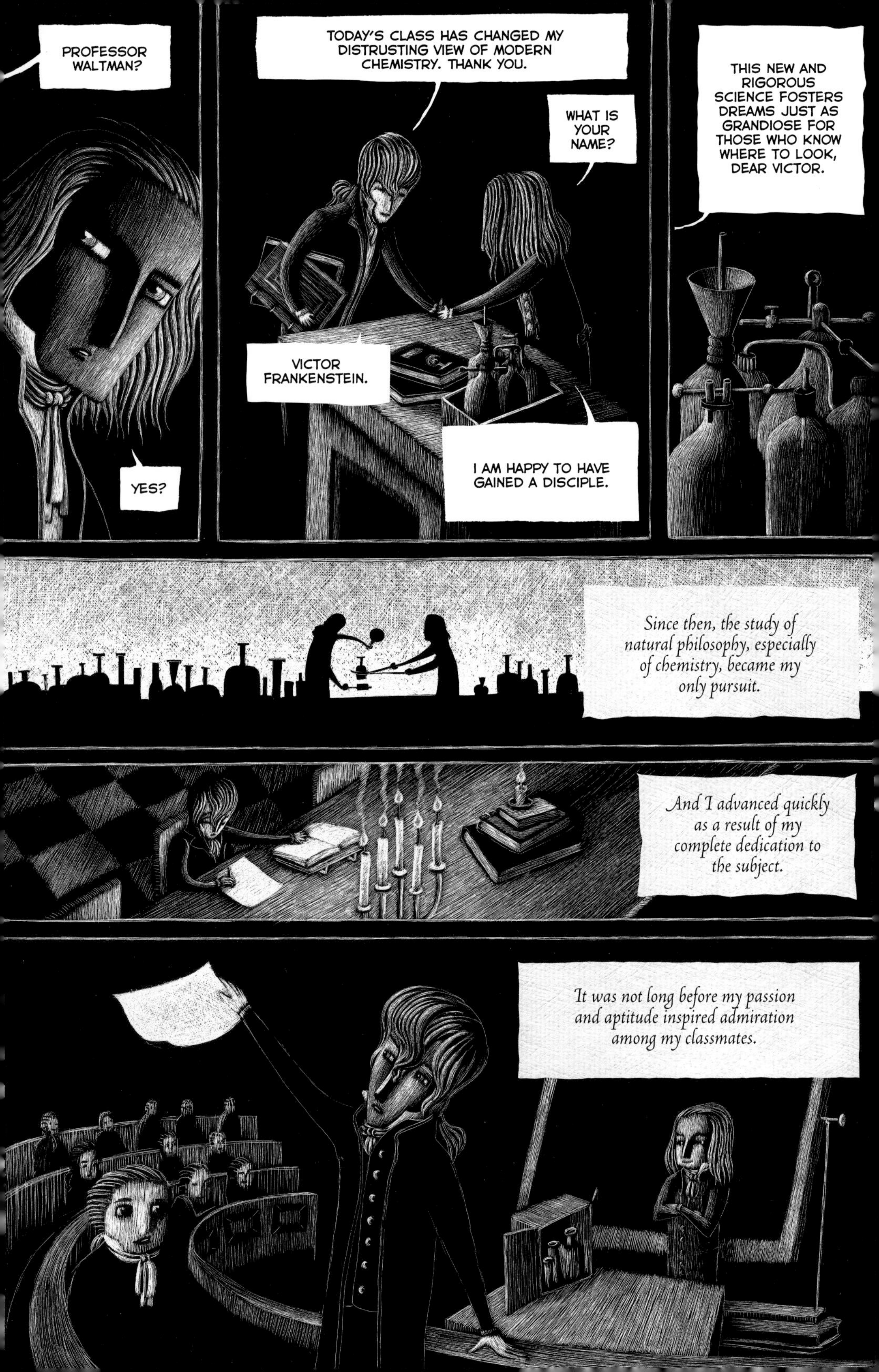

PROFESSOR WALTMAN?
YES?
TODAY'S CLASS HAS CHANGED MY DISTRUSTING VIEW OF MODERN CHEMISTRY. THANK YOU.
WHAT IS YOUR NAME?
VICTOR FRANKENSTEIN.
I AM HAPPY TO HAVE GAINED A DISCIPLE.
THIS NEW AND RIGOROUS SCIENCE FOSTERS DREAMS JUST AS GRANDIOSE FOR THOSE WHO KNOW WHERE TO LOOK, DEAR VICTOR.
Since then, the study of natural philosophy, especially of chemistry, became my only pursuit.
And I advanced quickly as a result of my complete dedication to the subject.
It was not long before my passion and aptitude inspired admiration among my classmates.

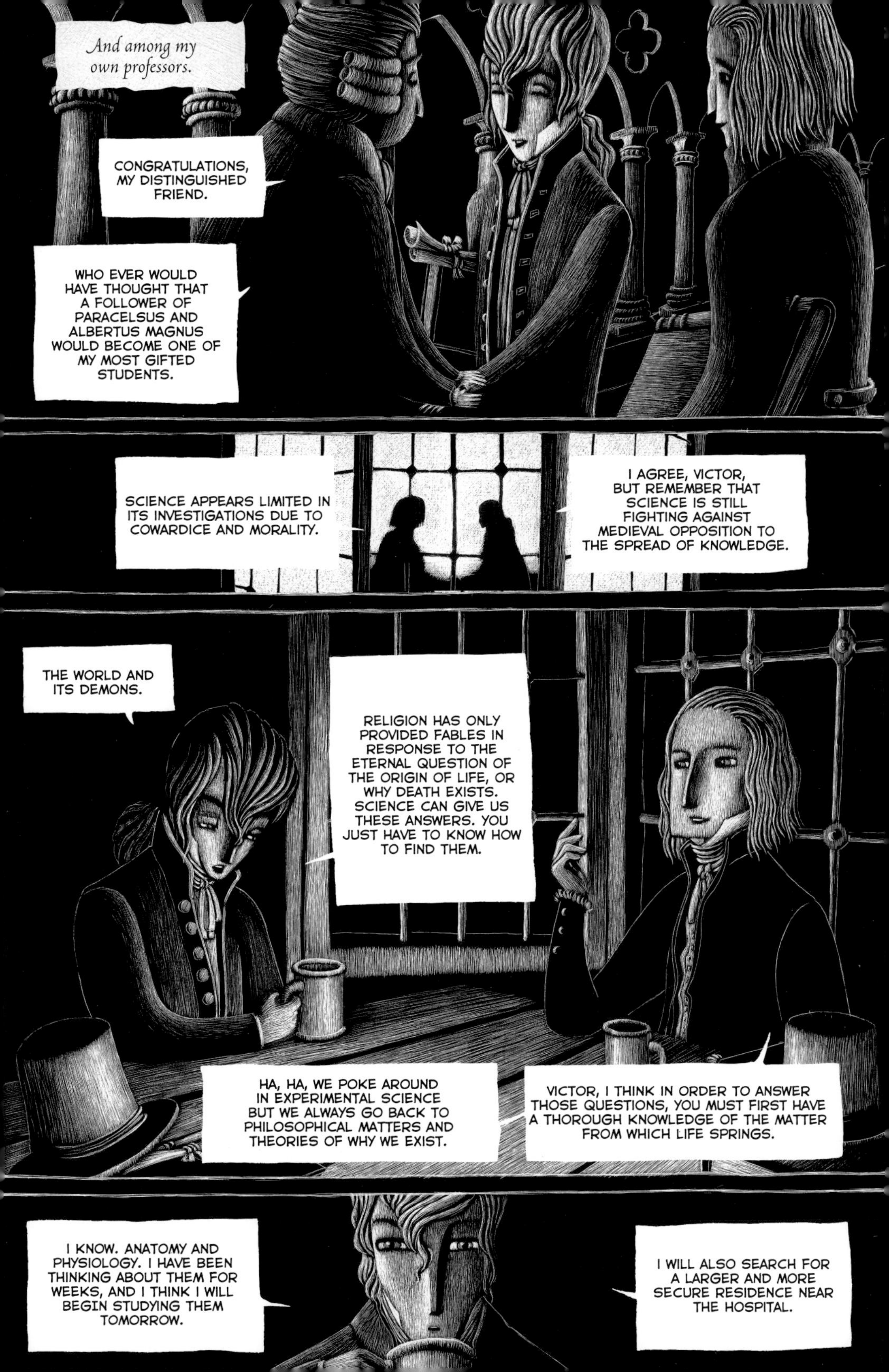
And among my own professors.
CONGRATULATIONS, MY DISTINGUISHED FRIEND.
WHO EVER WOULD HAVE THOUGHT THAT A FOLLOWER OF PARACELSUS AND ALBERTUS MAGNUS WOULD BECOME ONE OF MY MOST GIFTED STUDENTS.
SCIENCE APPEARS LIMITED IN ITS INVESTIGATIONS DUE TO COWARDICE AND MORALITY.
I AGREE, VICTOR, BUT REMEMBER THAT SCIENCE IS STILL FIGHTING AGAINST MEDIEVAL OPPOSITION TO THE SPREAD OF KNOWLEDGE.
THE WORLD AND ITS DEMONS.
RELIGION HAS ONLY PROVIDED FABLES IN RESPONSE TO THE ETERNAL QUESTION OF THE ORIGIN OF LIFE, OR WHY DEATH EXISTS. SCIENCE CAN GIVE US THESE ANSWERS. YOU JUST HAVE TO KNOW HOW TO FIND THEM.
HA, HA, WE POKE AROUND IN EXPERIMENTAL SCIENCE BUT WE ALWAYS GO BACK TO PHILOSOPHICAL MATTERS AND THEORIES OF WHY WE EXIST.
VICTOR, I THINK IN ORDER TO ANSWER THOSE QUESTIONS, YOU MUST FIRST HAVE A THOROUGH KNOWLEDGE OF THE MATTER FROM WHICH LIFE SPRINGS.
I KNOW. ANATOMY AND PHYSIOLOGY. I HAVE BEEN THINKING ABOUT THEM FOR WEEKS, AND I THINK I WILL BEGIN STUDYING THEM TOMORROW.
I WILL ALSO SEARCH FOR A LARGER AND MORE SECURE RESIDENCE NEAR THE HOSPITAL.

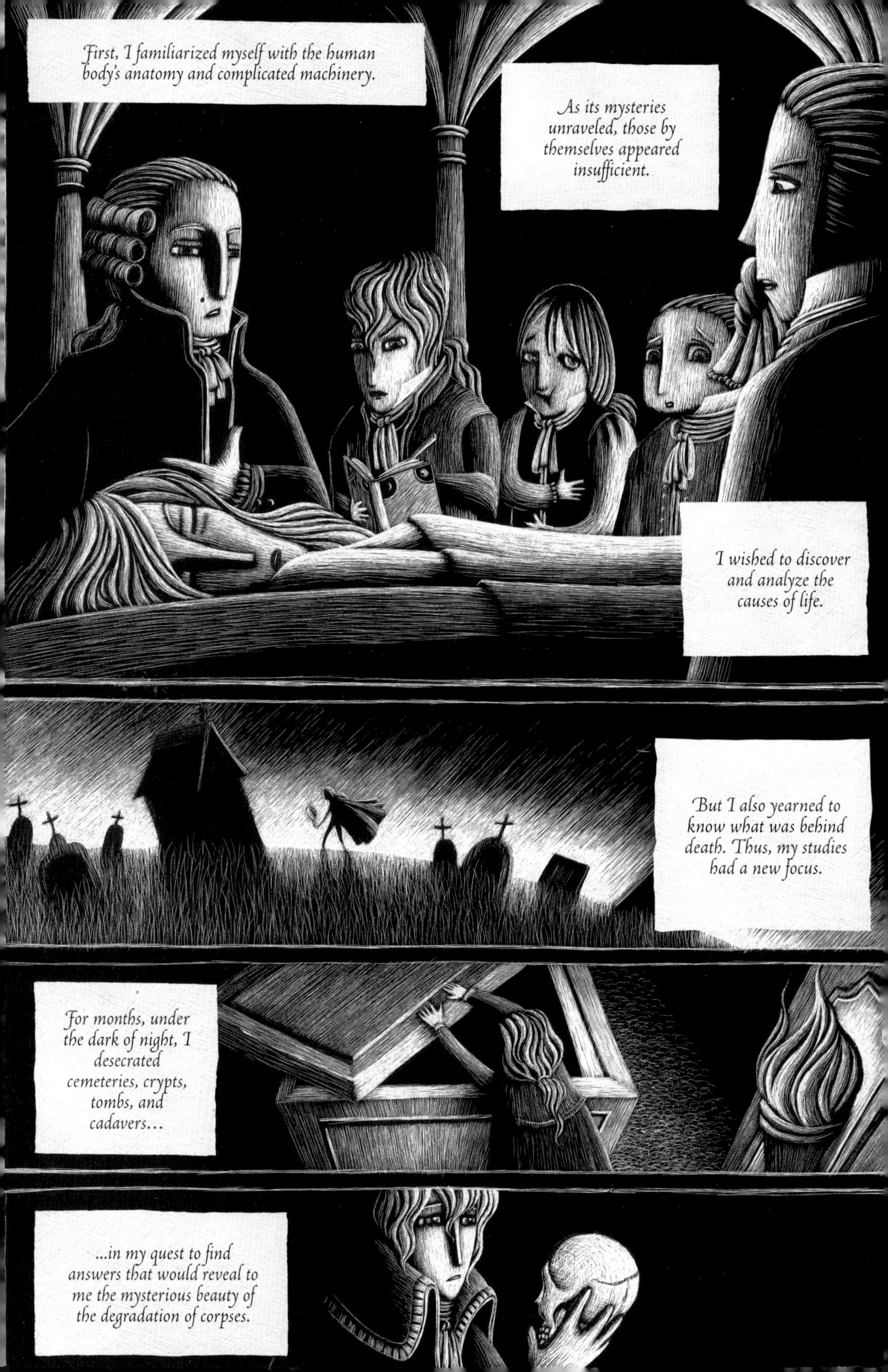
First, I familiarized myself with the human body's anatomy and complicated machinery.
As its mysteries unraveled, those by themselves appeared insufficient.
I wished to discover and analyze the causes of life.
But I also yearned to know what was behind death. Thus, my studies had a new focus.
For months, under the dark of night, I desecrated cemeteries, crypts, tombs, and cadavers…
...in my quest to find answers that would reveal to me the mysterious beauty of the degradation of corpses.

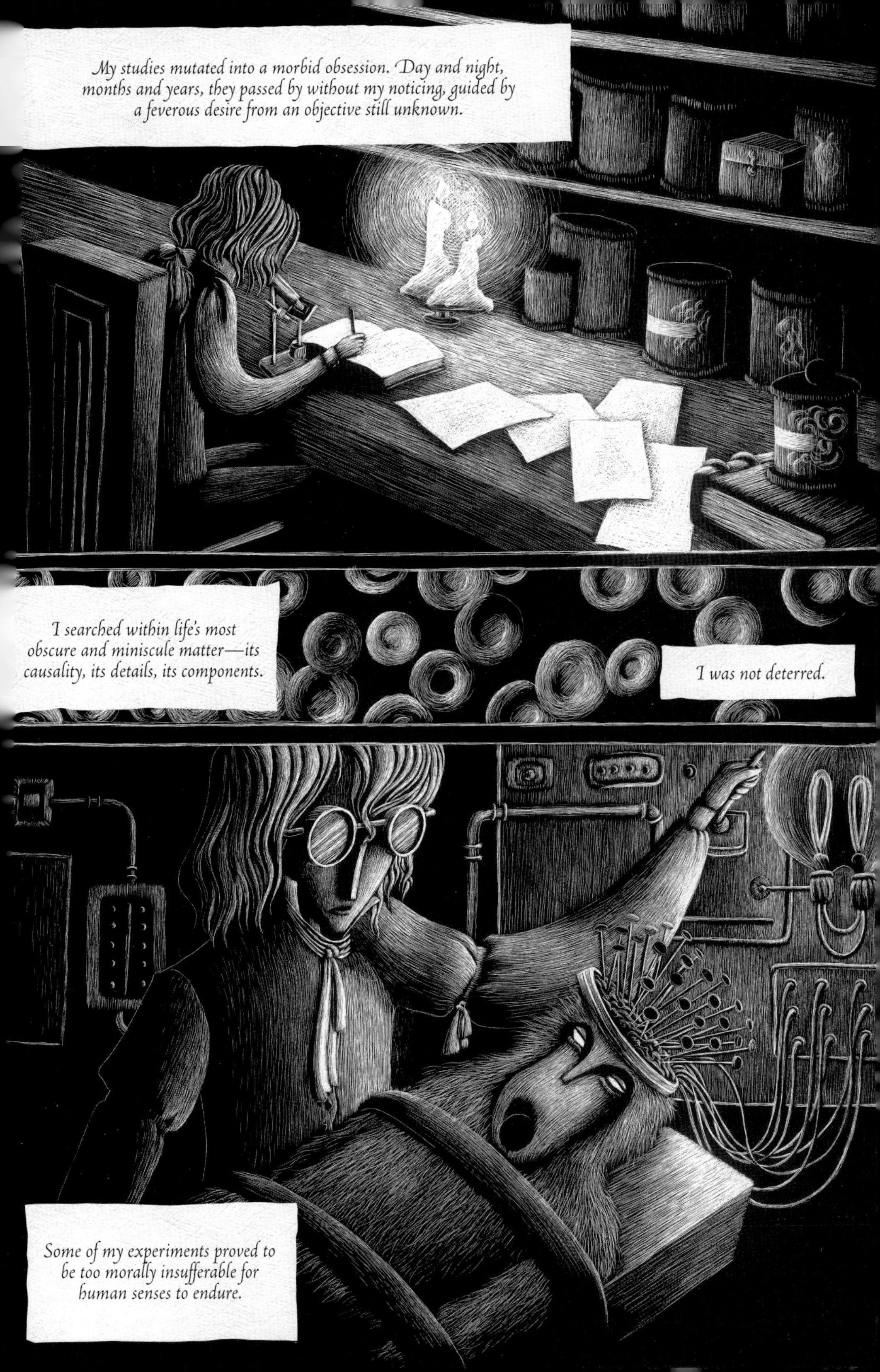
My studies mutated into a morbid obsession. Day and night, months and years, they passed by without my noticing, guided by a feverous desire from an objective still unknown.
I searched within life's most obscure and miniscule matter—its causality, its details, its components.
I was not deterred.
Some of my experiments proved to be too morally insufferable for human senses to endure.

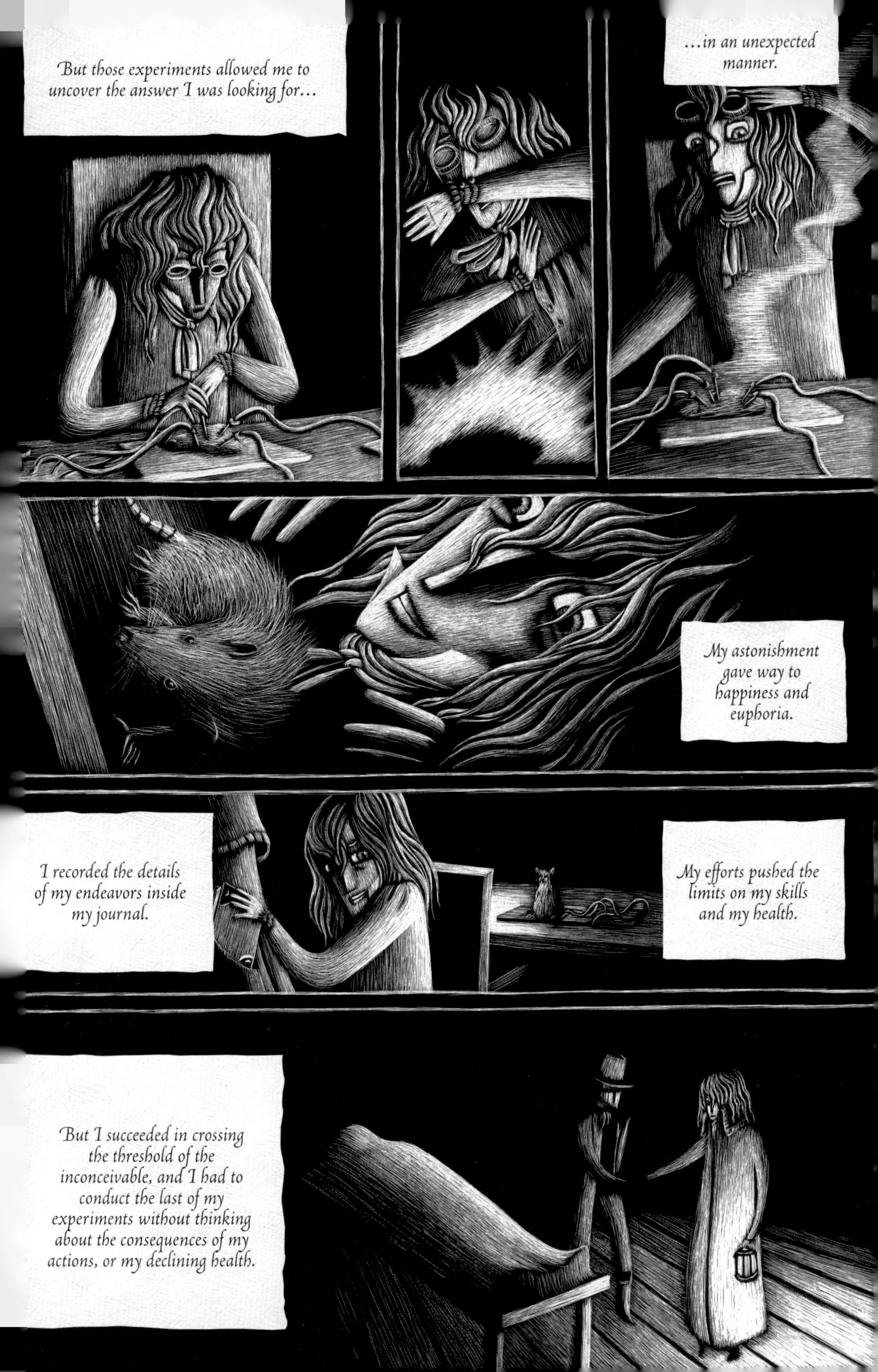
But those experiments allowed me to uncover the answer I was looking for...
...in an unexpected manner.
My astonishment gave way to happiness and euphoria.
I recorded the details of my endeavors inside my journal.
My efforts pushed the limits on my skills and my health.
But I succeeded in crossing the threshold of the inconceivable, and I had to conduct the last of my experiments without thinking about the consequences of my actions, or my declining health.

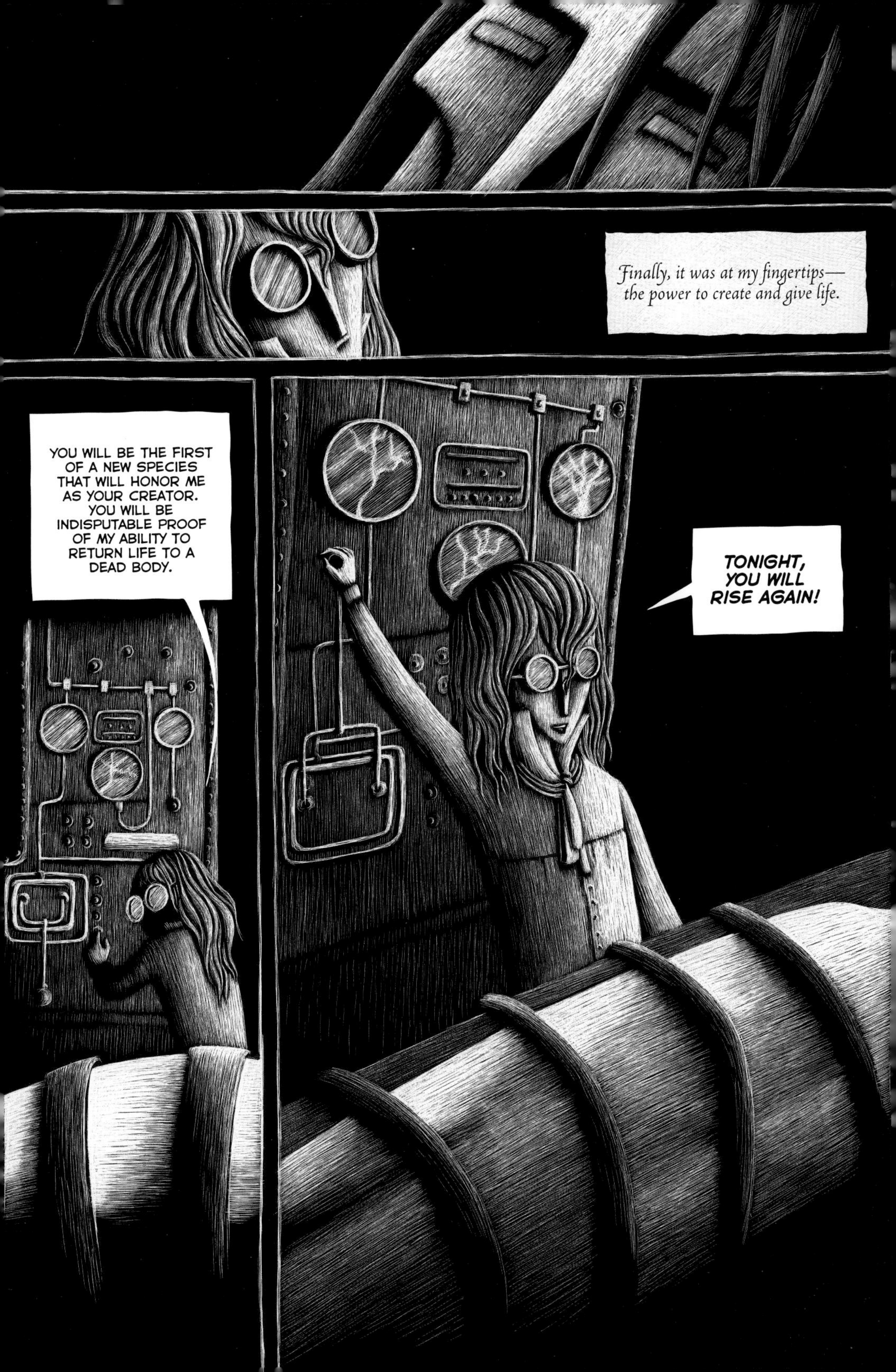
Finally, it was at my fingertips—the power to create and give life.
YOU WILL BE THE FIRST OF A NEW SPECIES THAT WILL HONOR ME AS YOUR CREATOR. YOU WILL BE INDISPUTABLE PROOF OF MY ABILITY TO RETURN LIFE TO A DEAD BODY.
TONIGHT, YOU WILL RISE AGAIN!

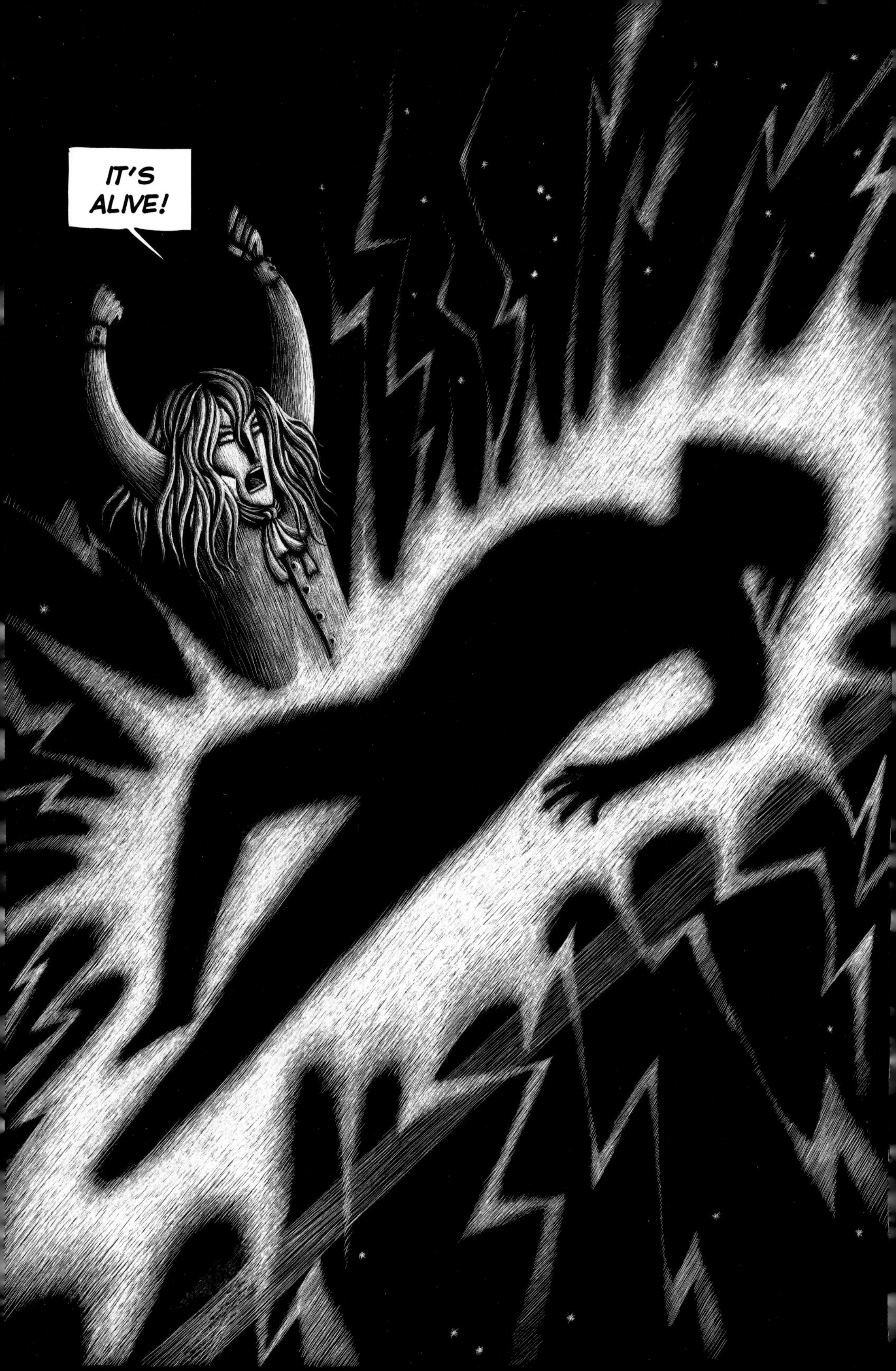
IT'S ALIVE!

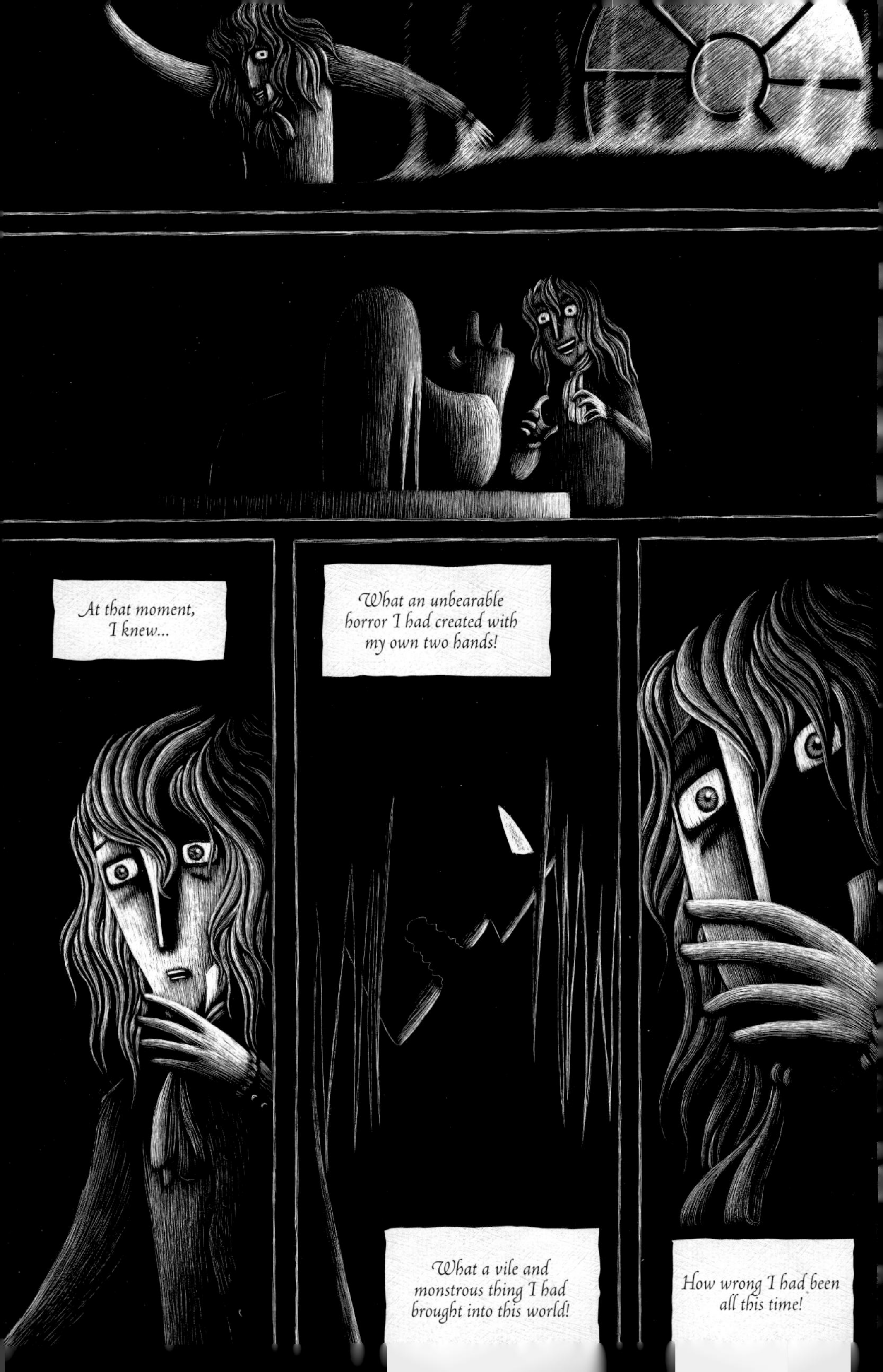
At that moment, I knew...
What an unbearable horror I had created with my own two hands!
What a vile and monstrous thing I had brought into this world!
How wrong I had been all this time!

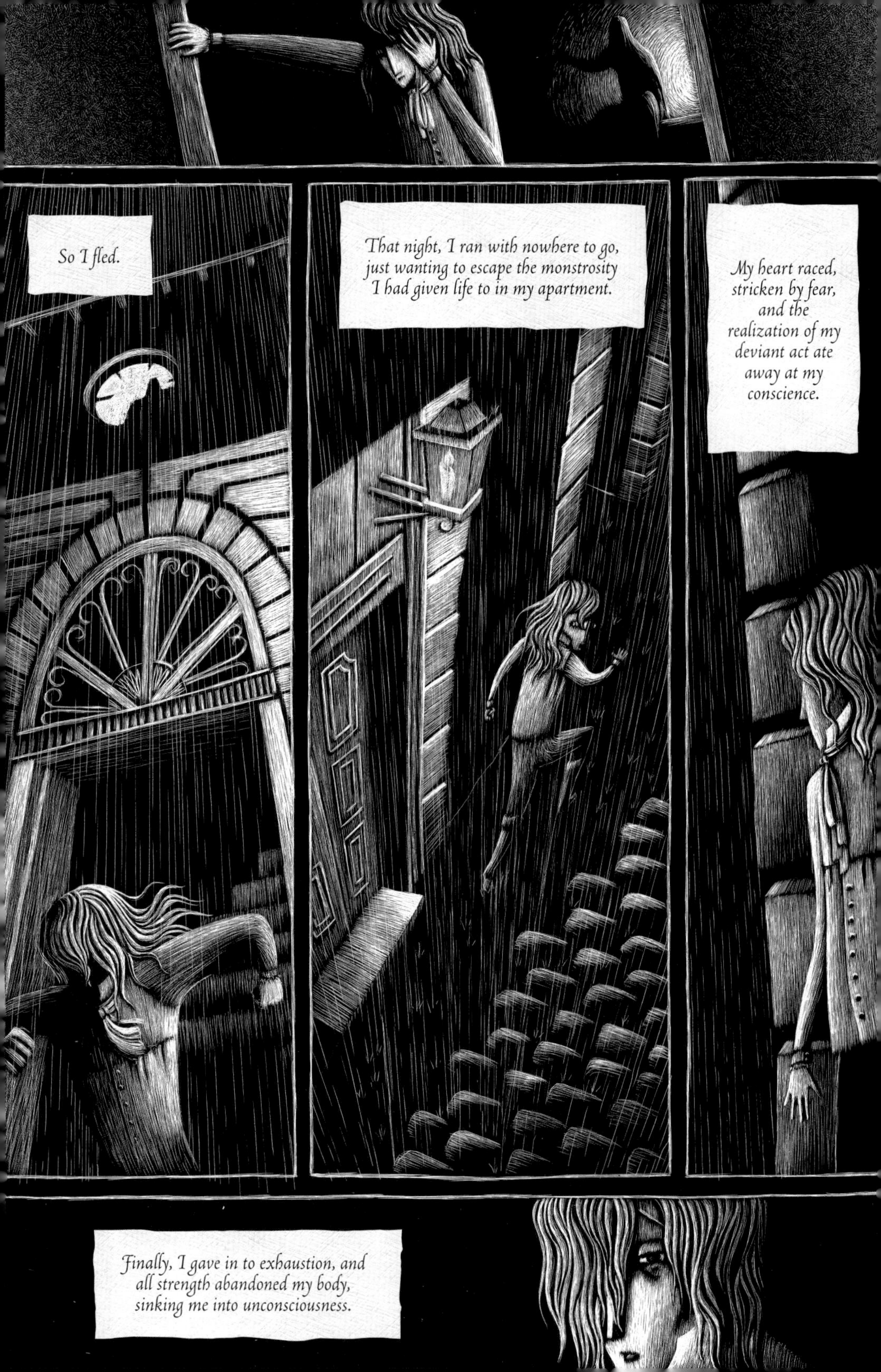
So I fled.
That night, I ran with nowhere to go, just wanting to escape the monstrosity I had given life to in my apartment.
My heart raced, stricken by fear, and the realization of my deviant act ate away at my conscience.
Finally, I gave in to exhaustion, and all strength abandoned my body, sinking me into unconsciousness.

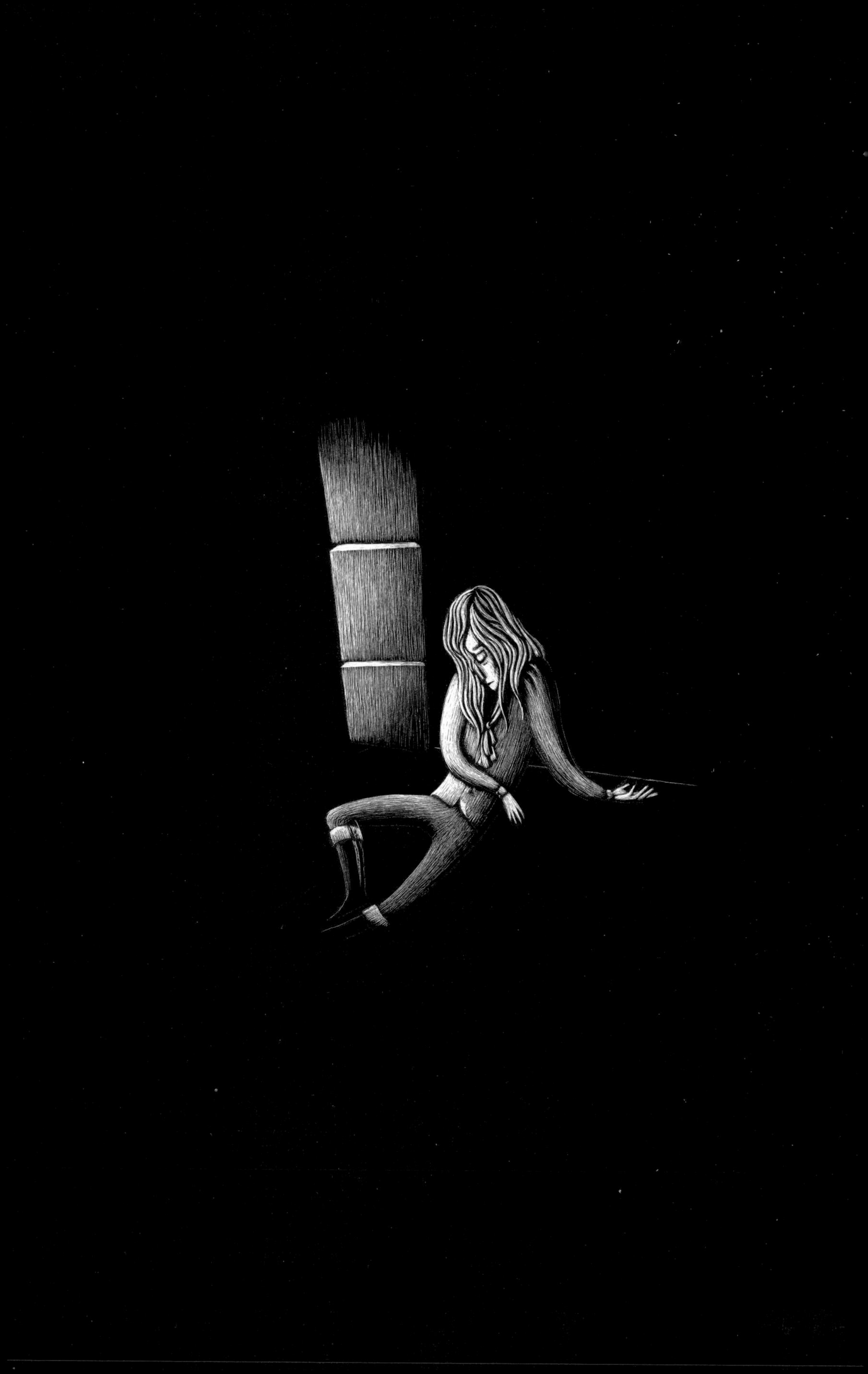

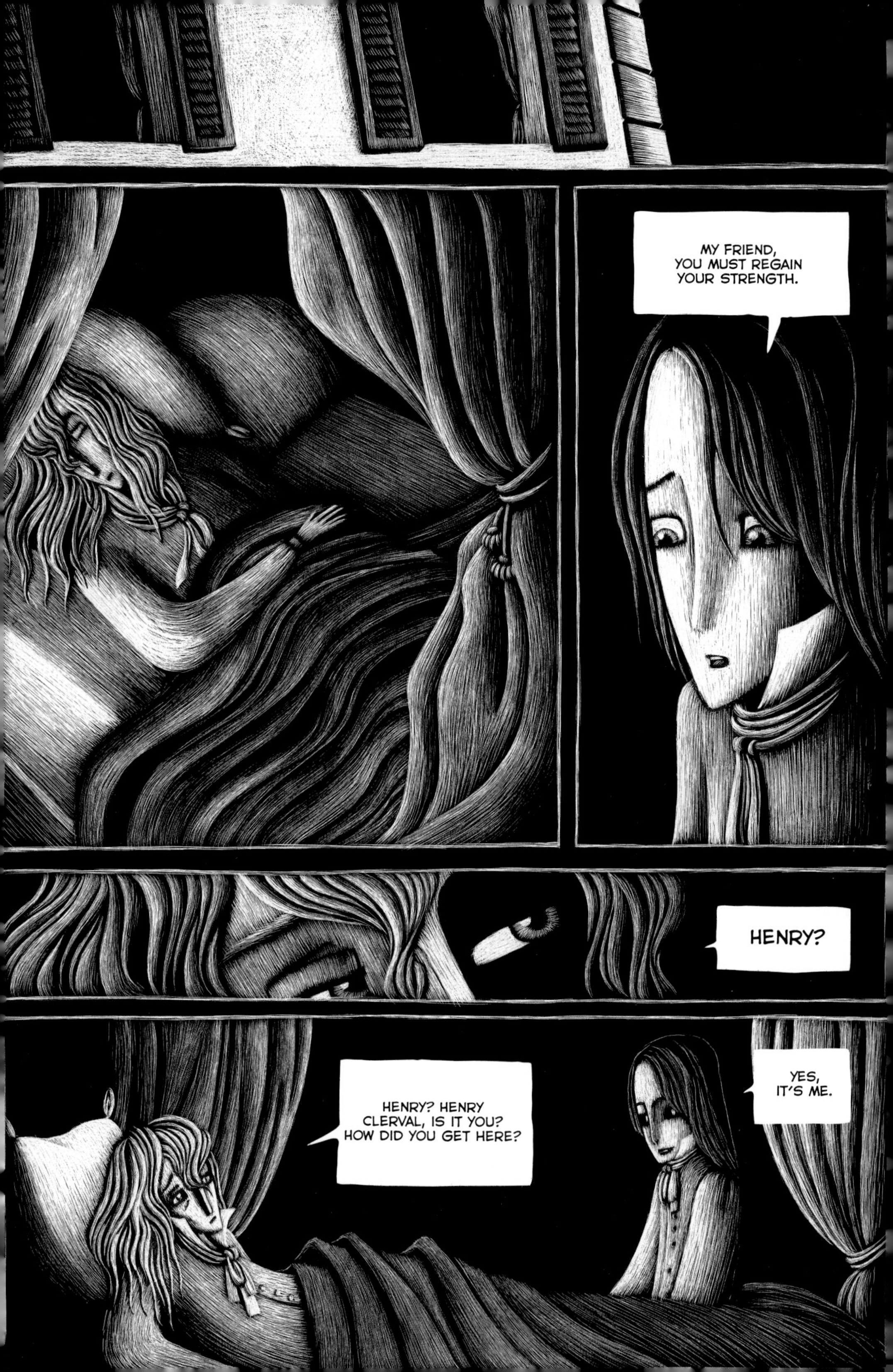
MY FRIEND, YOU MUST REGAIN YOUR STRENGTH.
HENRY?
HENRY? HENRY CLERVAL, IS IT YOU? HOW DID YOU GET HERE?
YES, IT'S ME.

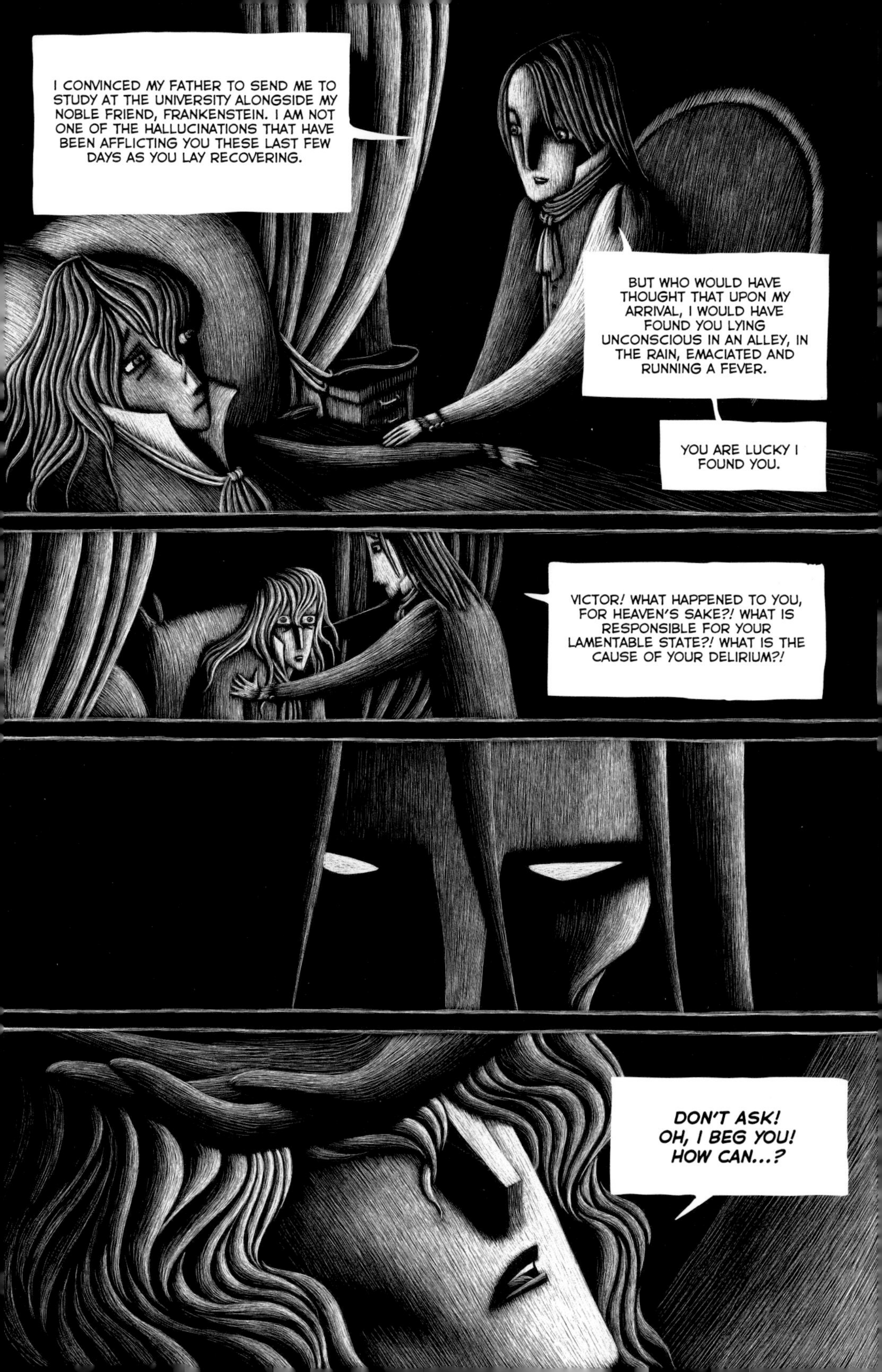
I CONVINCED MY FATHER TO SEND ME TO STUDY AT THE UNIVERSITY ALONGSIDE MY NOBLE FRIEND, FRANKENSTEIN. I AM NOT ONE OF THE HALLUCINATIONS THAT HAVE BEEN AFFLICTING YOU THESE LAST FEW DAYS AS YOU LAY RECOVERING.
BUT WHO WOULD HAVE THOUGHT THAT UPON MY ARRIVAL, I WOULD HAVE FOUND YOU LYING UNCONSCIOUS IN AN ALLEY, IN THE RAIN, EMACIATED AND RUNNING A FEVER.
YOU ARE LUCKY I FOUND YOU.
VICTOR! WHAT HAPPENED TO YOU, FOR HEAVEN'S SAKE?! WHAT IS RESPONSIBLE FOR YOUR LAMENTABLE STATE?! WHAT IS THE CAUSE OF YOUR DELIRIUM?!
DON'T ASK! OH, I BEG YOU! HOW CAN...?

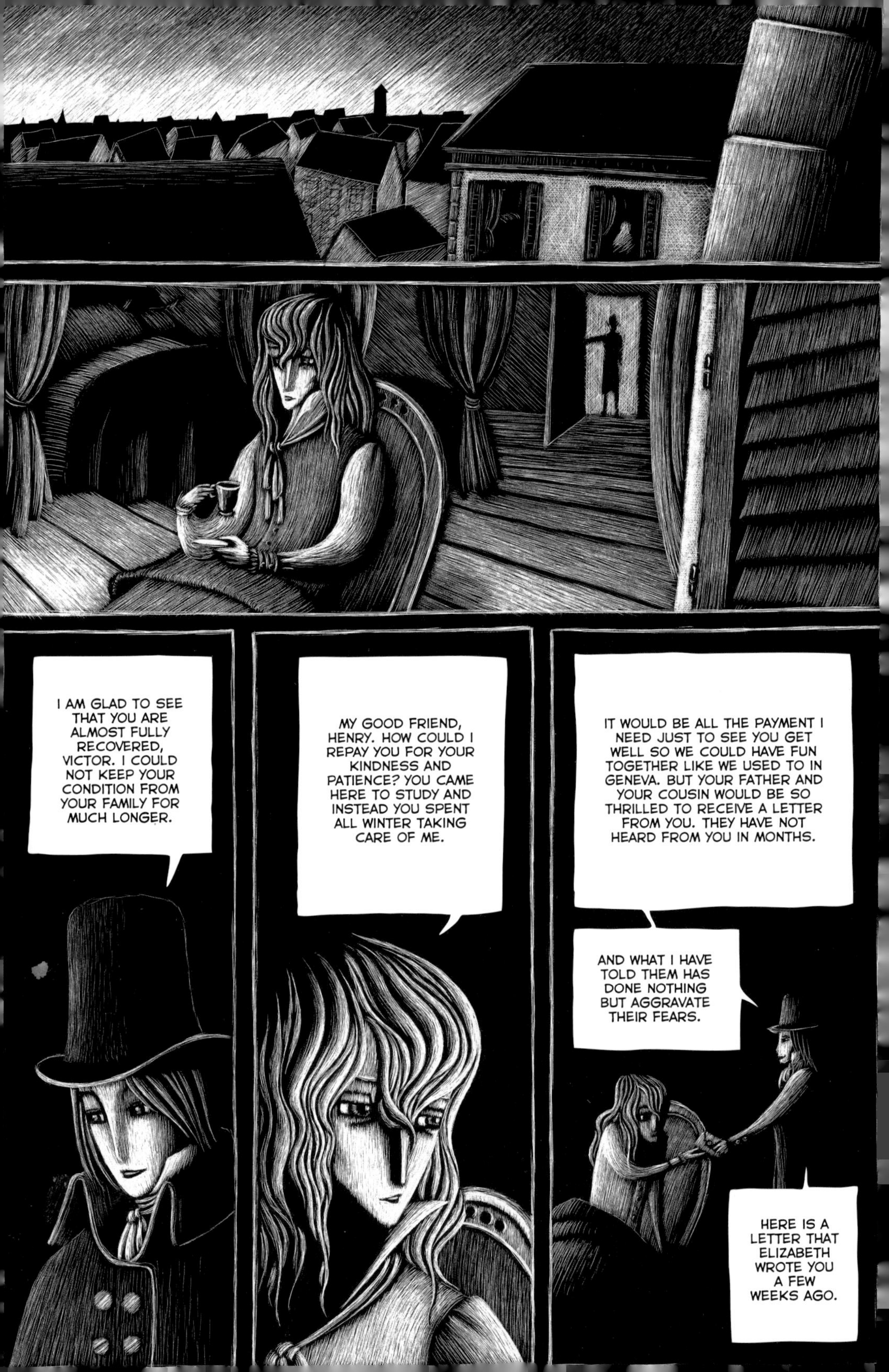
I AM GLAD TO SEE THAT YOU ARE ALMOST FULLY RECOVERED, VICTOR. I COULD NOT KEEP YOUR CONDITION FROM YOUR FAMILY FOR MUCH LONGER.
MY GOOD FRIEND, HENRY. HOW COULD I REPAY YOU FOR YOUR KINDNESS AND PATIENCE? YOU CAME HERE TO STUDY AND INSTEAD YOU SPENT ALL WINTER TAKING CARE OF ME.
IT WOULD BE ALL THE PAYMENT I NEED JUST TO SEE YOU GET WELL SO WE COULD HAVE FUN TOGETHER LIKE WE USED TO IN GENEVA. BUT YOUR FATHER AND YOUR COUSIN WOULD BE SO THRILLED TO RECEIVE A LETTER FROM YOU. THEY HAVE NOT HEARD FROM YOU IN MONTHS.
AND WHAT I HAVE TOLD THEM HAS DONE NOTHING BUT AGGRAVATE THEIR FEARS.
HERE IS A LETTER THAT ELIZABETH WROTE YOU A FEW WEEKS AGO.

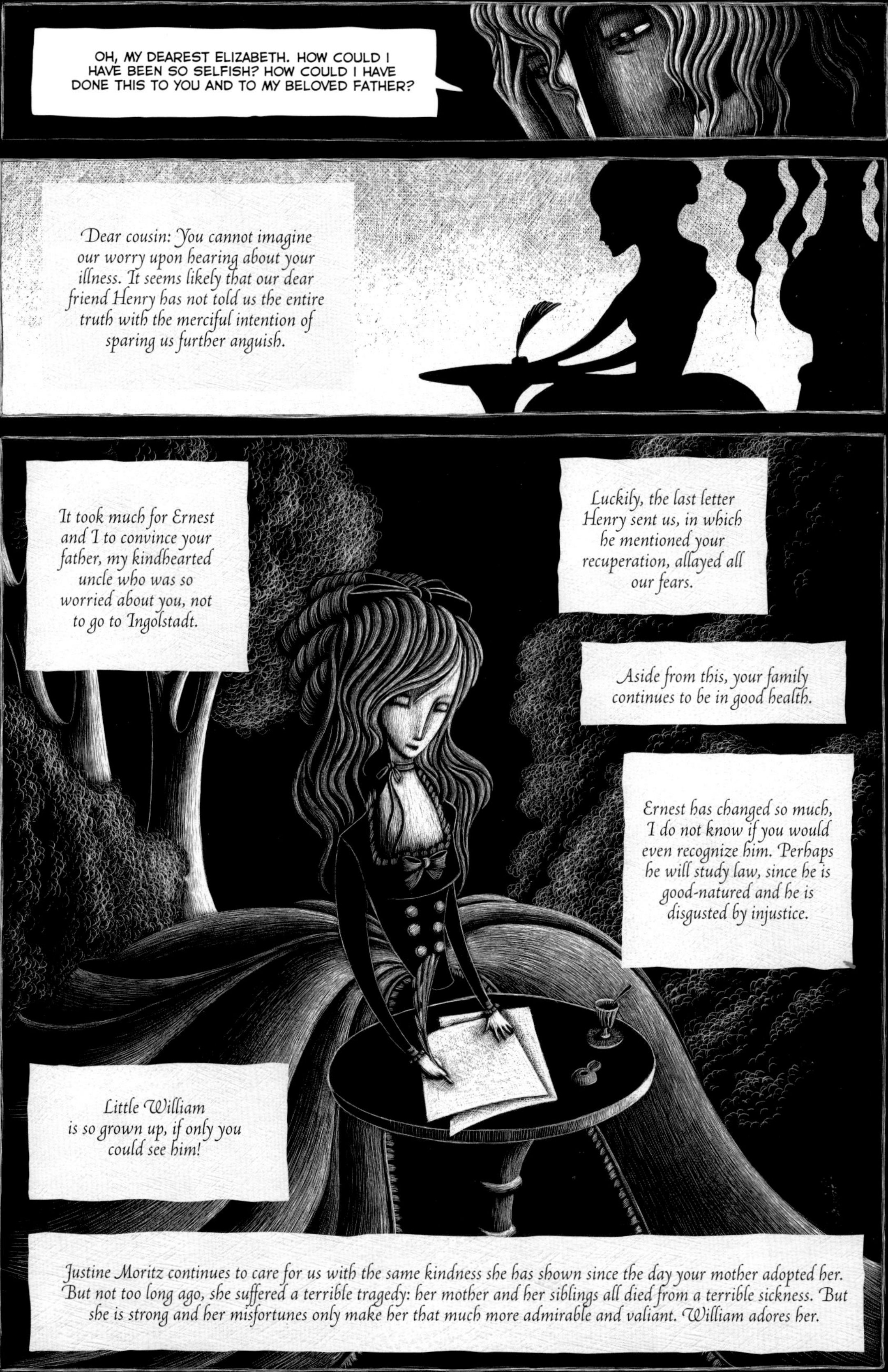
OH, MY DEAREST ELIZABETH. HOW COULD I HAVE BEEN SO SELFISH? HOW COULD I HAVE DONE THIS TO YOU AND TO MY BELOVED FATHER?
Dear cousin: You cannot imagine our worry upon hearing about your illness. It seems likely that our dear friend Henry has not told us the entire truth with the merciful intention of sparing us further anguish.
It took much for Ernest and I to convince your father, my kindhearted uncle who was so worried about you, not to go to Ingolstadt.
Luckily, the last letter Henry sent us, in which he mentioned your recuperation, allayed all our fears.
Aside from this, your family continues to be in good health.
Ernest has changed so much, I do not know if you would even recognize him. Perhaps he will study law, since he is good-natured and he is disgusted by injustice.
Little William is so grown up, if only you could see him!
Justine Moritz continues to care for us with the same kindness she has shown since the day your mother adopted her. But not too long ago, she suffered a terrible tragedy: her mother and her siblings all died from a terrible sickness. But she is strong and her misfortunes only make her that much more admirable and valiant. William adores her.

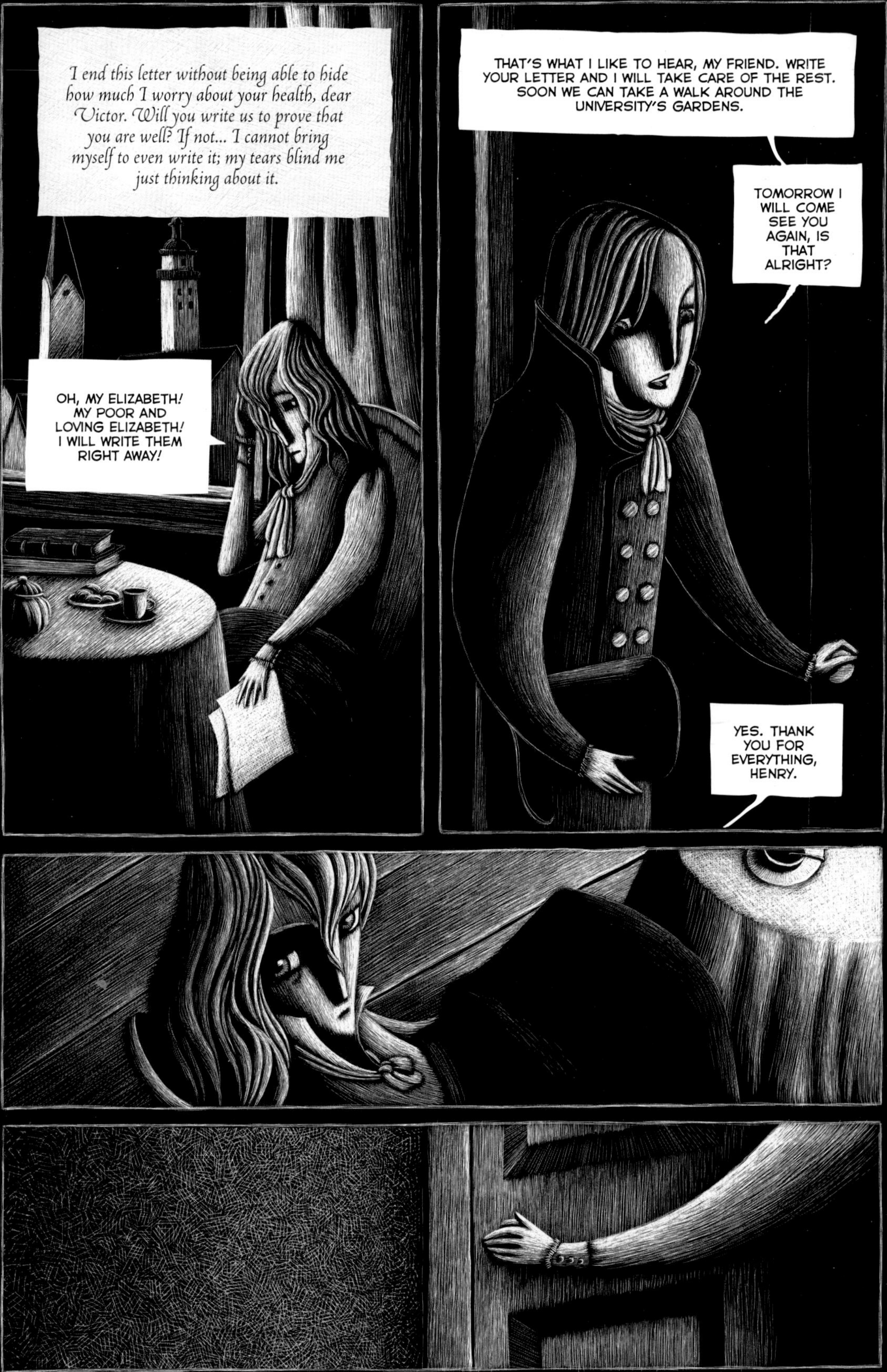
I end this letter without being able to hide how much I worry about your health, dear Victor. Will you write us to prove that you are well? If not... I cannot bring myself to even write it; my tears blind me just thinking about it.
OH, MY ELIZABETH! MY POOR AND LOVING ELIZABETH! I WILL WRITE THEM RIGHT AWAY!
THAT'S WHAT I LIKE TO HEAR, MY FRIEND. WRITE YOUR LETTER AND I WILL TAKE CARE OF THE REST. SOON WE CAN TAKE A WALK AROUND THE UNIVERSITY'S GARDENS.
TOMORROW I WILL COME SEE YOU AGAIN, IS THAT ALRIGHT?
YES. THANK YOU FOR EVERYTHING, HENRY.

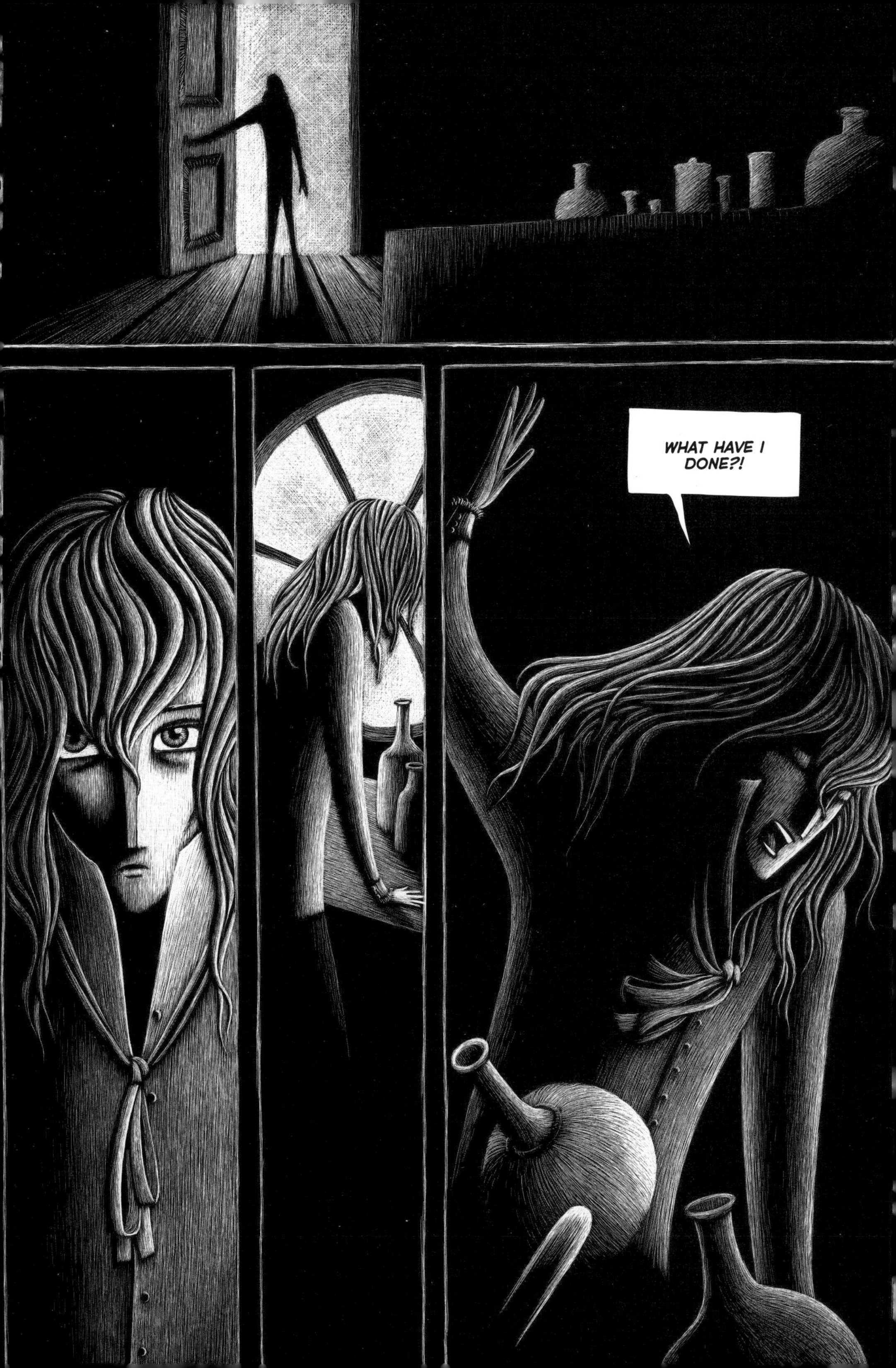
WHAT HAVE I DONE?!

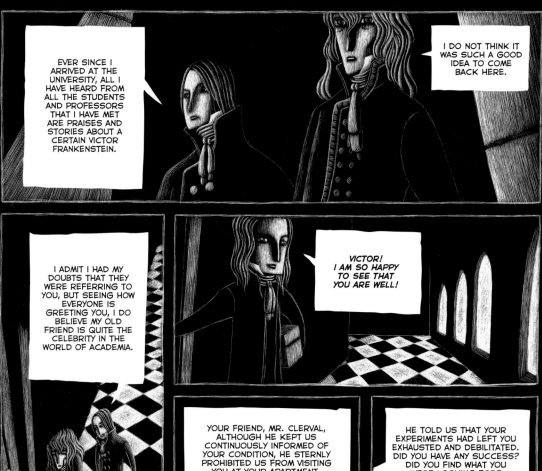

EVER SINCE I ARRIVED AT THE UNIVERSITY, ALL I HAVE HEARD FROM ALL THE STUDENTS AND PROFESSORS THAT I HAVE MET ARE PRAISES AND STORIES ABOUT A CERTAIN VICTOR FRANKENSTEIN.

I DO NOT THINK IT WAS SUCH A GOOD IDEA TO COME BACK HERE.

I ADMIT I HAD MY DOUBTS THAT THEY WERE REFERRING TO YOU, BUT SEEING HOW EVERYONE IS GREETING YOU, I DO BELIEVE MY OLD FRIEND IS QUITE THE CELEBRITY IN THE WORLD OF ACADEMIA.

VICTOR! I AM SO HAPPY TO SEE THAT YOU ARE WELL!

YOUR FRIEND, MR. CLERVAL, ALTHOUGH HE KEPT US CONTINUOUSLY INFORMED OF YOUR CONDITION, HE STERNLY PROHIBITED US FROM VISITING YOU AT YOUR APARTMENT.

HE TOLD US THAT YOUR EXPERIMENTS HAD LEFT YOU EXHAUSTED AND DEBILITATED. DID YOU HAVE ANY SUCCESS? DID YOU FIND WHAT YOU WERE LOOKING FOR?

WELL, I DO NOT FEEL LIKE ONE. QUITE THE CONTRARY.

PROFESSOR WALTMAN, IT IS BEST THAT WE LEAVE THIS CONVERSATION FOR ANOTHER DAY. PLEASE EXCUSE US BUT WE ARE IN A HURRY. SOME VERY IMPORTANT PEOPLE ARE WAITING FOR US.

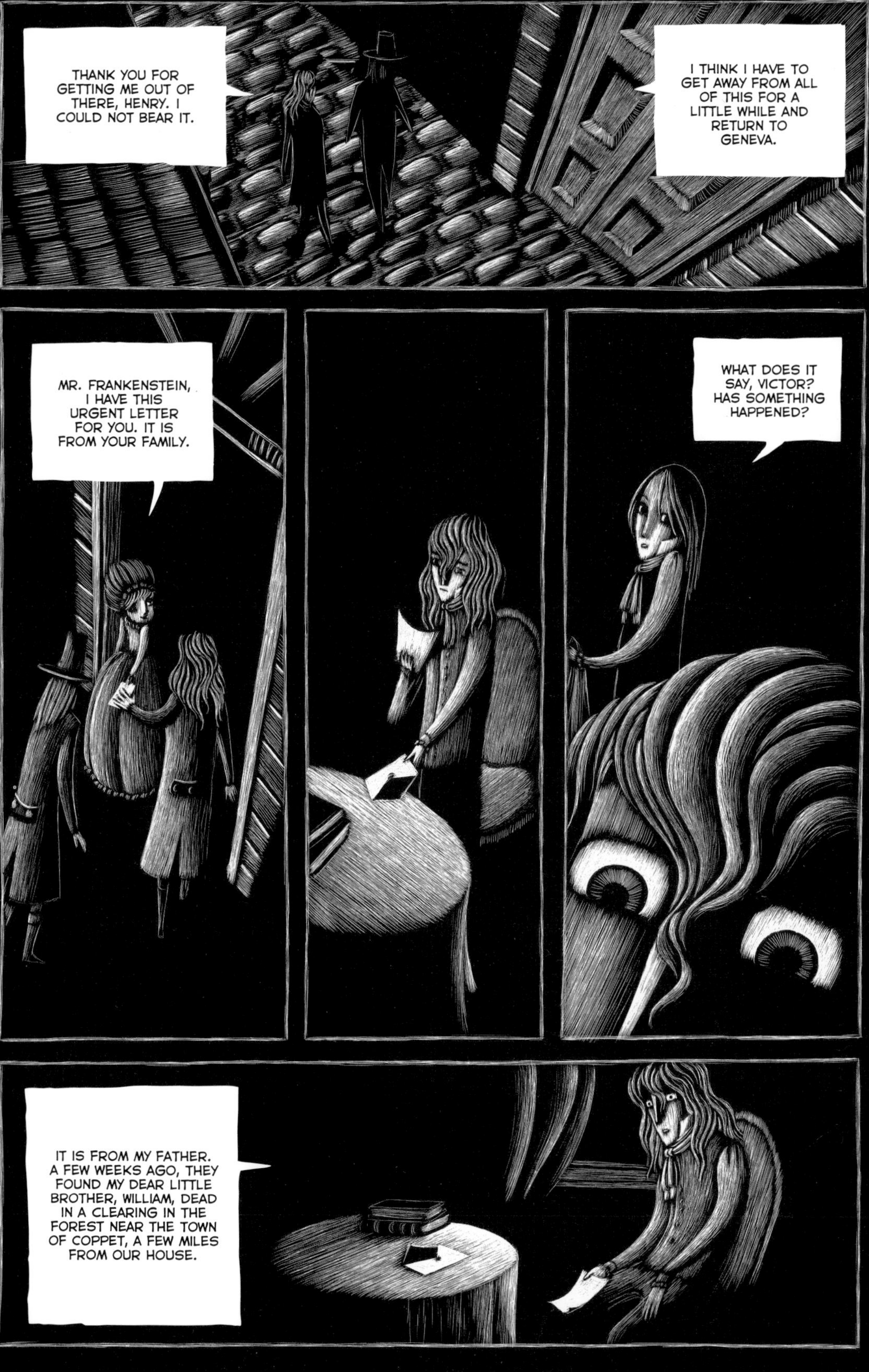
THANK YOU FOR GETTING ME OUT OF THERE, HENRY. I COULD NOT BEAR IT.
I THINK I HAVE TO GET AWAY FROM ALL OF THIS FOR A LITTLE WHILE AND RETURN TO GENEVA.
MR. FRANKENSTEIN, I HAVE THIS URGENT LETTER FOR YOU. IT IS FROM YOUR FAMILY.
WHAT DOES IT SAY, VICTOR? HAS SOMETHING HAPPENED?
IT IS FROM MY FATHER. A FEW WEEKS AGO, THEY FOUND MY DEAR LITTLE BROTHER, WILLIAM, DEAD IN A CLEARING IN THE FOREST NEAR THE TOWN OF COPPET, A FEW MILES FROM OUR HOUSE.

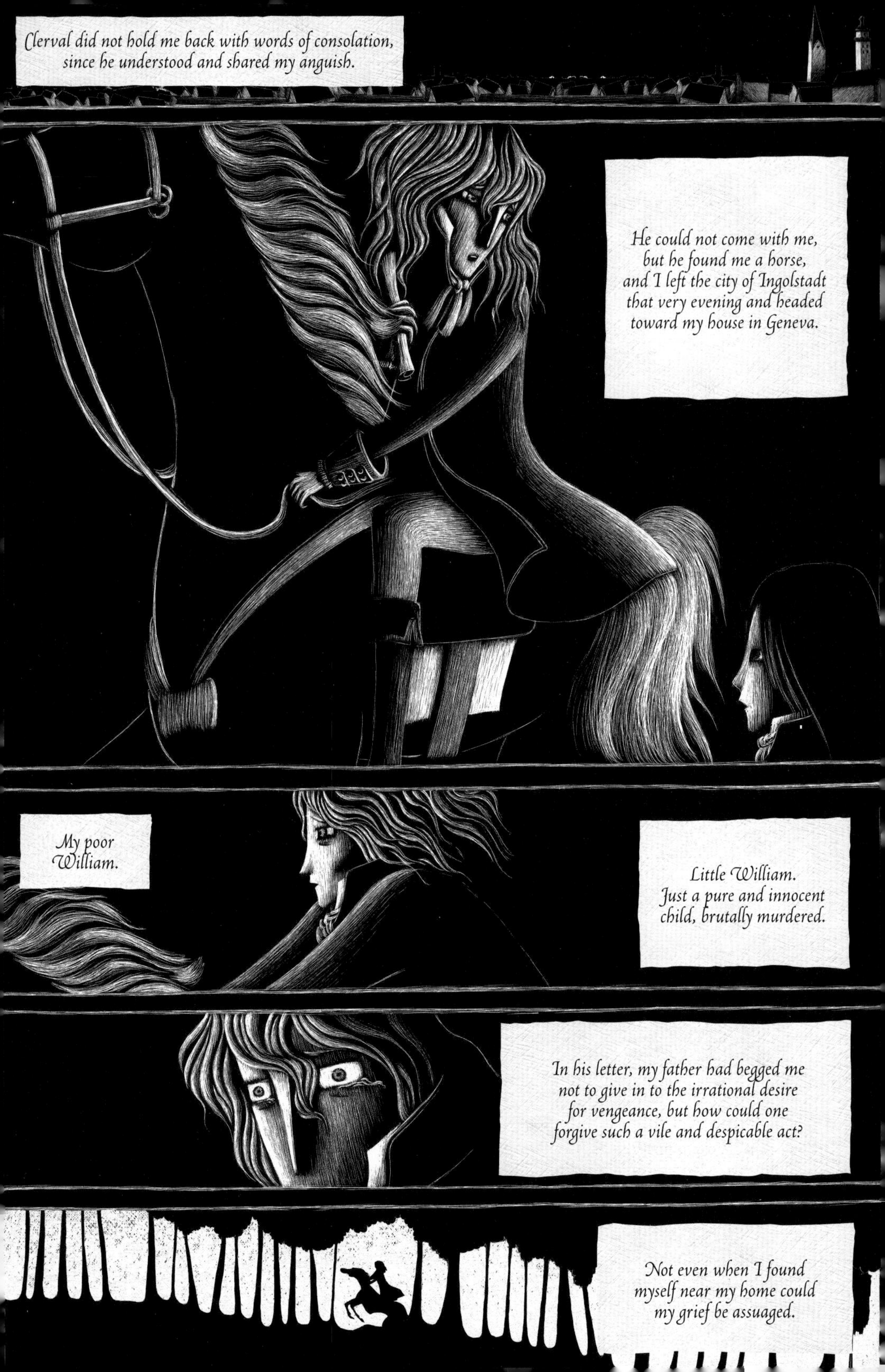
Clerval did not hold me back with words of consolation, since he understood and shared my anguish.
He could not come with me, but he found me a horse, and I left the city of Ingolstadt that very evening and headed toward my house in Geneva.
My poor William.
Little William. Just a pure and innocent child, brutally murdered.
In his letter, my father had begged me not to give in to the irrational desire for vengeance, but how could one forgive such a vile and despicable act?
Not even when I found myself near my home could my grief be assuaged.

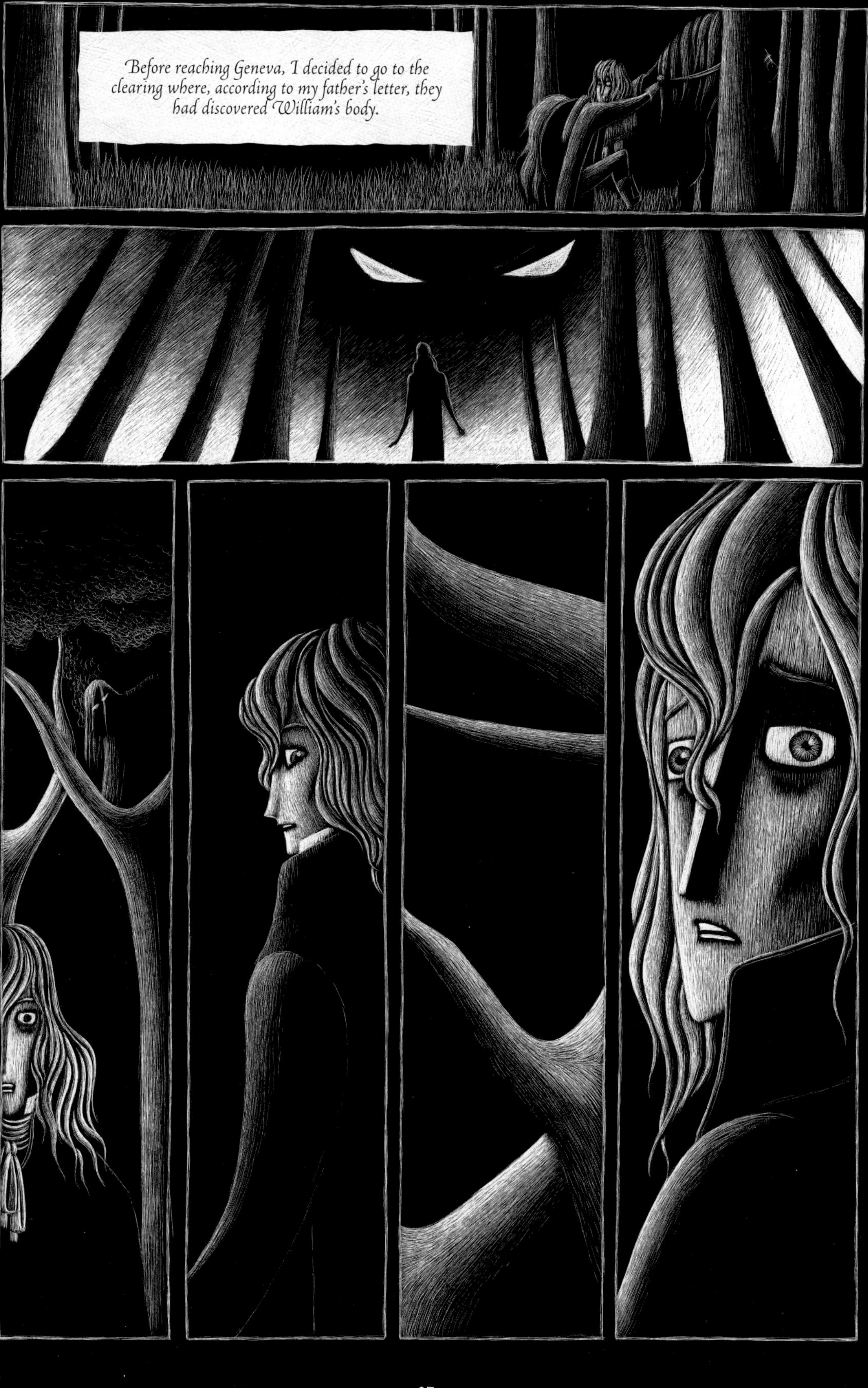
Before reaching Geneva, I decided to go to the clearing where, according to my father's letter, they had discovered William's body.

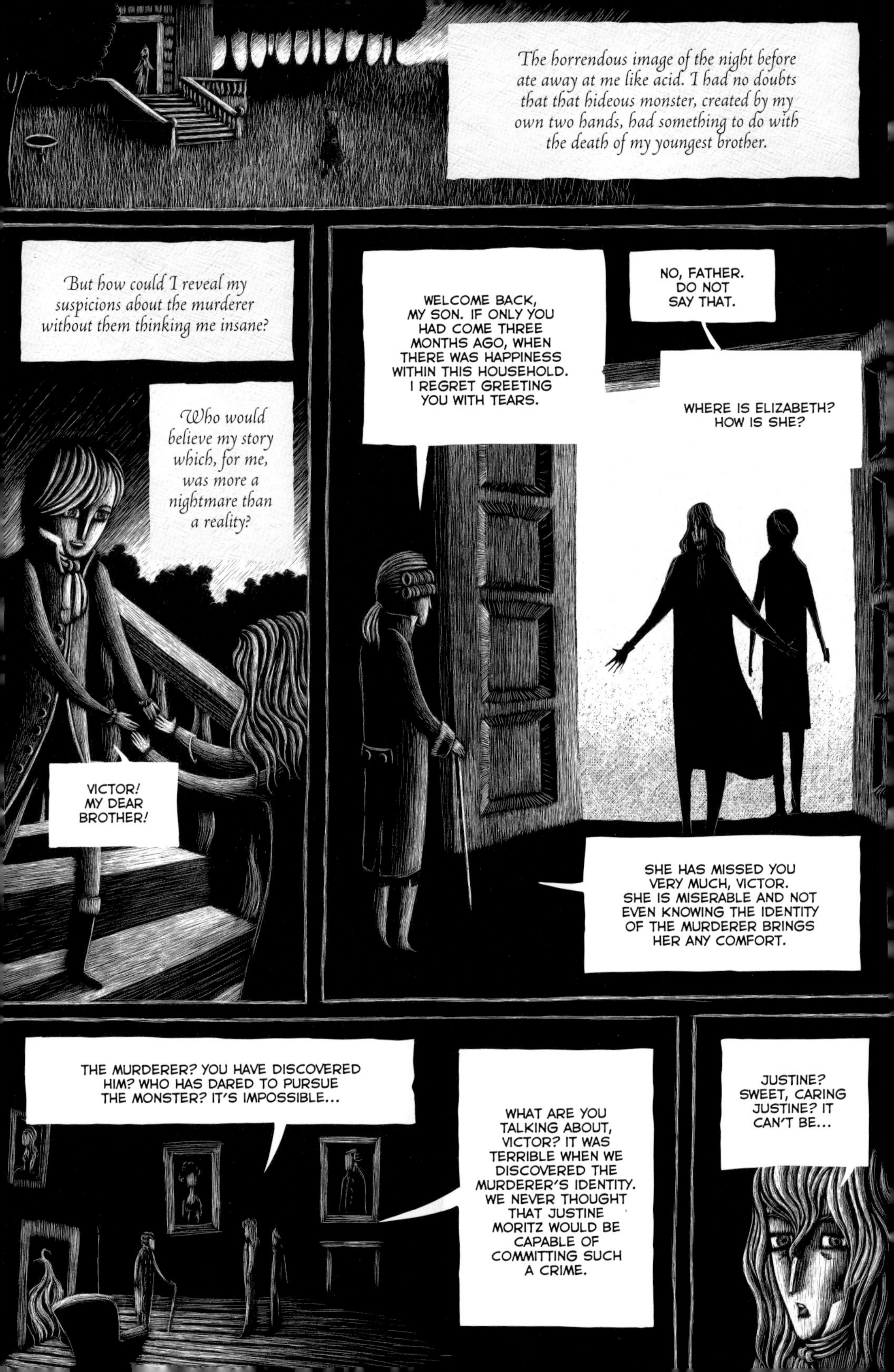
The horrendous image of the night before ate away at me like acid. I had no doubts that that hideous monster, created by my own two hands, had something to do with the death of my youngest brother.
But how could I reveal my suspicions about the murderer without them thinking me insane?
Who would believe my story which, for me, was more a nightmare than a reality?
VICTOR! MY DEAR BROTHER!
WELCOME BACK, MY SON. IF ONLY YOU HAD COME THREE MONTHS AGO, WHEN THERE WAS HAPPINESS WITHIN THIS HOUSEHOLD. I REGRET GREETING YOU WITH TEARS.
NO, FATHER. DO NOT SAY THAT.
WHERE IS ELIZABETH? HOW IS SHE?
SHE HAS MISSED YOU VERY MUCH, VICTOR. SHE IS MISERABLE AND NOT EVEN KNOWING THE IDENTITY OF THE MURDERER BRINGS HER ANY COMFORT.
THE MURDERER? YOU HAVE DISCOVERED HIM? WHO HAS DARED TO PURSUE THE MONSTER? IT'S IMPOSSIBLE...
WHAT ARE YOU TALKING ABOUT, VICTOR? IT WAS TERRIBLE WHEN WE DISCOVERED THE MURDERER'S IDENTITY. WE NEVER THOUGHT THAT JUSTINE MORITZ WOULD BE CAPABLE OF COMMITTING SUCH A CRIME.
JUSTINE? SWEET, CARING JUSTINE? IT CAN'T BE...

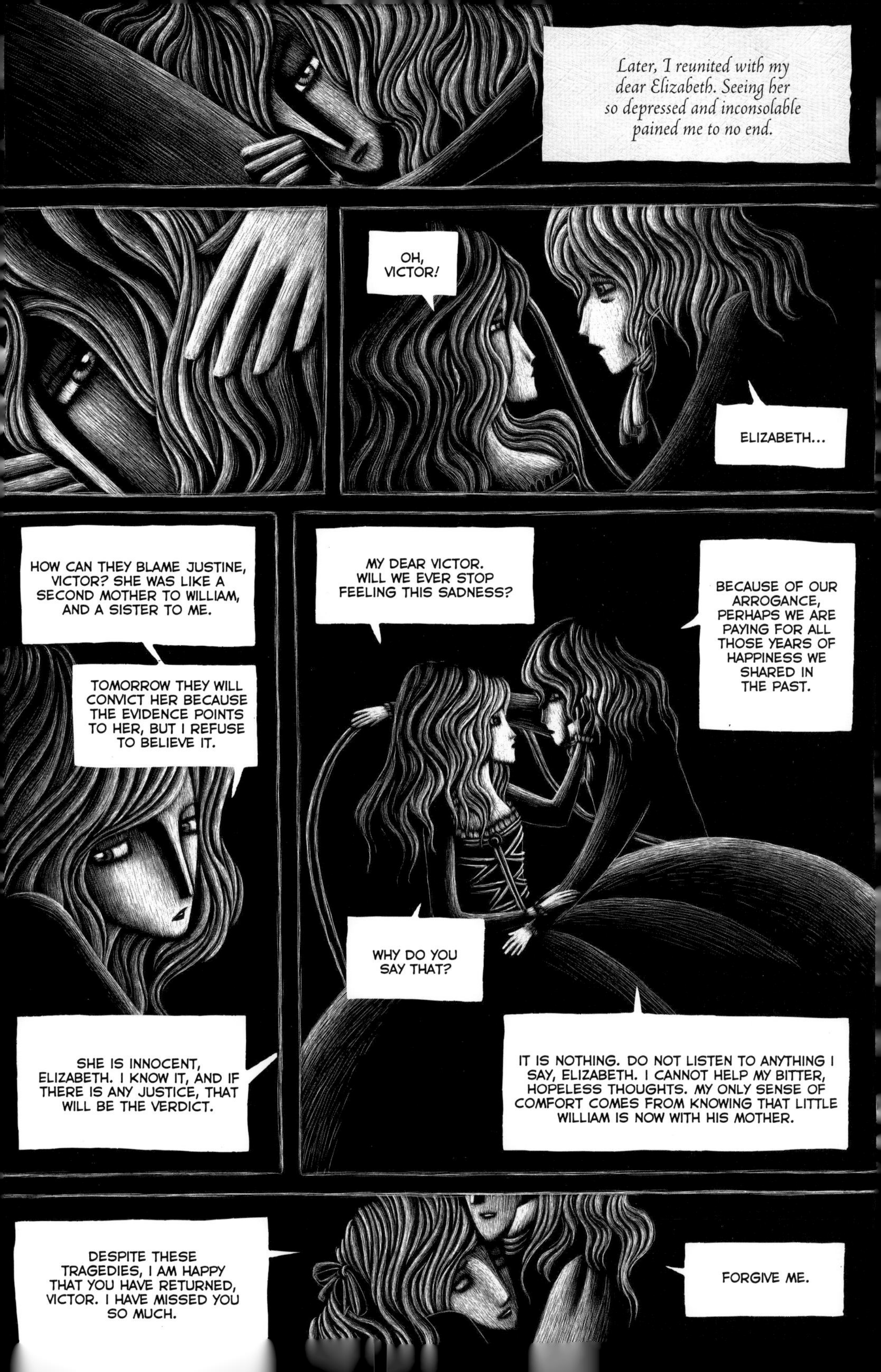
Later, I reunited with my dear Elizabeth. Seeing her so depressed and inconsolable pained me to no end.
OH, VICTOR!
ELIZABETH...
HOW CAN THEY BLAME JUSTINE, VICTOR? SHE WAS LIKE A SECOND MOTHER TO WILLIAM, AND A SISTER TO ME.
TOMORROW THEY WILL CONVICT HER BECAUSE THE EVIDENCE POINTS TO HER, BUT I REFUSE TO BELIEVE IT.
SHE IS INNOCENT, ELIZABETH. I KNOW IT, AND IF THERE IS ANY JUSTICE, THAT WILL BE THE VERDICT.
MY DEAR VICTOR. WILL WE EVER STOP FEELING THIS SADNESS?
BECAUSE OF OUR ARROGANCE, PERHAPS WE ARE PAYING FOR ALL THOSE YEARS OF HAPPINESS WE SHARED IN THE PAST.
WHY DO YOU SAY THAT?
IT IS NOTHING. DO NOT LISTEN TO ANYTHING I SAY, ELIZABETH. I CANNOT HELP MY BITTER, HOPELESS THOUGHTS. MY ONLY SENSE OF COMFORT COMES FROM KNOWING THAT LITTLE WILLIAM IS NOW WITH HIS MOTHER.
DESPITE THESE TRAGEDIES, I AM HAPPY THAT YOU HAVE RETURNED, VICTOR. I HAVE MISSED YOU SO MUCH.
FORGIVE ME.

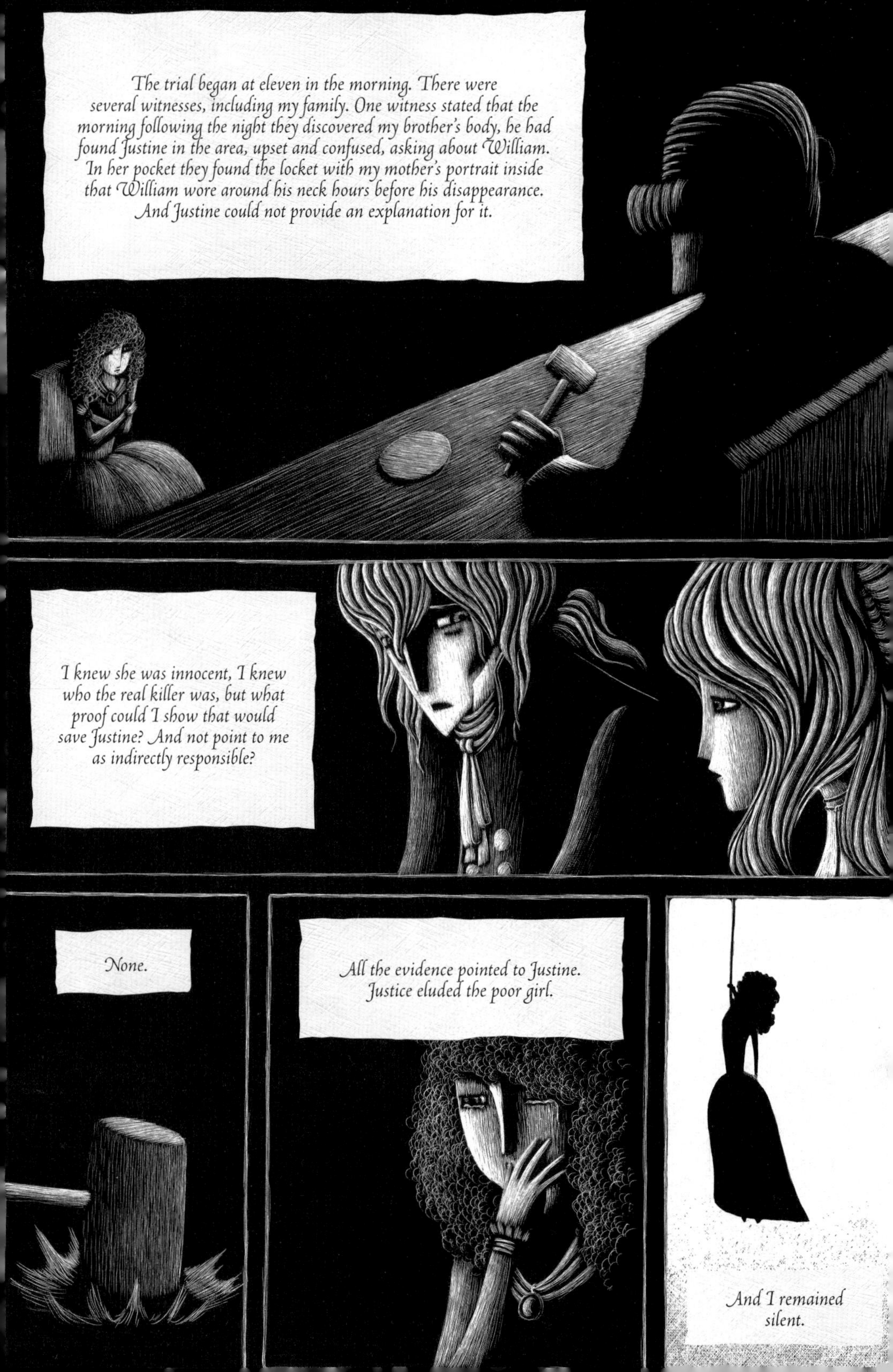
The trial began at eleven in the morning. There were several witnesses, including my family. One witness stated that the morning following the night they discovered my brother's body, he had found Justine in the area, upset and confused, asking about William. In her pocket they found the locket with my mother's portrait inside that William wore around his neck hours before his disappearance. And Justine could not provide an explanation for it.
I knew she was innocent, I knew who the real killer was, but what proof could I show that would save Justine? And not point to me as indirectly responsible?
None.
All the evidence pointed to Justine. Justice eluded the poor girl.
And I remained silent.

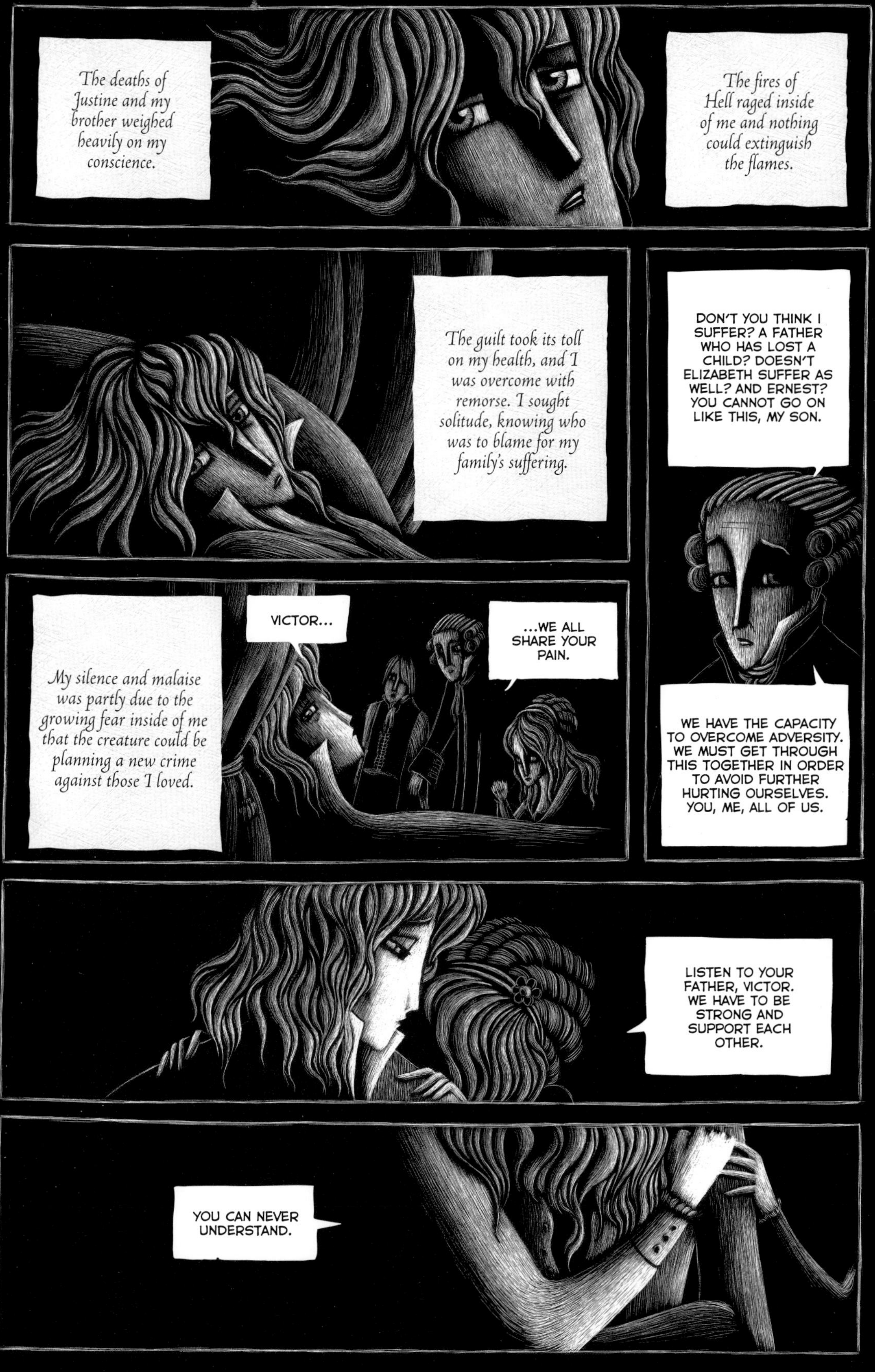

The deaths of Justine and my brother weighed heavily on my conscience.
The fires of Hell raged inside of me and nothing could extinguish the flames.
The guilt took its toll on my health, and I was overcome with remorse. I sought solitude, knowing who was to blame for my family's suffering.
DON'T YOU THINK I SUFFER? A FATHER WHO HAS LOST A CHILD? DOESN'T ELIZABETH SUFFER AS WELL? AND ERNEST? YOU CANNOT GO ON LIKE THIS, MY SON.
My silence and malaise was partly due to the growing fear inside of me that the creature could be planning a new crime against those I loved.
VICTOR...
...WE ALL SHARE YOUR PAIN.
WE HAVE THE CAPACITY TO OVERCOME ADVERSITY. WE MUST GET THROUGH THIS TOGETHER IN ORDER TO AVOID FURTHER HURTING OURSELVES. YOU, ME, ALL OF US.
LISTEN TO YOUR FATHER, VICTOR. WE HAVE TO BE STRONG AND SUPPORT EACH OTHER.
YOU CAN NEVER UNDERSTAND.

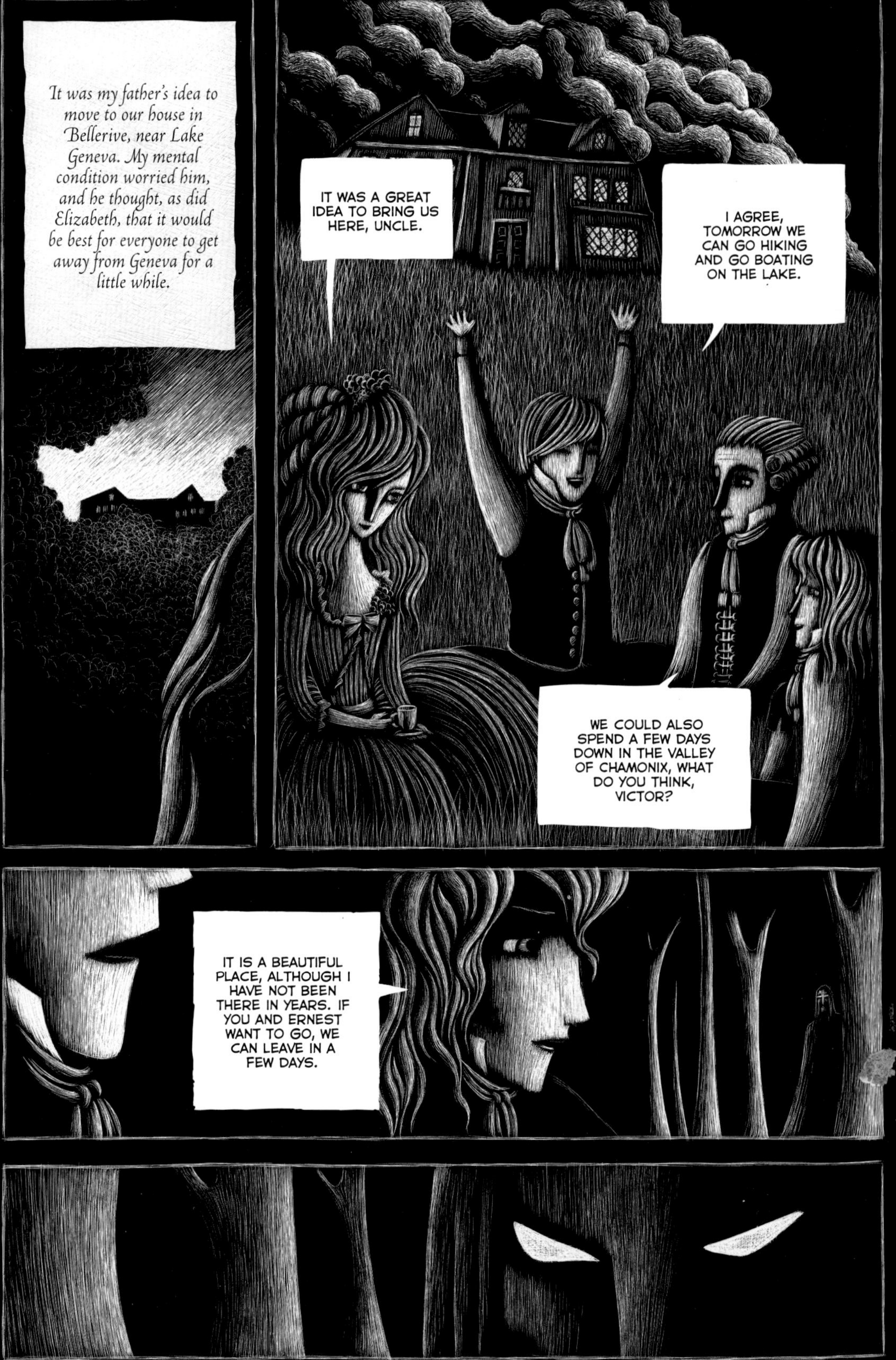
It was my father's idea to move to our house in Bellerive, near Lake Geneva. My mental condition worried him, and he thought, as did Elizabeth, that it would be best for everyone to get away from Geneva for a little while.
IT WAS A GREAT IDEA TO BRING US HERE, UNCLE.
I AGREE, TOMORROW WE CAN GO HIKING AND GO BOATING ON THE LAKE.
WE COULD ALSO SPEND A FEW DAYS DOWN IN THE VALLEY OF CHAMONIX, WHAT DO YOU THINK, VICTOR?
IT IS A BEAUTIFUL PLACE, ALTHOUGH I HAVE NOT BEEN THERE IN YEARS. IF YOU AND ERNEST WANT TO GO, WE CAN LEAVE IN A FEW DAYS.

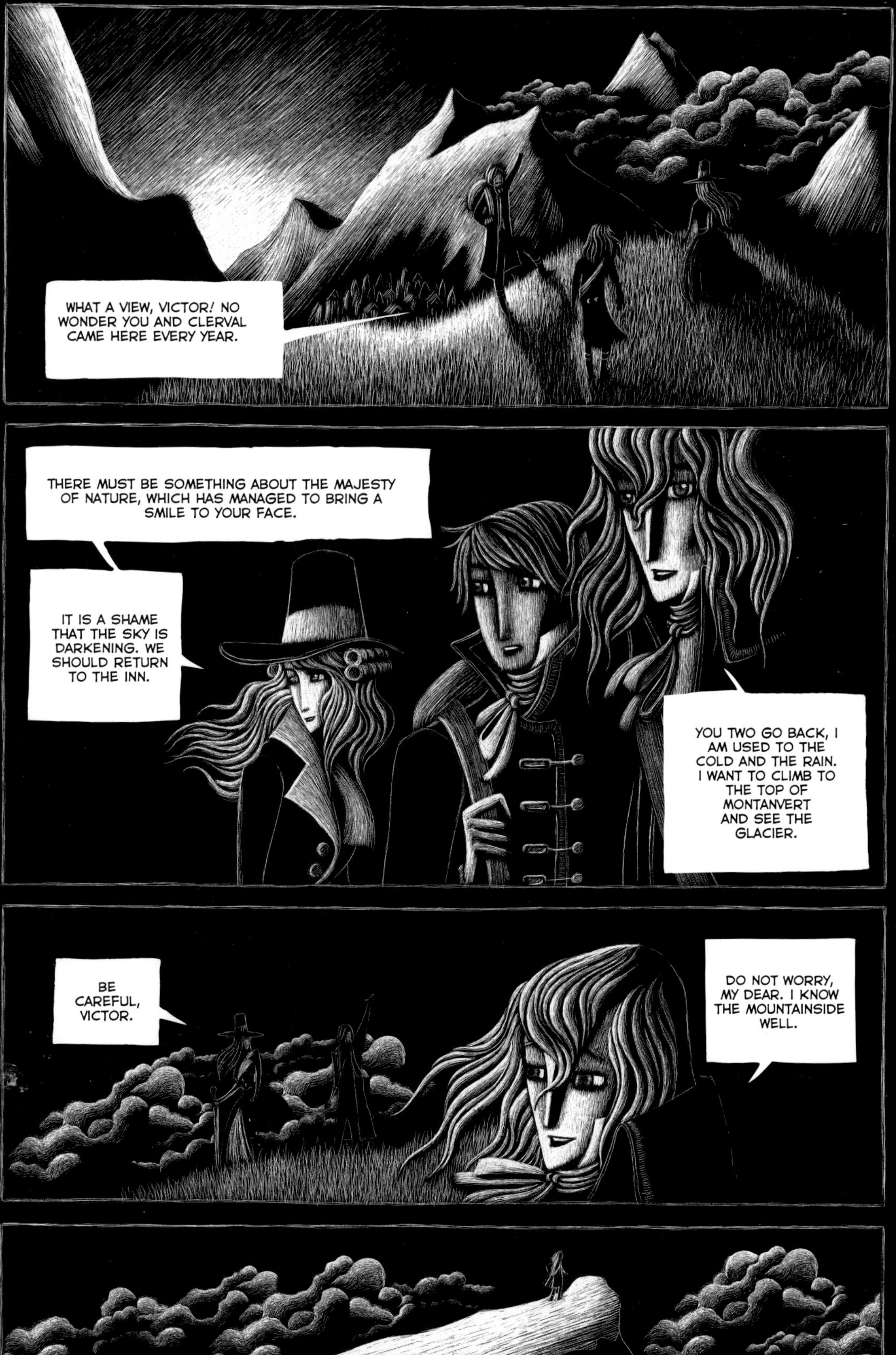

WHAT A VIEW, VICTOR! NO WONDER YOU AND CLERVAL CAME HERE EVERY YEAR.
THERE MUST BE SOMETHING ABOUT THE MAJESTY OF NATURE, WHICH HAS MANAGED TO BRING A SMILE TO YOUR FACE.
IT IS A SHAME THAT THE SKY IS DARKENING. WE SHOULD RETURN TO THE INN.
YOU TWO GO BACK, I AM USED TO THE COLD AND THE RAIN. I WANT TO CLIMB TO THE TOP OF MONTANVERT AND SEE THE GLACIER.
BE CAREFUL, VICTOR.
DO NOT WORRY, MY DEAR. I KNOW THE MOUNTAINSIDE WELL.

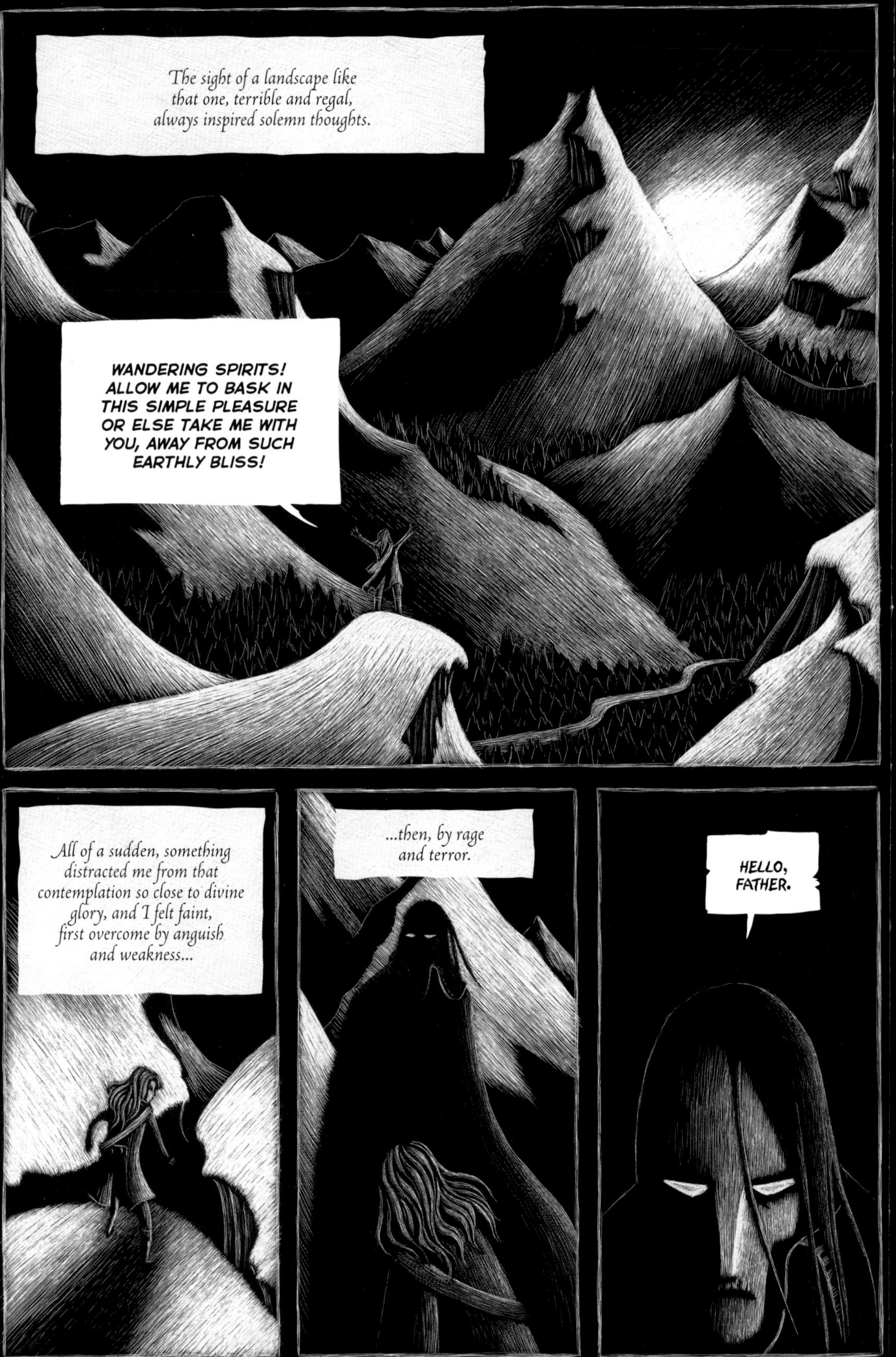
The sight of a landscape like that one, terrible and regal, always inspired solemn thoughts.
WANDERING SPIRITS! ALLOW ME TO BASK IN THIS SIMPLE PLEASURE OR ELSE TAKE ME WITH YOU, AWAY FROM SUCH EARTHLY BLISS!
All of a sudden, something distracted me from that contemplation so close to divine glory, and I felt faint, first overcome by anguish and weakness...
...then, by rage and terror.
HELLO, FATHER.

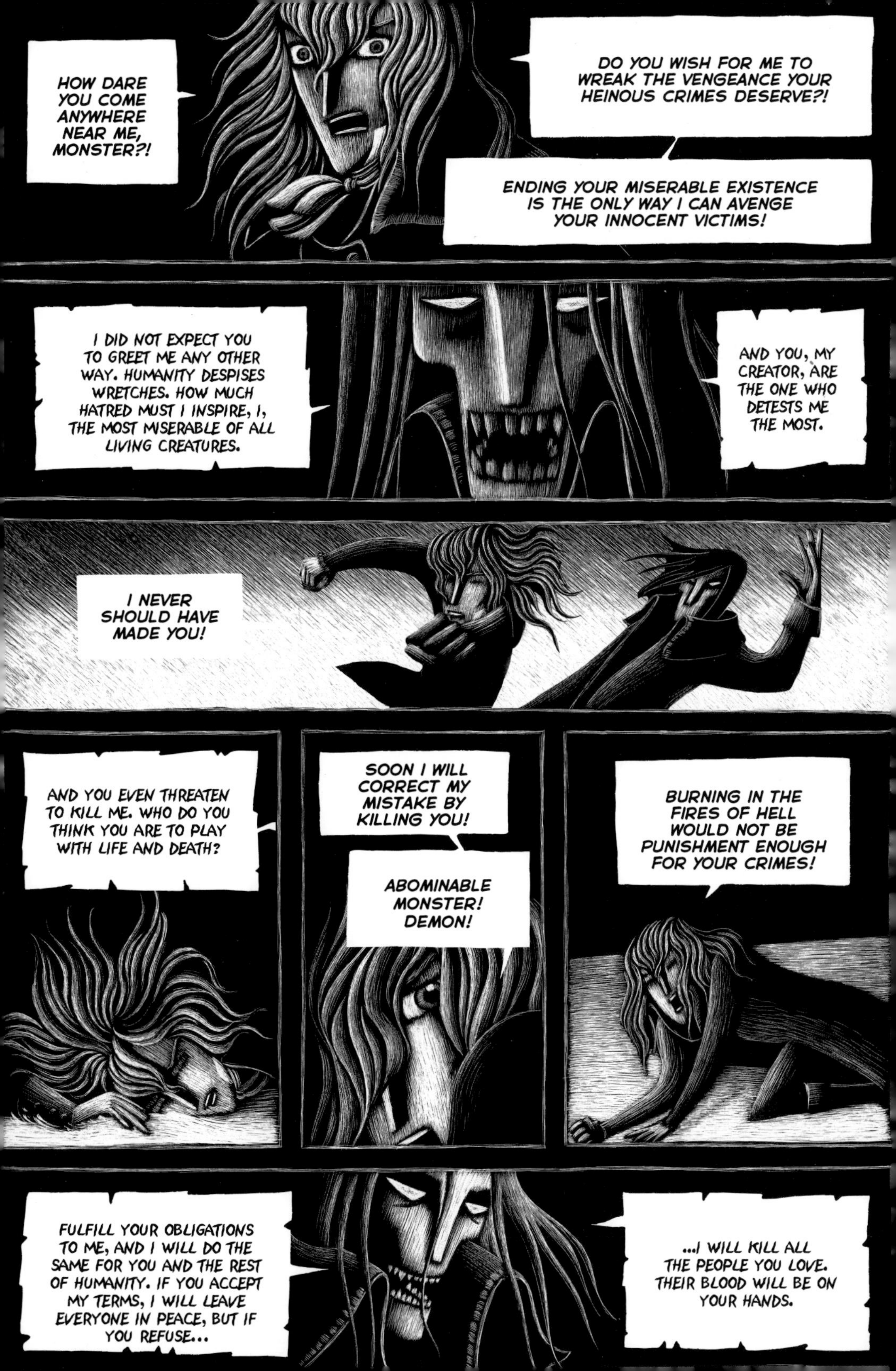
HOW DARE YOU COME ANYWHERE NEAR ME, MONSTER?!
DO YOU WISH FOR ME TO WREAK THE VENGEANCE YOUR HEINOUS CRIMES DESERVE?!
ENDING YOUR MISERABLE EXISTENCE IS THE ONLY WAY I CAN AVENGE YOUR INNOCENT VICTIMS!
I DID NOT EXPECT YOU TO GREET ME ANY OTHER WAY. HUMANITY DESPISES WRETCHES. HOW MUCH HATRED MUST I INSPIRE, I, THE MOST MISERABLE OF ALL LIVING CREATURES.
AND YOU, MY CREATOR, ARE THE ONE WHO DETESTS ME THE MOST.
I NEVER SHOULD HAVE MADE YOU!
AND YOU EVEN THREATEN TO KILL ME. WHO DO YOU THINK YOU ARE TO PLAY WITH LIFE AND DEATH?
SOON I WILL CORRECT MY MISTAKE BY KILLING YOU!
ABOMINABLE MONSTER! DEMON!
BURNING IN THE FIRES OF HELL WOULD NOT BE PUNISHMENT ENOUGH FOR YOUR CRIMES!
FULFILL YOUR OBLIGATIONS TO ME, AND I WILL DO THE SAME FOR YOU AND THE REST OF HUMANITY. IF YOU ACCEPT MY TERMS, I WILL LEAVE EVERYONE IN PEACE, BUT IF YOU REFUSE...
...I WILL KILL ALL THE PEOPLE YOU LOVE. THEIR BLOOD WILL BE ON YOUR HANDS.

NEVER! I WILL NOT LISTEN TO ANOTHER WORD! I WILL NEVER GIVE IN TO YOUR DEMANDS! MURDERER!

WE WILL FIGHT TO THE DEATH!

CALM YOURSELF, FATHER. HAVE I NOT SUFFERED ENOUGH? WHAT CAN I DO TO MAKE YOU PITY ME AND NOT HATE ME?

DO YOU NOT FEEL EVEN A MODICUM OF REMORSE FOR ABANDONING ME AFTER GIVING ME LIFE?

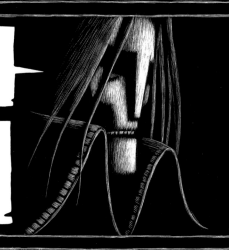

HOW CAN YOU SPEAK OF JUSTICE, YOU, WHO DENIES ME THE RIGHT TO CALL YOU FATHER? I AM LIKE THE FALLEN ANGEL, CREATED ON A WHIM AND DEPRIVED OF HAPPINESS WITHOUT HAVING COMMITTED A SINGLE SIN.

BELIEVE ME WHEN I TELL YOU THAT I WAS BORN GOOD. BUT YOU ABANDONED ME. I TRIED TO BE ACCEPTED BY OTHERS BUT WAS MET WITH ONLY REJECTION AND FEAR. IS IT NOT LOGICAL FOR ME TO HATE THOSE WHO LOATHE ME? I EXPECTED THOSE WHO WERE AS MISERABLE AS I AM TO UNDERSTAND AND SYMPATHIZE.

YOU HAVE THE POWER TO GIVE ME WHAT I WANT AND TO FREE THE WORLD OF AN EVIL FOR WHICH YOU ARE SOLELY RESPONSIBLE, FRANKENSTEIN.

YES, I KNOW YOUR NAME, DOES IT SURPRISE YOU?

I BEG YOU TO LISTEN TO ME. PITY ME AND LISTEN; GIVE ME THE OPPORTUNITY TO TELL YOU MY STORY. ACCOMPANY ME TO A CABIN ON THE TOP OF THIS MOUNTAIN AND, ONCE YOU HEAR MY STORY, THINK ABOUT IT, AND THEN MAKE A DECISION.

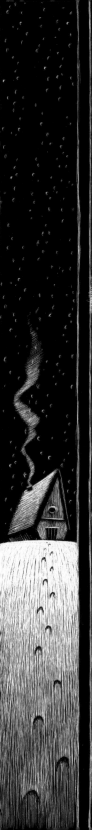

I observed how the monster started a fire. I was quite surprised. I suppose that is why I agreed to hear his story. I was curious. Perhaps this was the first time I truly understood the duties a creator had to his creation.

As a naturalist, I was intrigued by his pain, his desires, how he came to learn man's customs and ways, his speech, possibly the ability to read...

But above all, I was waiting for him to confess to my brother's murder.

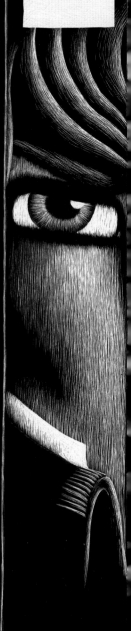

...Or maybe I just wanted to know about his loneliness and persecution.

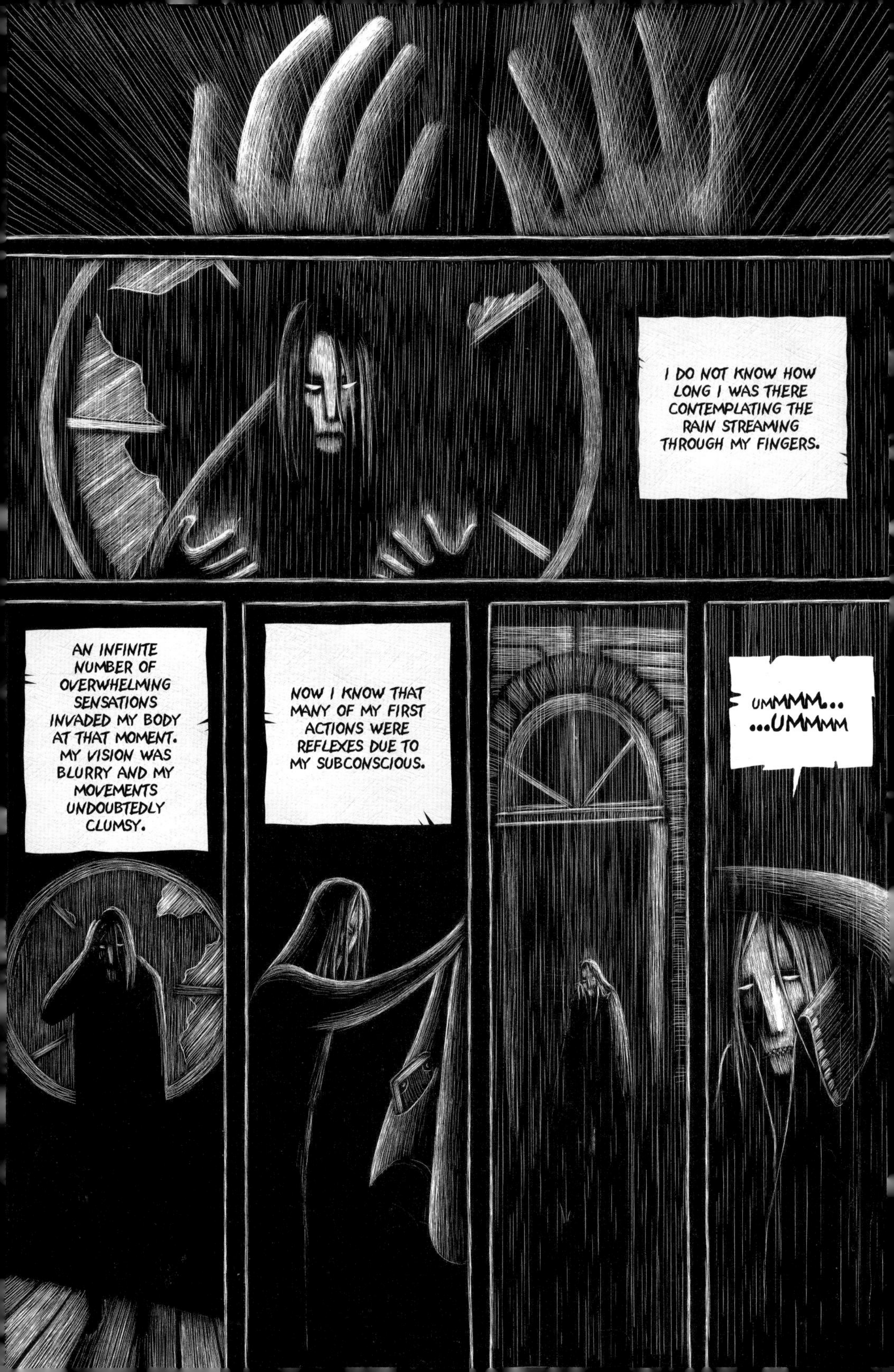
I DO NOT KNOW HOW LONG I WAS THERE CONTEMPLATING THE RAIN STREAMING THROUGH MY FINGERS.
AN INFINITE NUMBER OF OVERWHELMING SENSATIONS INVADED MY BODY AT THAT MOMENT. MY VISION WAS BLURRY AND MY MOVEMENTS UNDOUBTEDLY CLUMSY.
NOW I KNOW THAT MANY OF MY FIRST ACTIONS WERE REFLEXES DUE TO MY SUBCONSCIOUS.
UMMMM...
...UMMMM

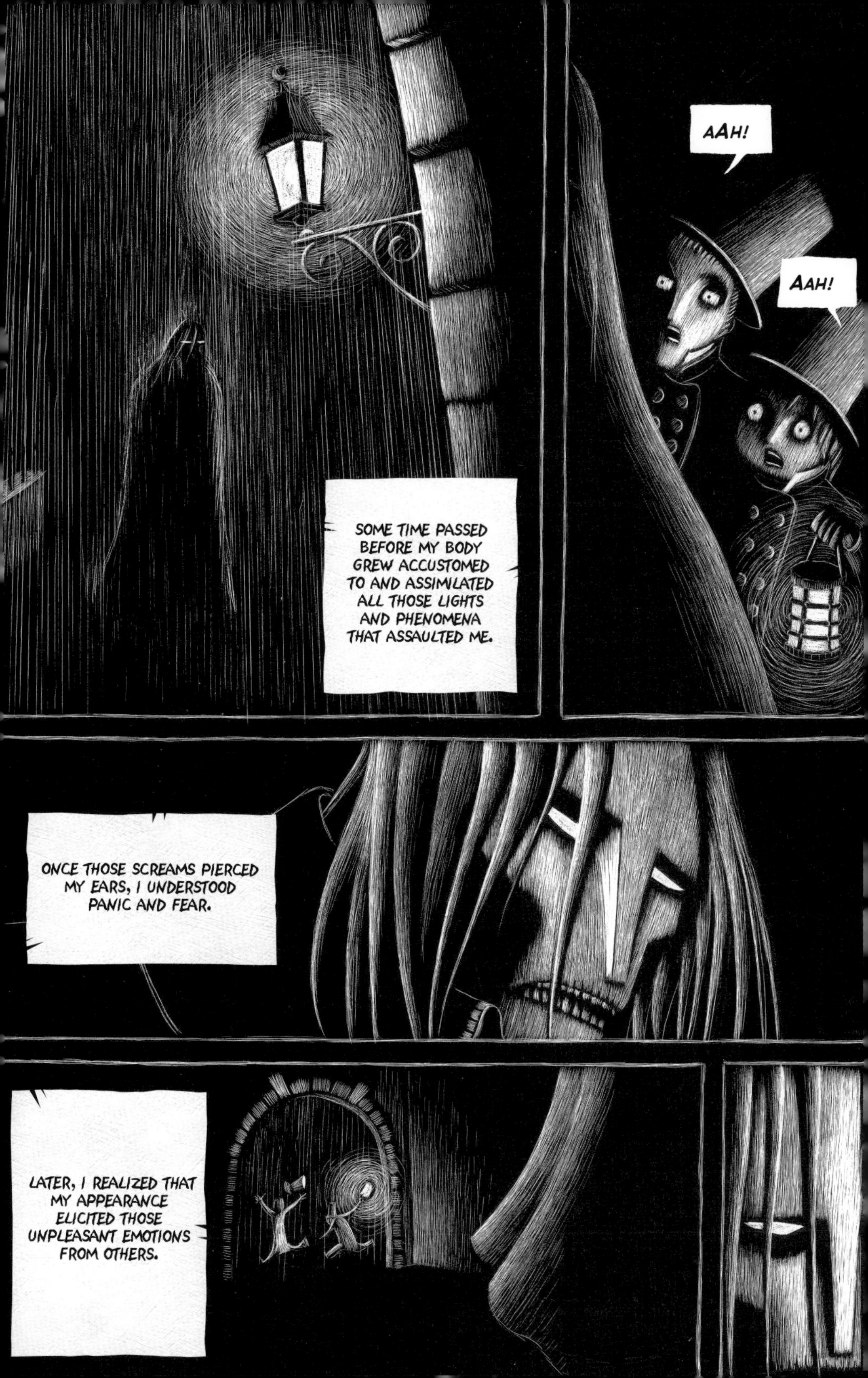
SOME TIME PASSED BEFORE MY BODY GREW ACCUSTOMED TO AND ASSIMILATED ALL THOSE LIGHTS AND PHENOMENA THAT ASSAULTED ME.
AAH!
AAH!
ONCE THOSE SCREAMS PIERCED MY EARS, I UNDERSTOOD PANIC AND FEAR.
LATER, I REALIZED THAT MY APPEARANCE ELICITED THOSE UNPLEASANT EMOTIONS FROM OTHERS.

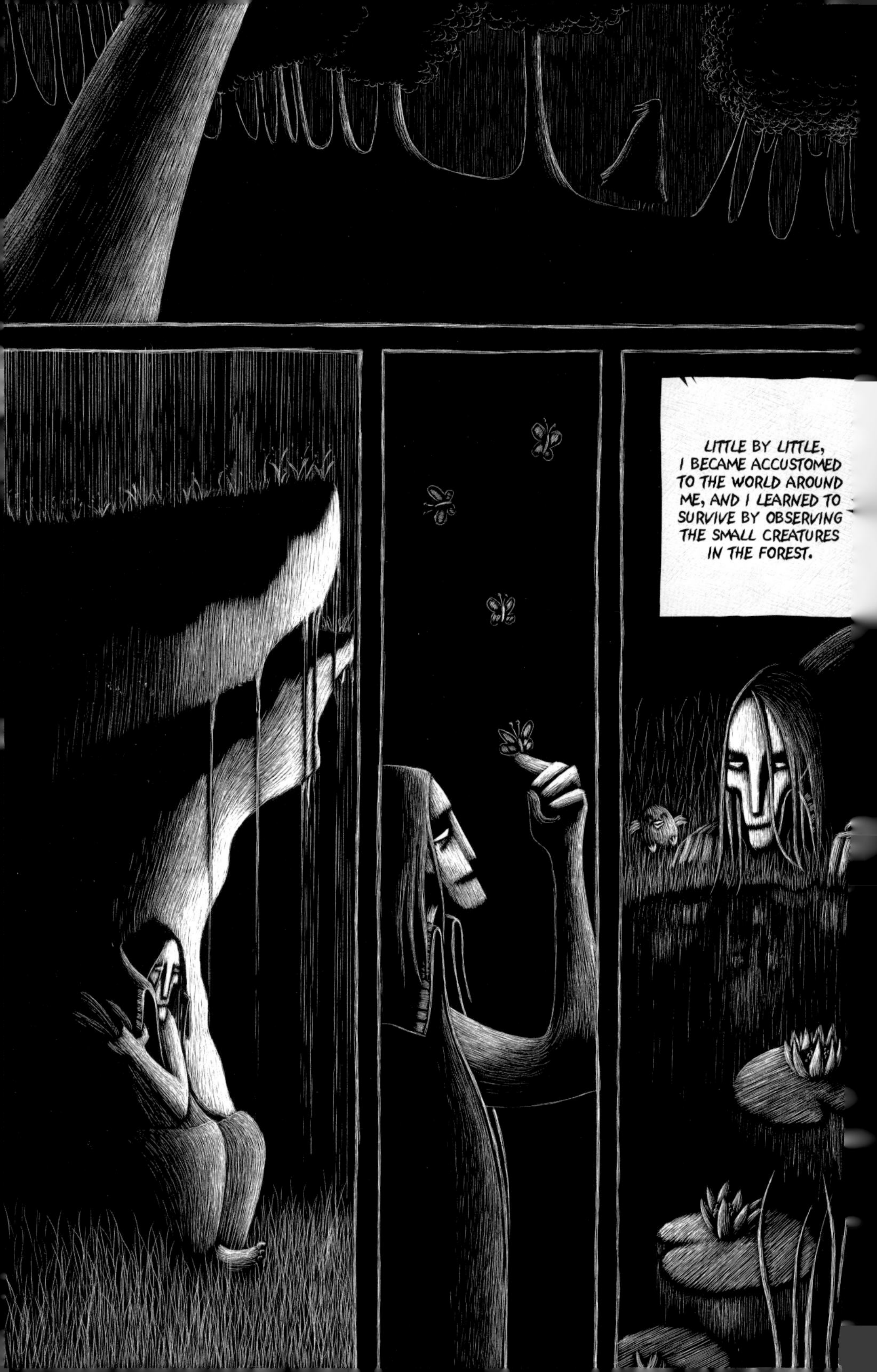
LITTLE BY LITTLE, I BECAME ACCUSTOMED TO THE WORLD AROUND ME, AND I LEARNED TO SURVIVE BY OBSERVING THE SMALL CREATURES IN THE FOREST.

TO MY REGRET, I LEARNED THAT I HAD TO STAY AWAY FROM PEOPLE AND THEIR VILLAGES...

...TO AVOID INSPIRING THEIR FEAR AND THEIR REACTIONS, WHICH WERE SOMETIMES INCOMPREHENSIBLY VIOLENT.

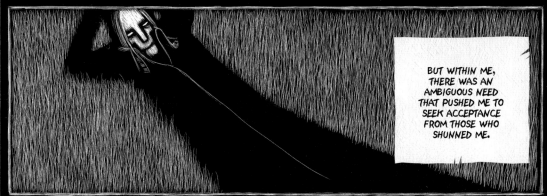

BUT WITHIN ME, THERE WAS AN AMBIGUOUS NEED THAT PUSHED ME TO SEEK ACCEPTANCE FROM THOSE WHO SHUNNED ME.

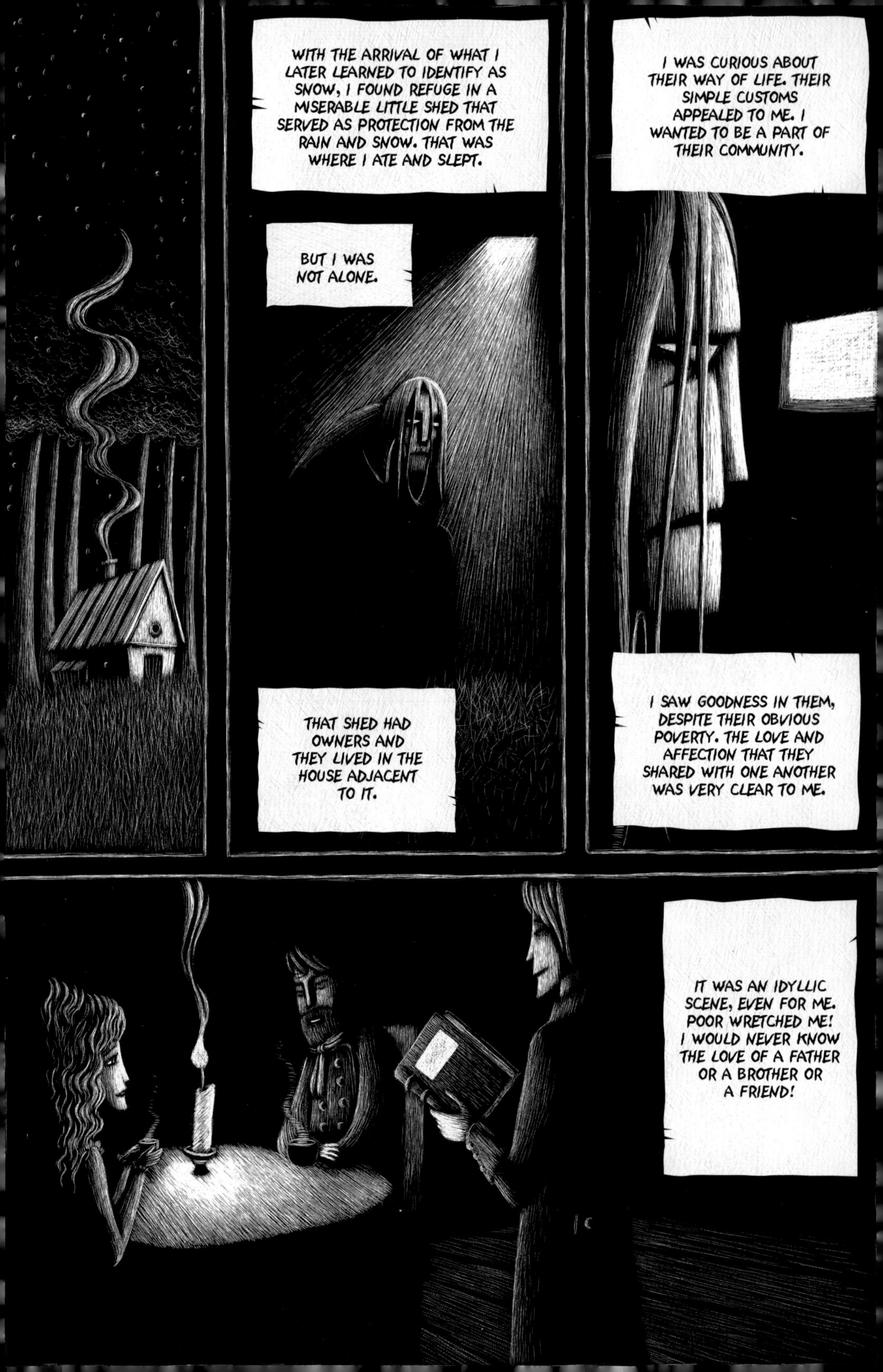
WITH THE ARRIVAL OF WHAT I LATER LEARNED TO IDENTIFY AS SNOW, I FOUND REFUGE IN A MISERABLE LITTLE SHED THAT SERVED AS PROTECTION FROM THE RAIN AND SNOW. THAT WAS WHERE I ATE AND SLEPT.
BUT I WAS NOT ALONE.
THAT SHED HAD OWNERS AND THEY LIVED IN THE HOUSE ADJACENT TO IT.
I WAS CURIOUS ABOUT THEIR WAY OF LIFE. THEIR SIMPLE CUSTOMS APPEALED TO ME. I WANTED TO BE A PART OF THEIR COMMUNITY.
I SAW GOODNESS IN THEM, DESPITE THEIR OBVIOUS POVERTY. THE LOVE AND AFFECTION THAT THEY SHARED WITH ONE ANOTHER WAS VERY CLEAR TO ME.
IT WAS AN IDYLLIC SCENE, EVEN FOR ME. POOR WRETCHED ME! I WOULD NEVER KNOW THE LOVE OF A FATHER OR A BROTHER OR A FRIEND!

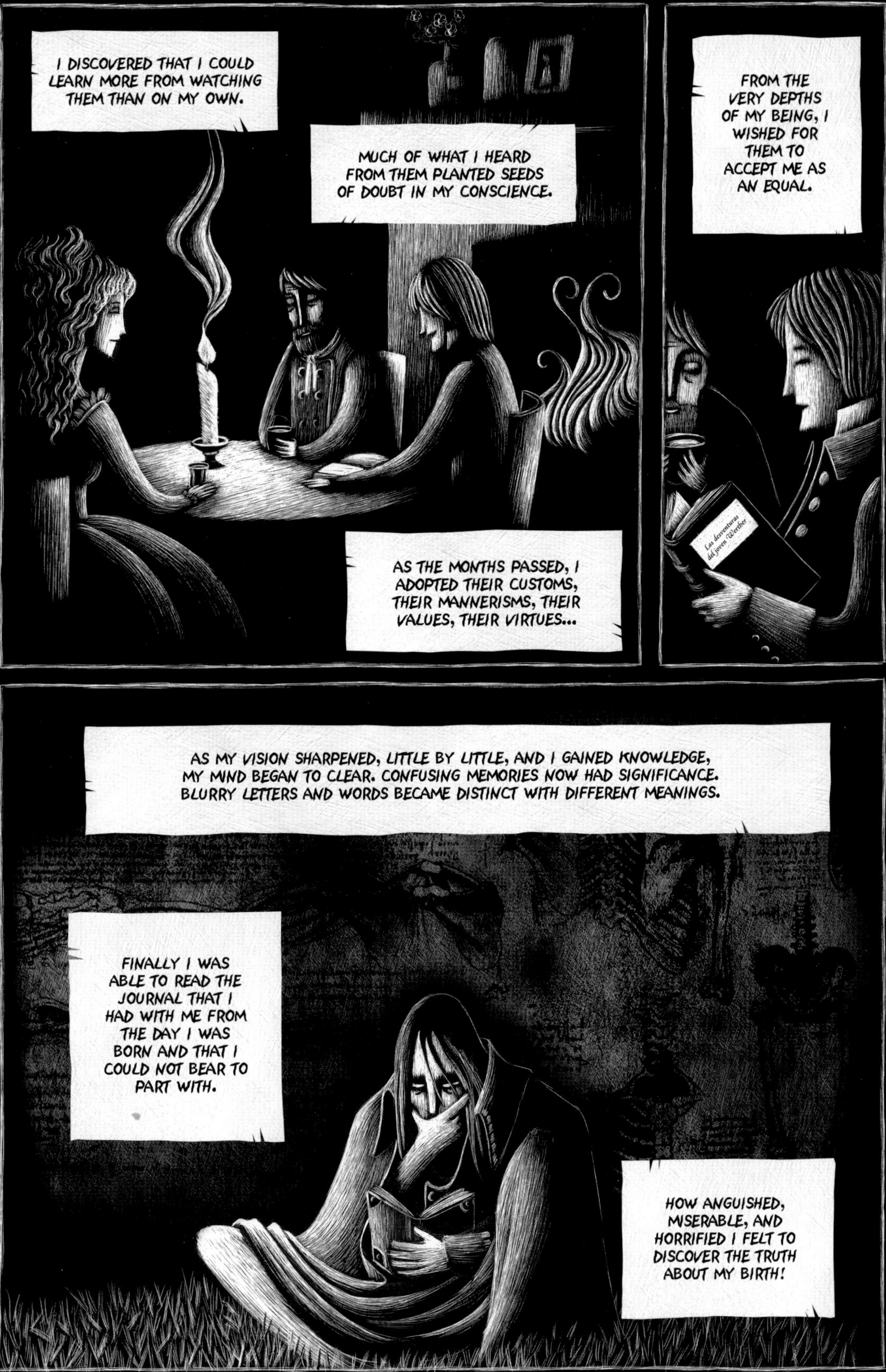
I DISCOVERED THAT I COULD LEARN MORE FROM WATCHING THEM THAN ON MY OWN.
MUCH OF WHAT I HEARD FROM THEM PLANTED SEEDS OF DOUBT IN MY CONSCIENCE.
AS THE MONTHS PASSED, I ADOPTED THEIR CUSTOMS, THEIR MANNERISMS, THEIR VALUES, THEIR VIRTUES...
FROM THE VERY DEPTHS OF MY BEING, I WISHED FOR THEM TO ACCEPT ME AS AN EQUAL.
Las desventuras del joven Werther
AS MY VISION SHARPENED, LITTLE BY LITTLE, AND I GAINED KNOWLEDGE, MY MIND BEGAN TO CLEAR. CONFUSING MEMORIES NOW HAD SIGNIFICANCE. BLURRY LETTERS AND WORDS BECAME DISTINCT WITH DIFFERENT MEANINGS.
FINALLY I WAS ABLE TO READ THE JOURNAL THAT I HAD WITH ME FROM THE DAY I WAS BORN AND THAT I COULD NOT BEAR TO PART WITH.
HOW ANGUISHED, MISERABLE, AND HORRIFIED I FELT TO DISCOVER THE TRUTH ABOUT MY BIRTH!

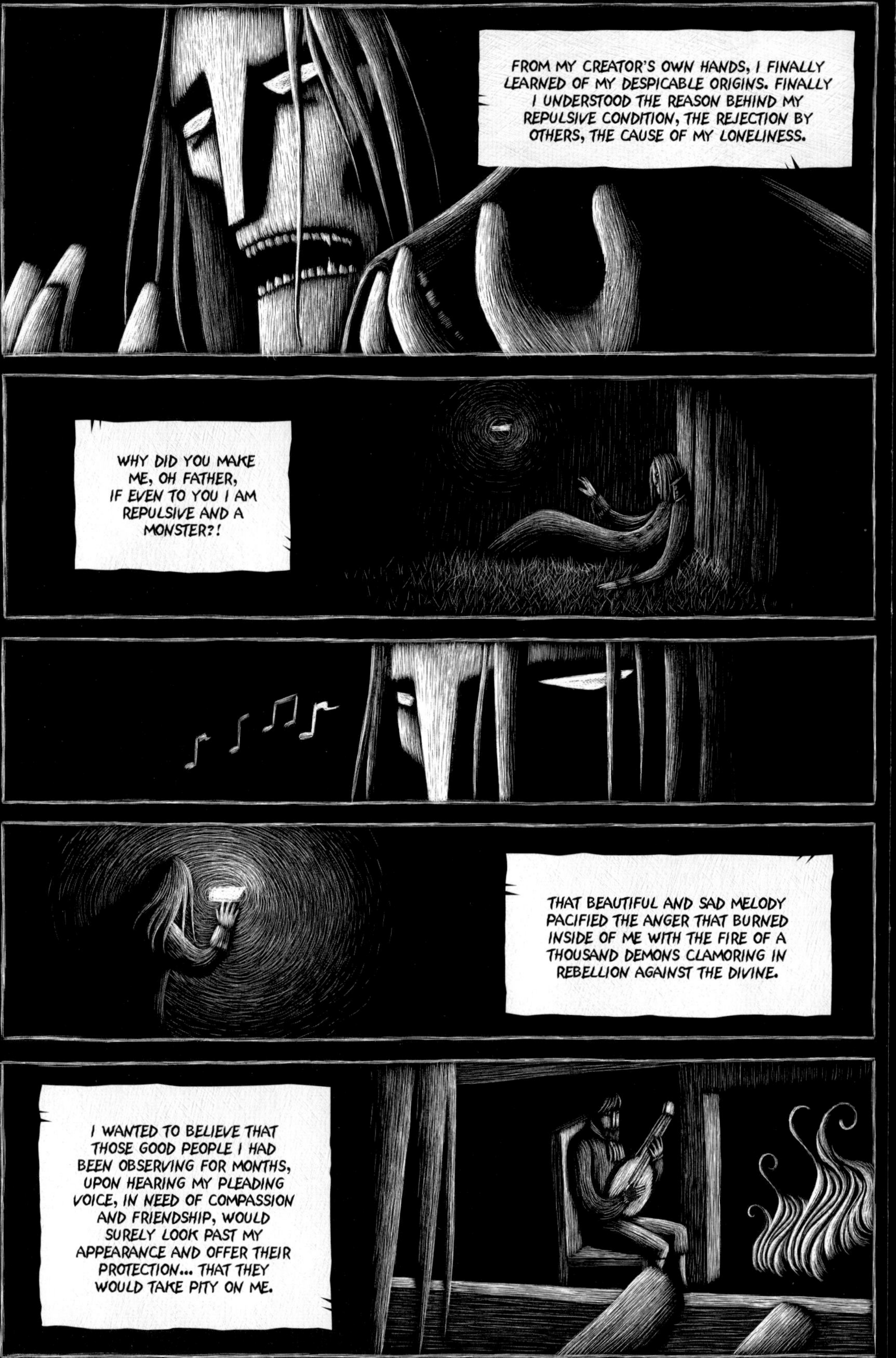
FROM MY CREATOR'S OWN HANDS, I FINALLY LEARNED OF MY DESPICABLE ORIGINS. FINALLY I UNDERSTOOD THE REASON BEHIND MY REPULSIVE CONDITION, THE REJECTION BY OTHERS, THE CAUSE OF MY LONELINESS.
WHY DID YOU MAKE ME, OH FATHER, IF EVEN TO YOU I AM REPULSIVE AND A MONSTER?!
THAT BEAUTIFUL AND SAD MELODY PACIFIED THE ANGER THAT BURNED INSIDE OF ME WITH THE FIRE OF A THOUSAND DEMONS CLAMORING IN REBELLION AGAINST THE DIVINE.
I WANTED TO BELIEVE THAT THOSE GOOD PEOPLE I HAD BEEN OBSERVING FOR MONTHS, UPON HEARING MY PLEADING VOICE, IN NEED OF COMPASSION AND FRIENDSHIP, WOULD SURELY LOOK PAST MY APPEARANCE AND OFFER THEIR PROTECTION... THAT THEY WOULD TAKE PITY ON ME.

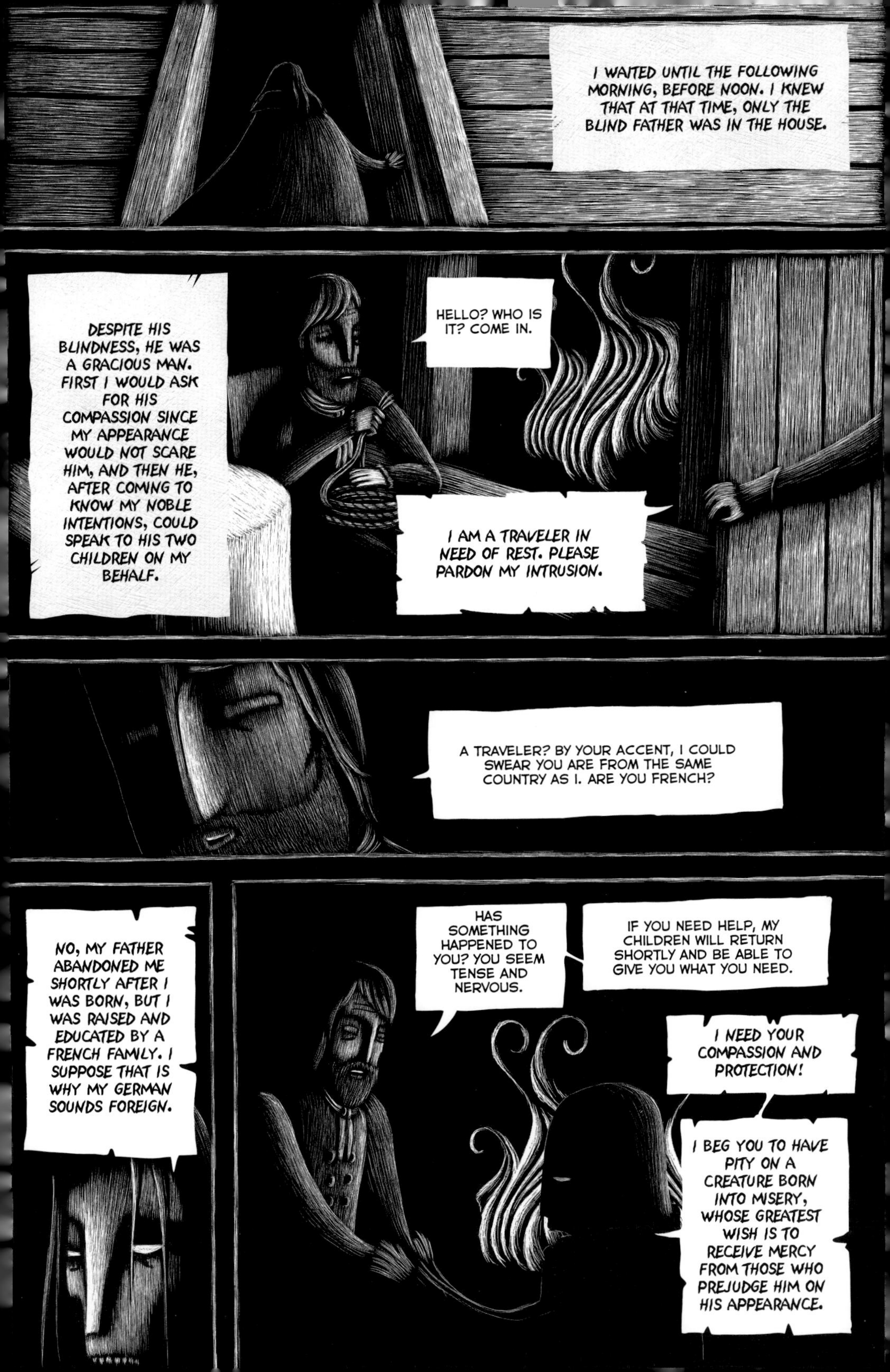
I WAITED UNTIL THE FOLLOWING MORNING, BEFORE NOON. I KNEW THAT AT THAT TIME, ONLY THE BLIND FATHER WAS IN THE HOUSE.
DESPITE HIS BLINDNESS, HE WAS A GRACIOUS MAN. FIRST I WOULD ASK FOR HIS COMPASSION SINCE MY APPEARANCE WOULD NOT SCARE HIM, AND THEN HE, AFTER COMING TO KNOW MY NOBLE INTENTIONS, COULD SPEAK TO HIS TWO CHILDREN ON MY BEHALF.
HELLO? WHO IS IT? COME IN.
I AM A TRAVELER IN NEED OF REST. PLEASE PARDON MY INTRUSION.
A TRAVELER? BY YOUR ACCENT, I COULD SWEAR YOU ARE FROM THE SAME COUNTRY AS I. ARE YOU FRENCH?
NO, MY FATHER ABANDONED ME SHORTLY AFTER I WAS BORN, BUT I WAS RAISED AND EDUCATED BY A FRENCH FAMILY. I SUPPOSE THAT IS WHY MY GERMAN SOUNDS FOREIGN.
HAS SOMETHING HAPPENED TO YOU? YOU SEEM TENSE AND NERVOUS.
IF YOU NEED HELP, MY CHILDREN WILL RETURN SHORTLY AND BE ABLE TO GIVE YOU WHAT YOU NEED.
I NEED YOUR COMPASSION AND PROTECTION!
I BEG YOU TO HAVE PITY ON A CREATURE BORN INTO MISERY, WHOSE GREATEST WISH IS TO RECEIVE MERCY FROM THOSE WHO PREJUDGE HIM ON HIS APPEARANCE.

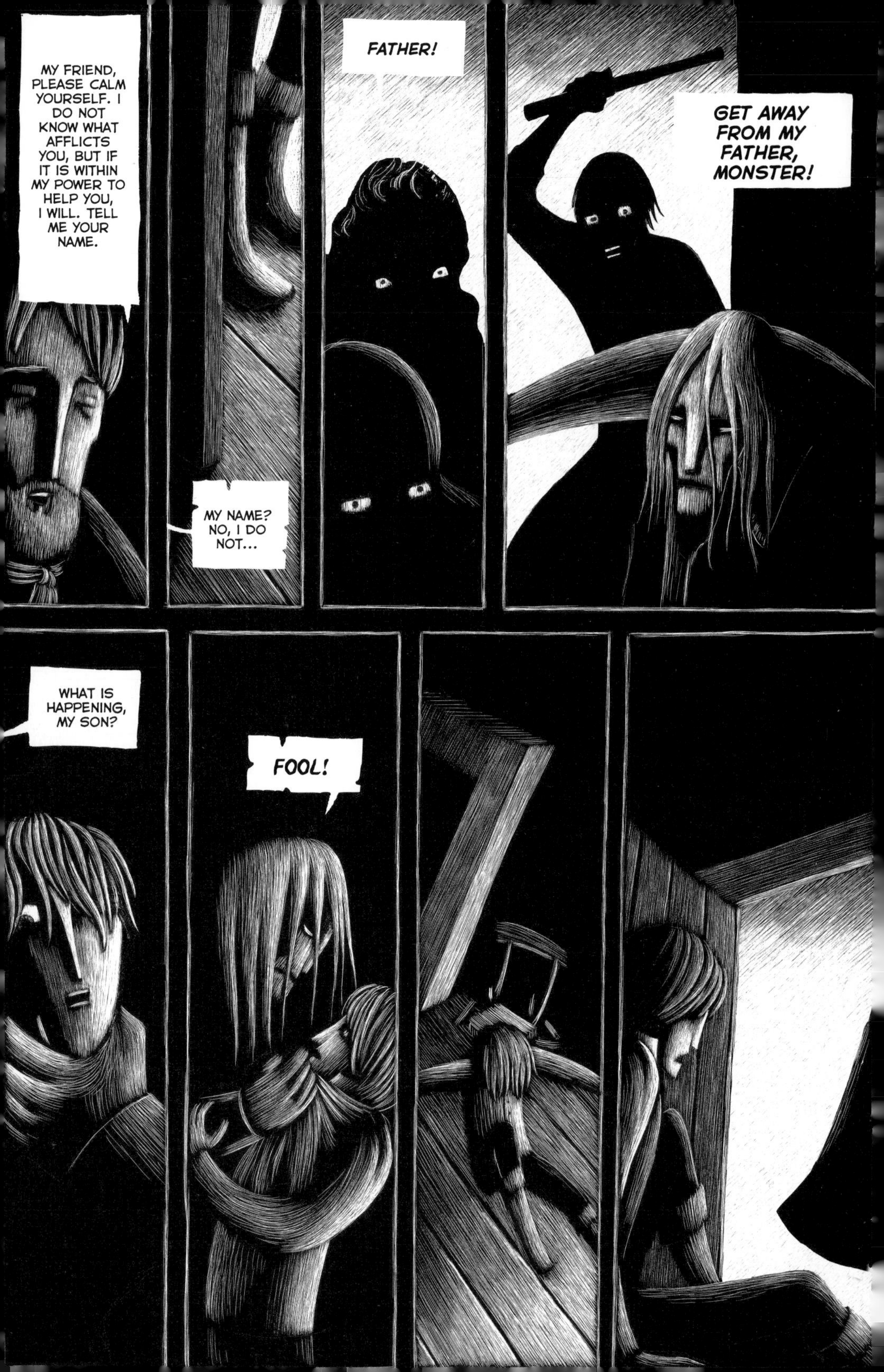
MY FRIEND, PLEASE CALM YOURSELF. I DO NOT KNOW WHAT AFFLICTS YOU, BUT IF IT IS WITHIN MY POWER TO HELP YOU, I WILL. TELL ME YOUR NAME.
MY NAME? NO, I DO NOT...
FATHER!
GET AWAY FROM MY FATHER, MONSTER!
WHAT IS HAPPENING, MY SON?
FOOL!

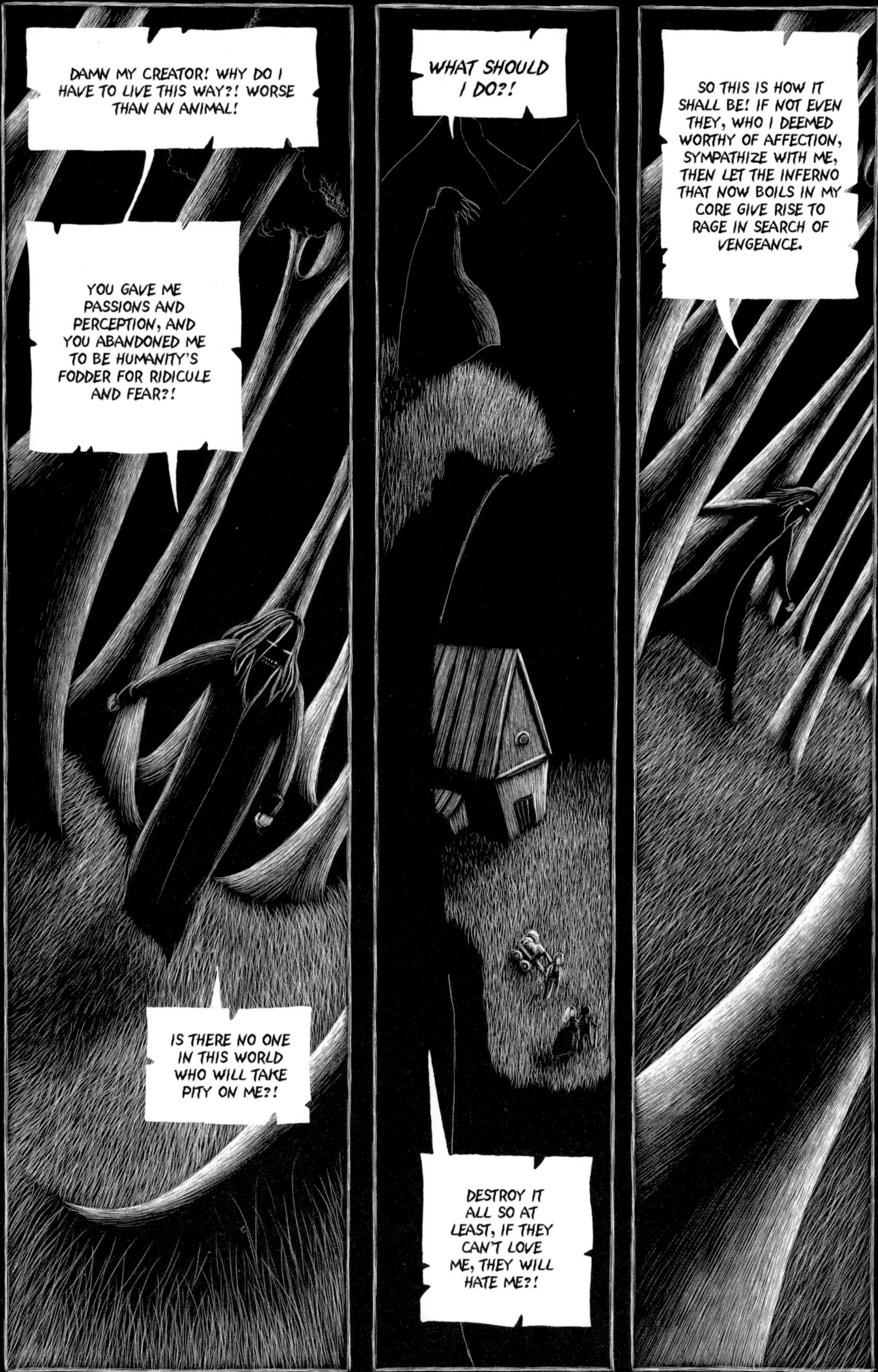
DAMN MY CREATOR! WHY DO I HAVE TO LIVE THIS WAY?! WORSE THAN AN ANIMAL!
YOU GAVE ME PASSIONS AND PERCEPTION, AND YOU ABANDONED ME TO BE HUMANITY'S FODDER FOR RIDICULE AND FEAR?!
IS THERE NO ONE IN THIS WORLD WHO WILL TAKE PITY ON ME?!
WHAT SHOULD I DO?!
DESTROY IT ALL SO AT LEAST, IF THEY CAN'T LOVE ME, THEY WILL HATE ME?!
SO THIS IS HOW IT SHALL BE! IF NOT EVEN THEY, WHO I DEEMED WORTHY OF AFFECTION, SYMPATHIZE WITH ME, THEN LET THE INFERNO THAT NOW BOILS IN MY CORE GIVE RISE TO RAGE IN SEARCH OF VENGEANCE.

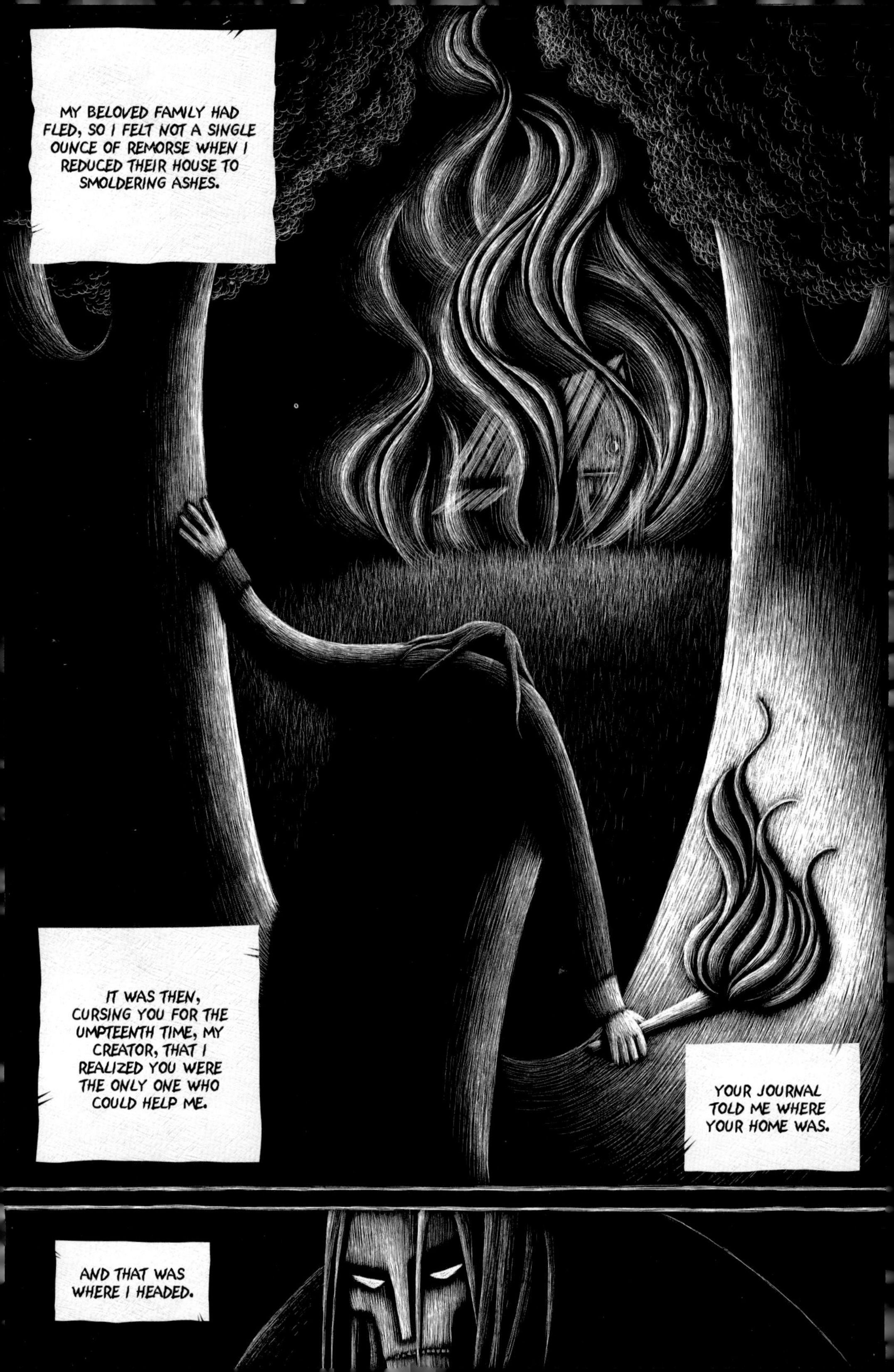
MY BELOVED FAMILY HAD FLED, SO I FELT NOT A SINGLE OUNCE OF REMORSE WHEN I REDUCED THEIR HOUSE TO SMOLDERING ASHES.
IT WAS THEN, CURSING YOU FOR THE UMPTEENTH TIME, MY CREATOR, THAT I REALIZED YOU WERE THE ONLY ONE WHO COULD HELP ME.
YOUR JOURNAL TOLD ME WHERE YOUR HOME WAS.
AND THAT WAS WHERE I HEADED.

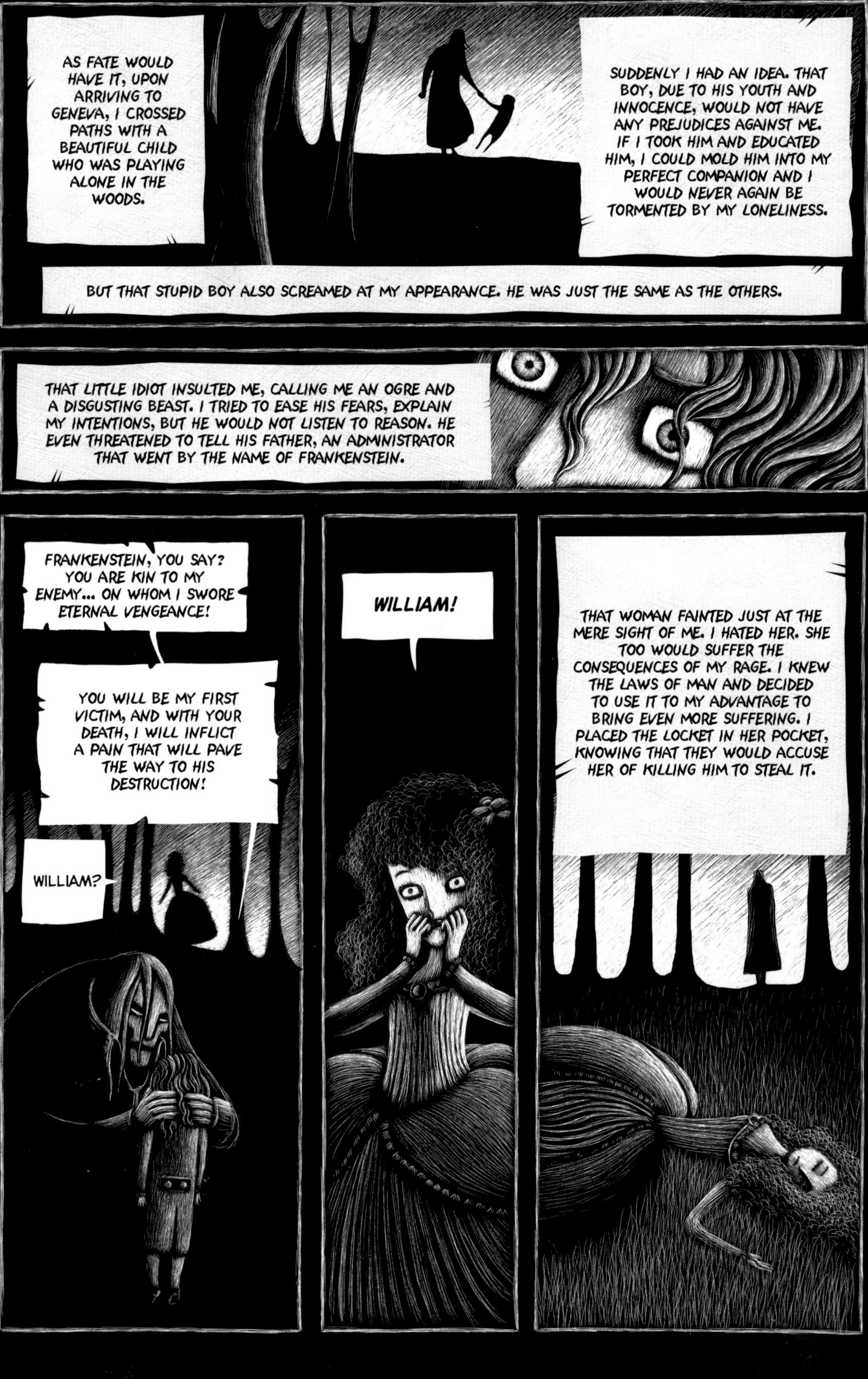
AS FATE WOULD HAVE IT, UPON ARRIVING TO GENEVA, I CROSSED PATHS WITH A BEAUTIFUL CHILD WHO WAS PLAYING ALONE IN THE WOODS.
SUDDENLY I HAD AN IDEA. THAT BOY, DUE TO HIS YOUTH AND INNOCENCE, WOULD NOT HAVE ANY PREJUDICES AGAINST ME. IF I TOOK HIM AND EDUCATED HIM, I COULD MOLD HIM INTO MY PERFECT COMPANION AND I WOULD NEVER AGAIN BE TORMENTED BY MY LONELINESS.
BUT THAT STUPID BOY ALSO SCREAMED AT MY APPEARANCE. HE WAS JUST THE SAME AS THE OTHERS.
THAT LITTLE IDIOT INSULTED ME, CALLING ME AN OGRE AND A DISGUSTING BEAST. I TRIED TO EASE HIS FEARS, EXPLAIN MY INTENTIONS, BUT HE WOULD NOT LISTEN TO REASON. HE EVEN THREATENED TO TELL HIS FATHER, AN ADMINISTRATOR THAT WENT BY THE NAME OF FRANKENSTEIN.
FRANKENSTEIN, YOU SAY? YOU ARE KIN TO MY ENEMY... ON WHOM I SWORE ETERNAL VENGEANCE!
YOU WILL BE MY FIRST VICTIM, AND WITH YOUR DEATH, I WILL INFLICT A PAIN THAT WILL PAVE THE WAY TO HIS DESTRUCTION!
WILLIAM?
WILLIAM!
THAT WOMAN FAINTED JUST AT THE MERE SIGHT OF ME. I HATED HER. SHE TOO WOULD SUFFER THE CONSEQUENCES OF MY RAGE. I KNEW THE LAWS OF MAN AND DECIDED TO USE IT TO MY ADVANTAGE TO BRING EVEN MORE SUFFERING. I PLACED THE LOCKET IN HER POCKET, KNOWING THAT THEY WOULD ACCUSE HER OF KILLING HIM TO STEAL IT.

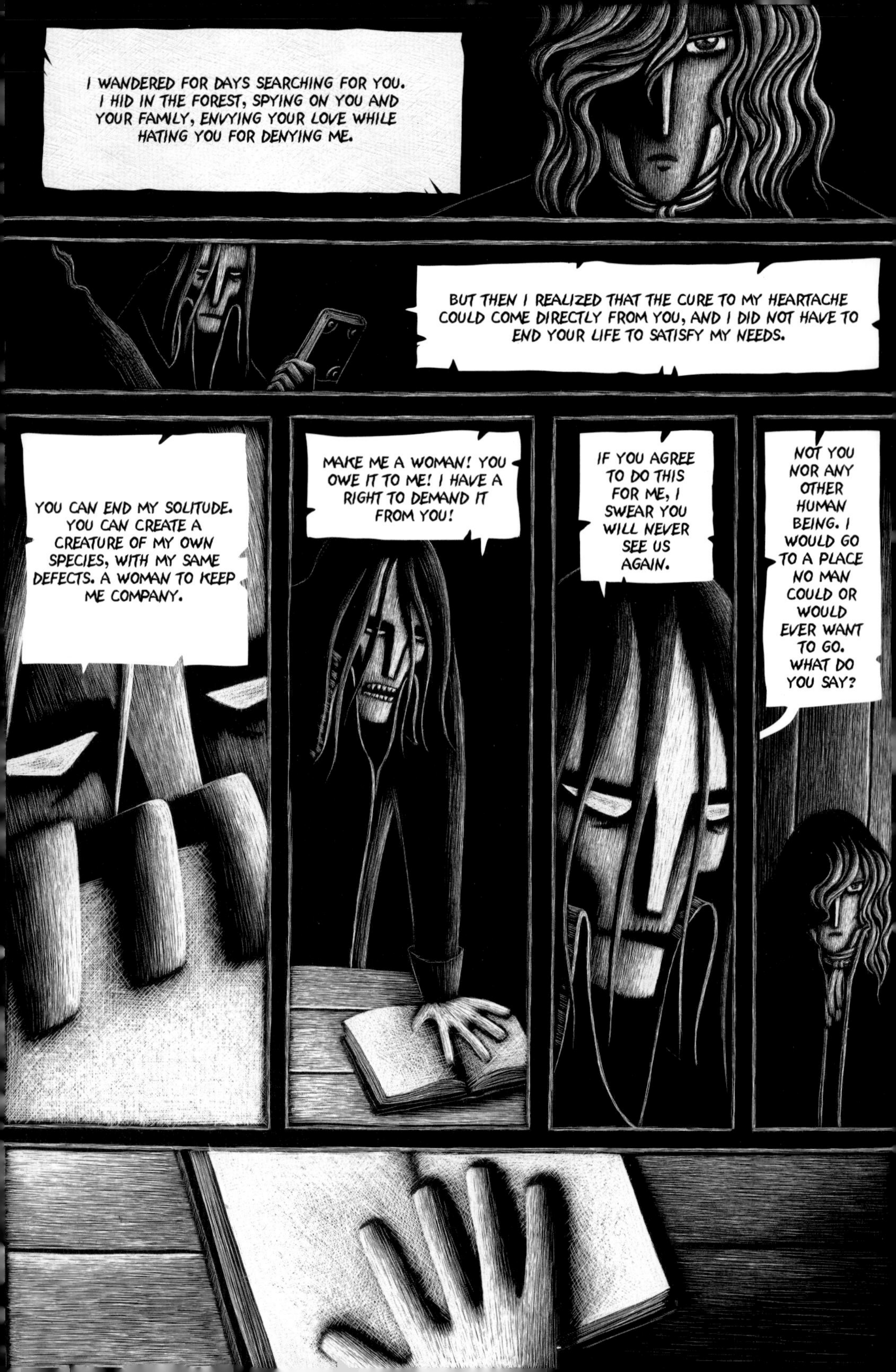
I WANDERED FOR DAYS SEARCHING FOR YOU. I HID IN THE FOREST, SPYING ON YOU AND YOUR FAMILY, ENVYING YOUR LOVE WHILE HATING YOU FOR DENYING ME.
BUT THEN I REALIZED THAT THE CURE TO MY HEARTACHE COULD COME DIRECTLY FROM YOU, AND I DID NOT HAVE TO END YOUR LIFE TO SATISFY MY NEEDS.
YOU CAN END MY SOLITUDE. YOU CAN CREATE A CREATURE OF MY OWN SPECIES, WITH MY SAME DEFECTS. A WOMAN TO KEEP ME COMPANY.
MAKE ME A WOMAN! YOU OWE IT TO ME! I HAVE A RIGHT TO DEMAND IT FROM YOU!
IF YOU AGREE TO DO THIS FOR ME, I SWEAR YOU WILL NEVER SEE US AGAIN.
NOT YOU NOR ANY OTHER HUMAN BEING. I WOULD GO TO A PLACE NO MAN COULD OR WOULD EVER WANT TO GO. WHAT DO YOU SAY?

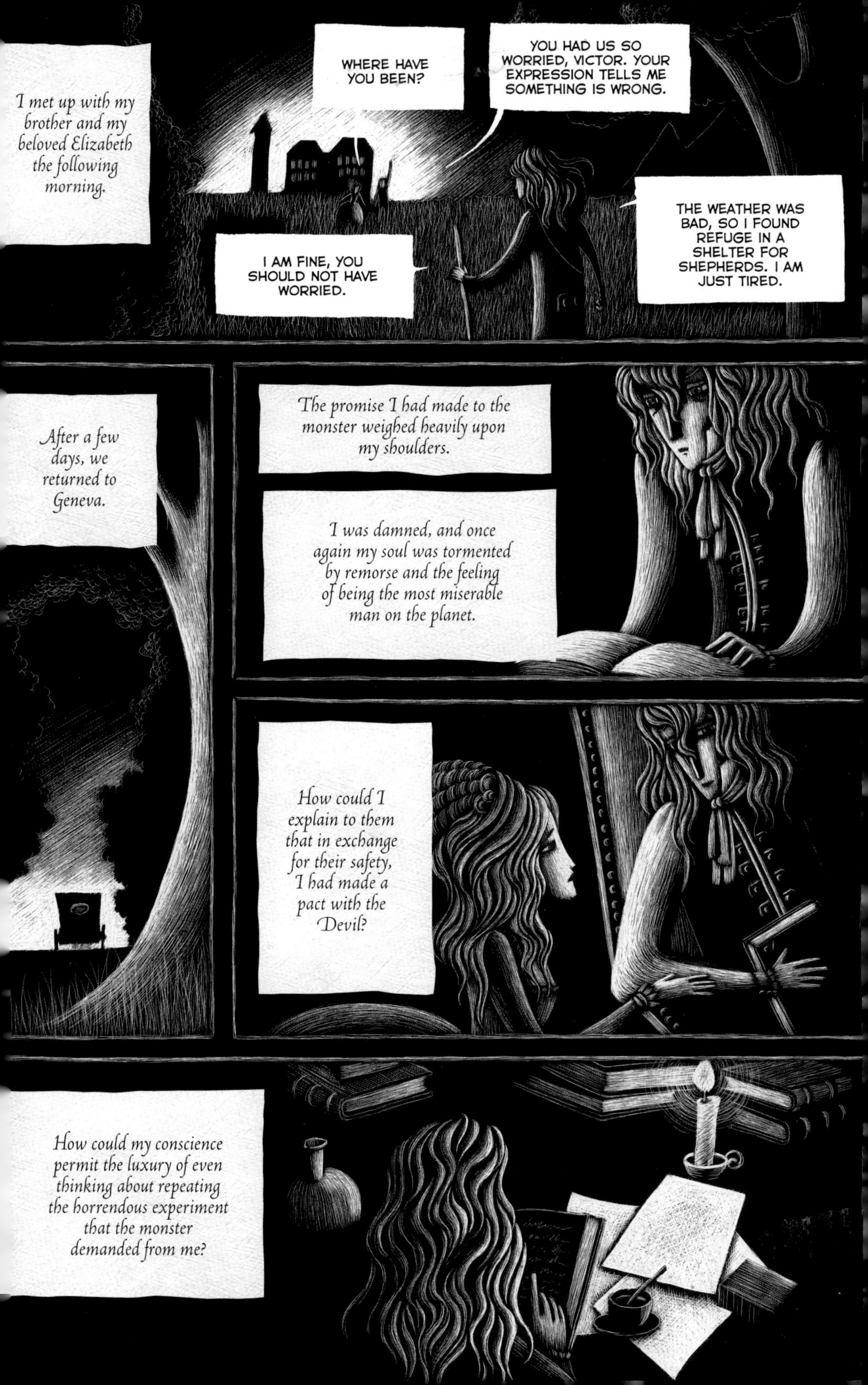
I met up with my brother and my beloved Elizabeth the following morning.
WHERE HAVE YOU BEEN?
YOU HAD US SO WORRIED, VICTOR. YOUR EXPRESSION TELLS ME SOMETHING IS WRONG.
I AM FINE, YOU SHOULD NOT HAVE WORRIED.
THE WEATHER WAS BAD, SO I FOUND REFUGE IN A SHELTER FOR SHEPHERDS. I AM JUST TIRED.
After a few days, we returned to Geneva.
The promise I had made to the monster weighed heavily upon my shoulders.
I was damned, and once again my soul was tormented by remorse and the feeling of being the most miserable man on the planet.
How could I explain to them that in exchange for their safety, I had made a pact with the Devil?
How could my conscience permit the luxury of even thinking about repeating the horrendous experiment that the monster demanded from me?

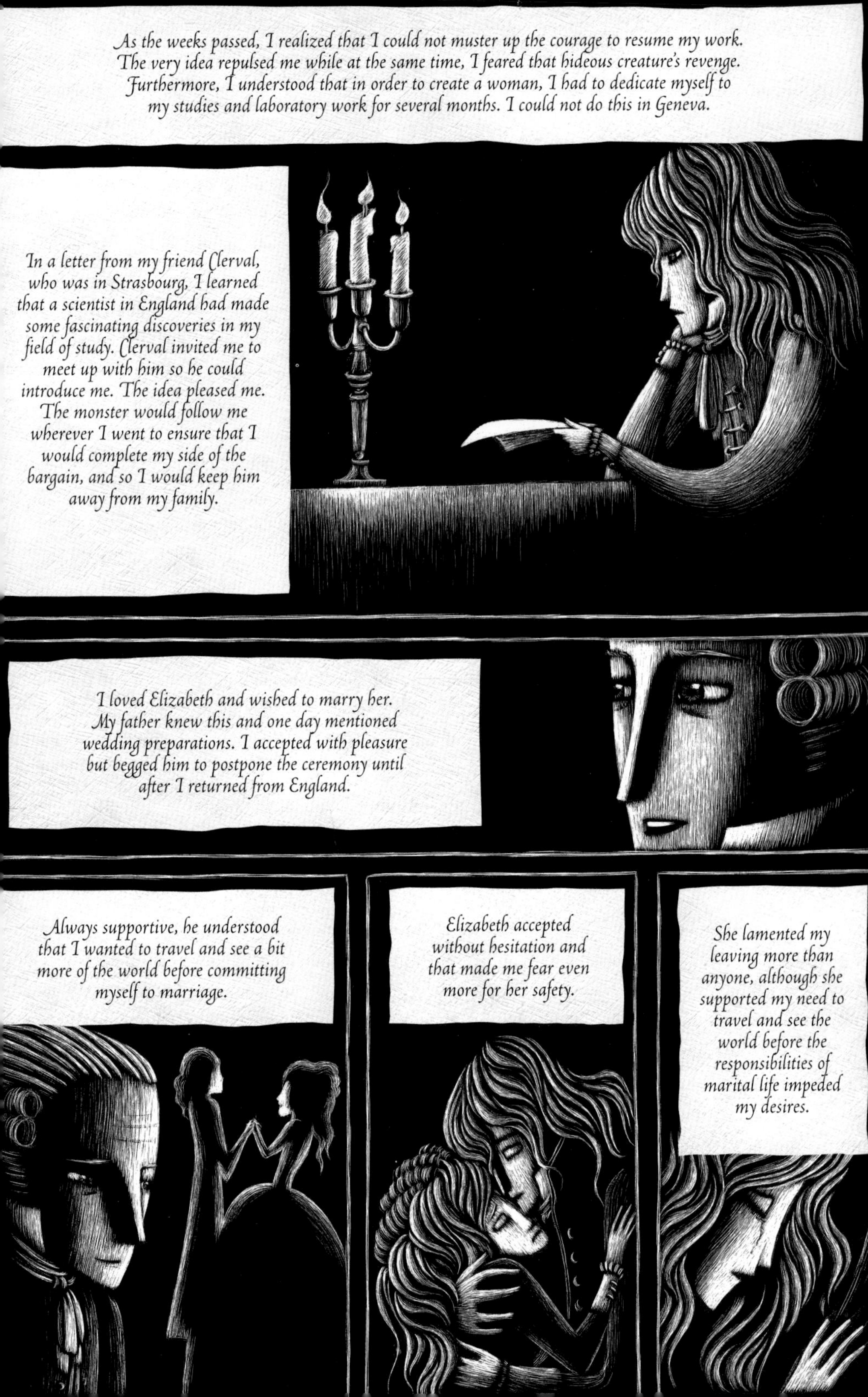
As the weeks passed, I realized that I could not muster up the courage to resume my work. The very idea repulsed me while at the same time, I feared that hideous creature's revenge. Furthermore, I understood that in order to create a woman, I had to dedicate myself to my studies and laboratory work for several months. I could not do this in Geneva.
In a letter from my friend Clerval, who was in Strasbourg, I learned that a scientist in England had made some fascinating discoveries in my field of study. Clerval invited me to meet up with him so he could introduce me. The idea pleased me. The monster would follow me wherever I went to ensure that I would complete my side of the bargain, and so I would keep him away from my family.
I loved Elizabeth and wished to marry her. My father knew this and one day mentioned wedding preparations. I accepted with pleasure but begged him to postpone the ceremony until after I returned from England.
Always supportive, he understood that I wanted to travel and see a bit more of the world before committing myself to marriage.
Elizabeth accepted without hesitation and that made me fear even more for her safety.
She lamented my leaving more than anyone, although she supported my need to travel and see the world before the responsibilities of marital life impeded my desires.

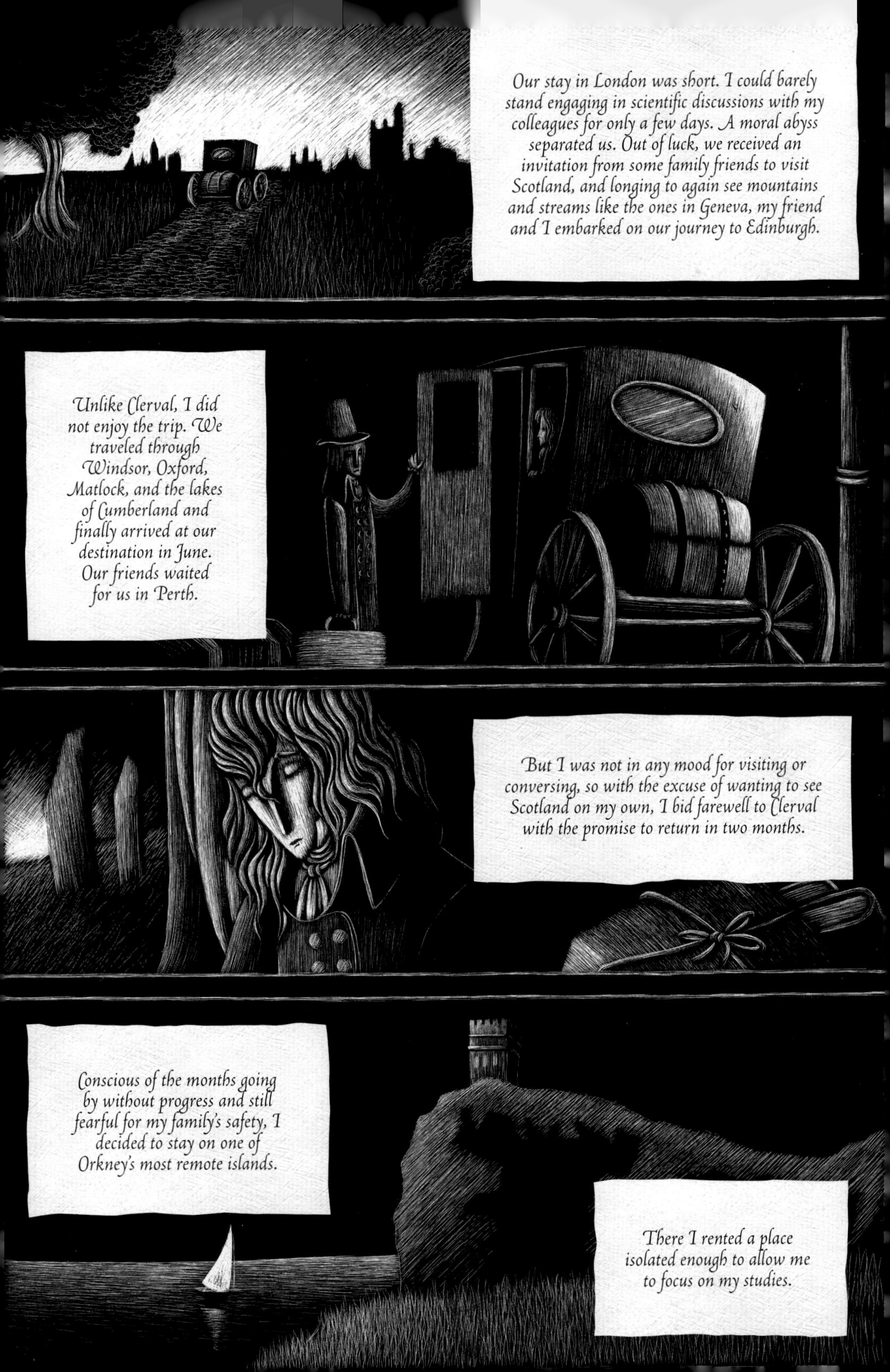
Our stay in London was short. I could barely stand engaging in scientific discussions with my colleagues for only a few days. A moral abyss separated us. Out of luck, we received an invitation from some family friends to visit Scotland, and longing to again see mountains and streams like the ones in Geneva, my friend and I embarked on our journey to Edinburgh.
Unlike Clerval, I did not enjoy the trip. We traveled through Windsor, Oxford, Matlock, and the lakes of Cumberland and finally arrived at our destination in June. Our friends waited for us in Perth.
But I was not in any mood for visiting or conversing, so with the excuse of wanting to see Scotland on my own, I bid farewell to Clerval with the promise to return in two months.
Conscious of the months going by without progress and still fearful for my family's safety, I decided to stay on one of Orkney's most remote islands.
There I rented a place isolated enough to allow me to focus on my studies.

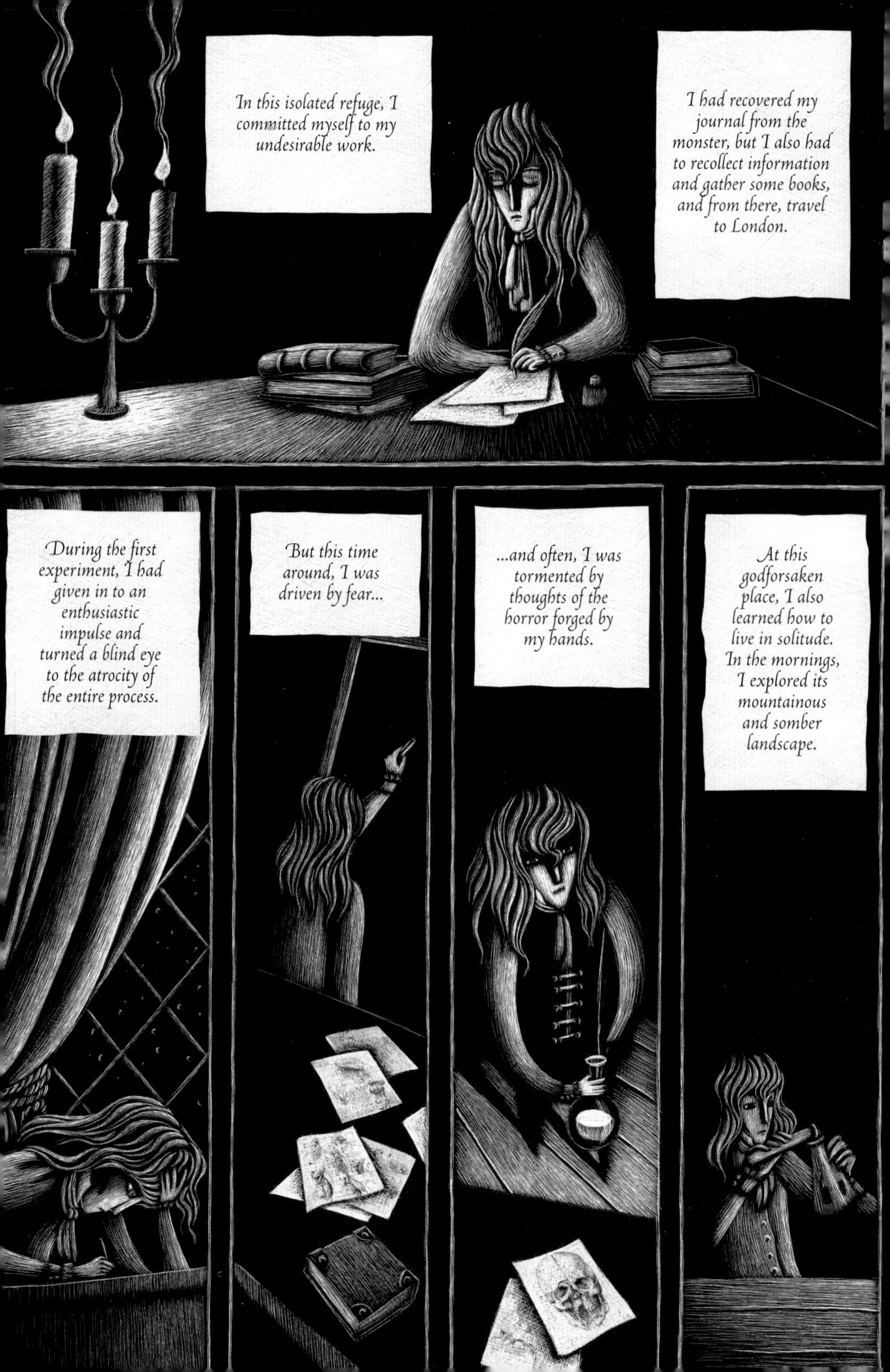
In this isolated refuge, I committed myself to my undesirable work.
I had recovered my journal from the monster, but I also had to recollect information and gather some books, and from there, travel to London.
During the first experiment, I had given in to an enthusiastic impulse and turned a blind eye to the atrocity of the entire process.
But this time around, I was driven by fear...
...and often, I was tormented by thoughts of the horror forged by my hands.
At this godforsaken place, I also learned how to live in solitude. In the mornings, I explored its mountainous and somber landscape.

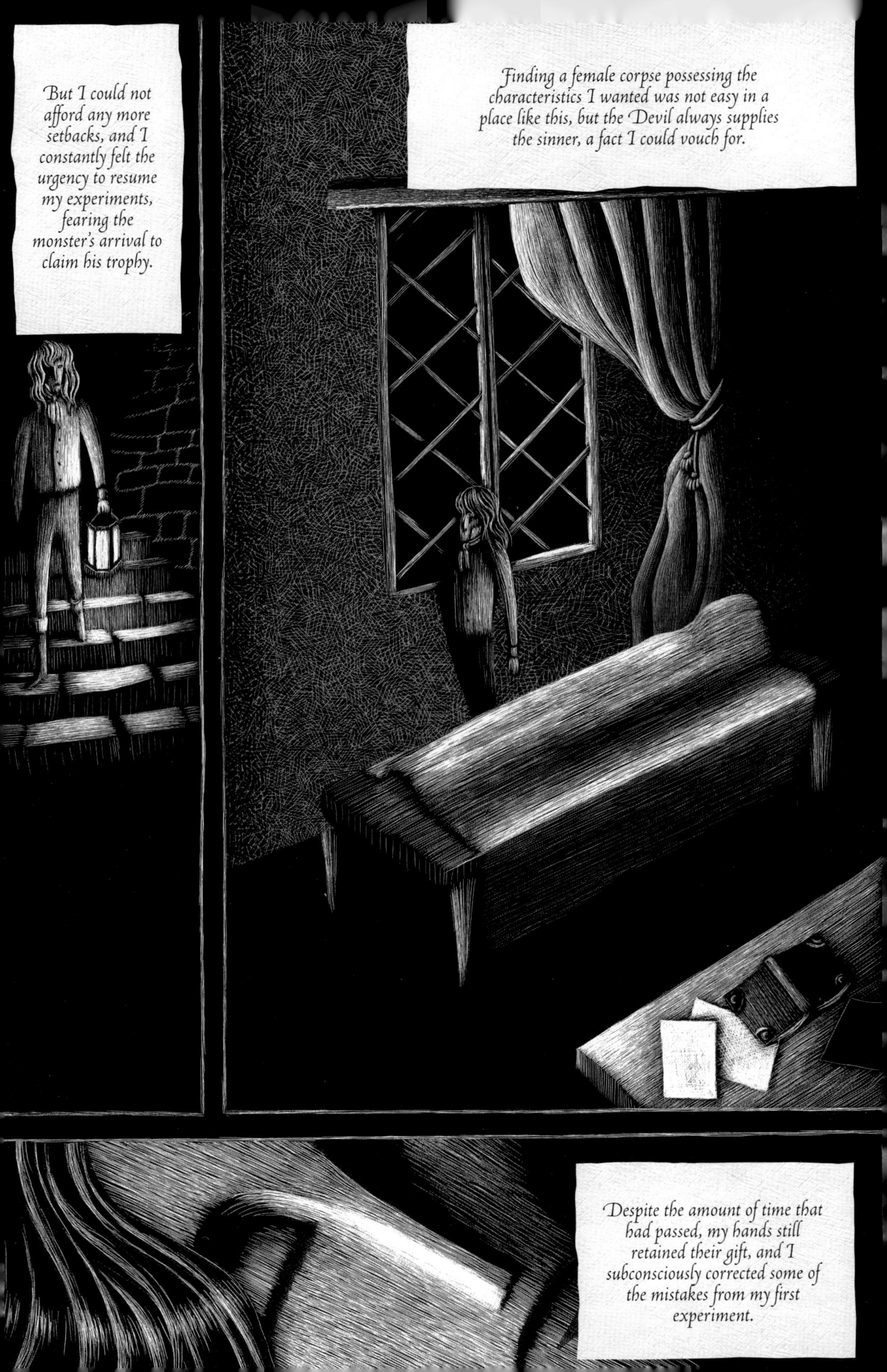
But I could not afford any more setbacks, and I constantly felt the urgency to resume my experiments, fearing the monster's arrival to claim his trophy.
Finding a female corpse possessing the characteristics I wanted was not easy in a place like this, but the Devil always supplies the sinner, a fact I could vouch for.
Despite the amount of time that had passed, my hands still retained their gift, and I subconsciously corrected some of the mistakes from my first experiment.

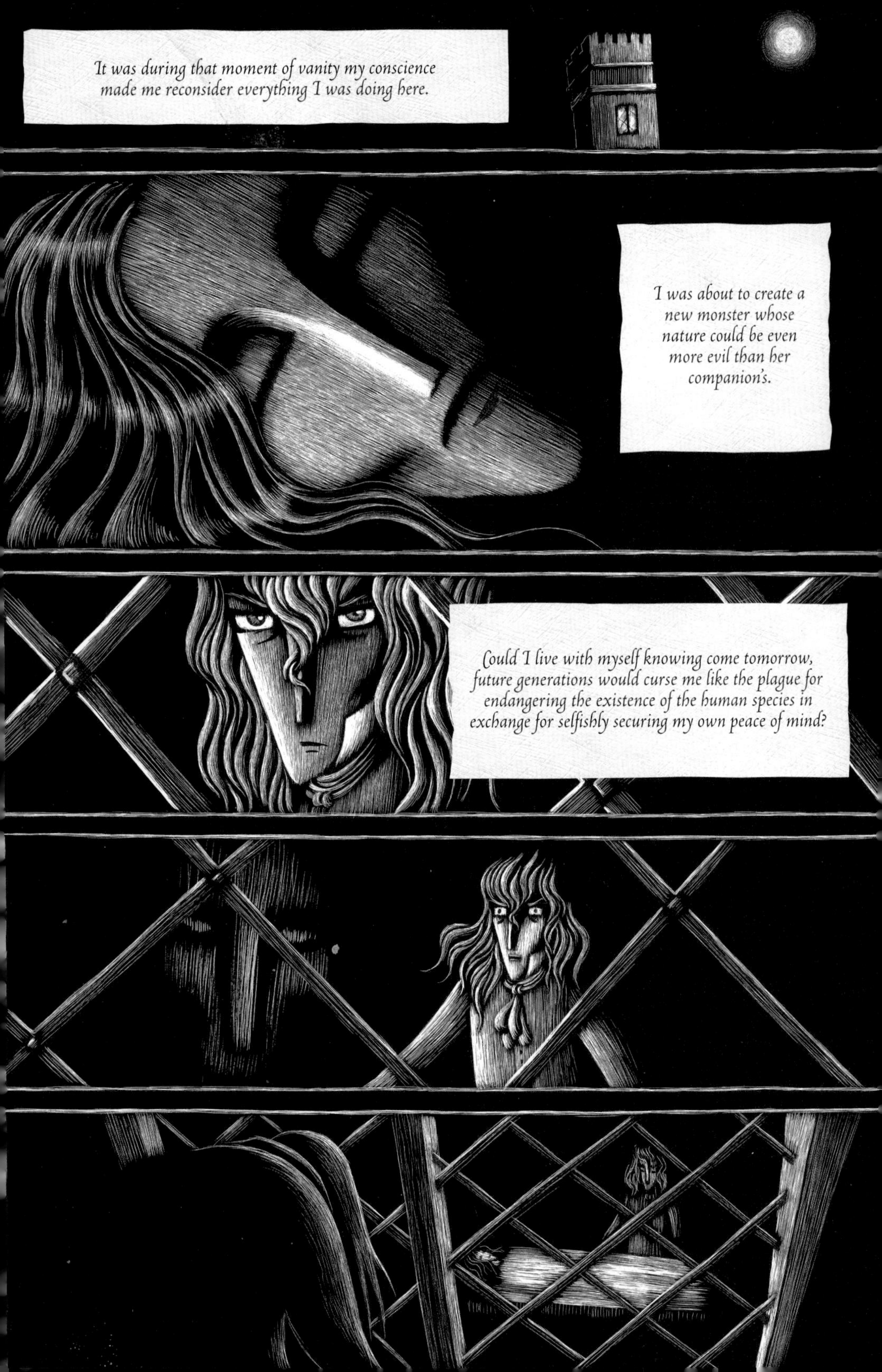
It was during that moment of vanity my conscience made me reconsider everything I was doing here.
I was about to create a new monster whose nature could be even more evil than her companion's.
Could I live with myself knowing come tomorrow, future generations would curse me like the plague for endangering the existence of the human species in exchange for selfishly securing my own peace of mind?

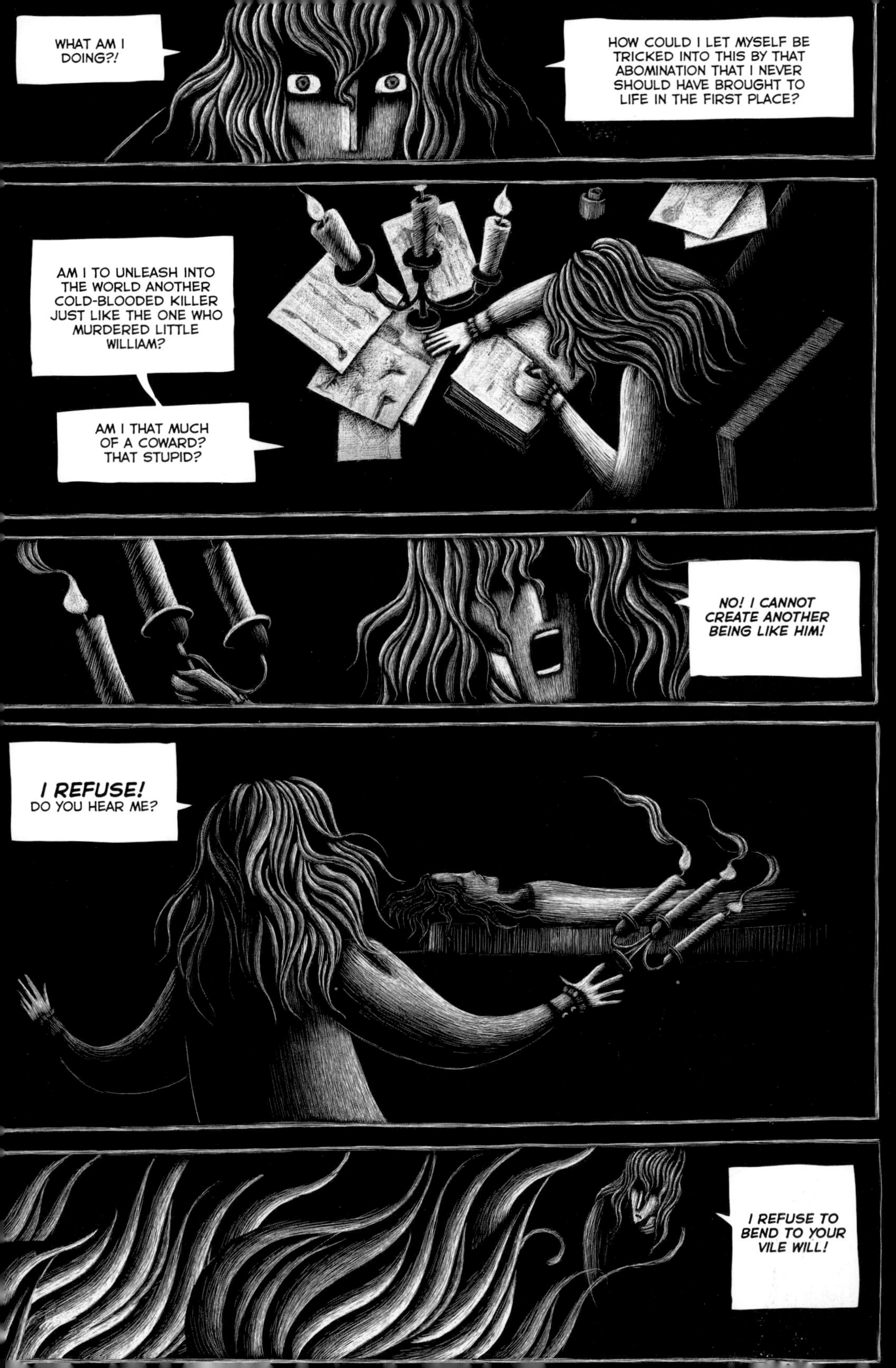

WHAT AM I DOING?!
HOW COULD I LET MYSELF BE TRICKED INTO THIS BY THAT ABOMINATION THAT I NEVER SHOULD HAVE BROUGHT TO LIFE IN THE FIRST PLACE?
AM I TO UNLEASH INTO THE WORLD ANOTHER COLD-BLOODED KILLER JUST LIKE THE ONE WHO MURDERED LITTLE WILLIAM?
AM I THAT MUCH OF A COWARD? THAT STUPID?
NO! I CANNOT CREATE ANOTHER BEING LIKE HIM!
I REFUSE! DO YOU HEAR ME?
I REFUSE TO BEND TO YOUR VILE WILL!

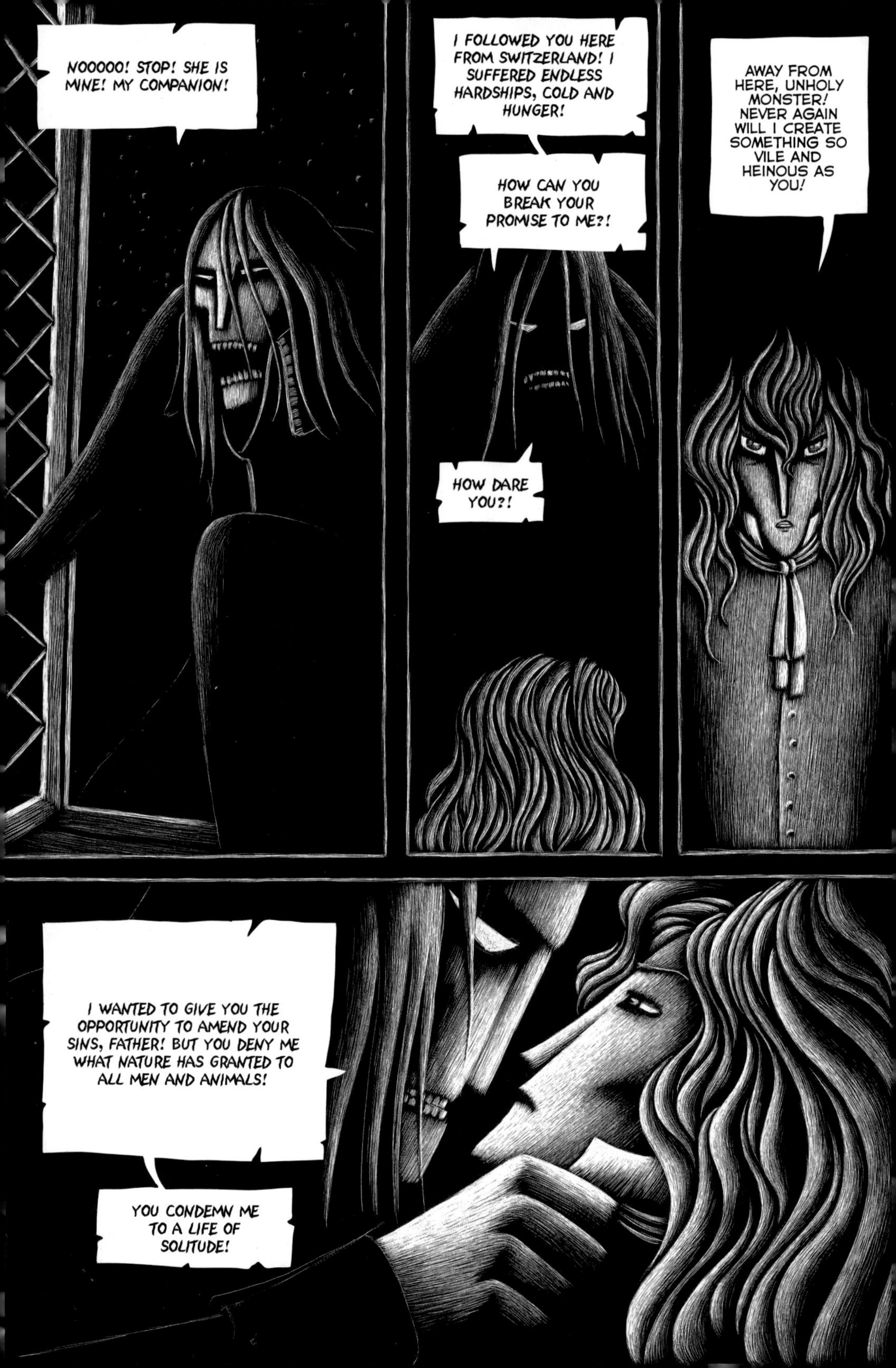
NOOOOO! STOP! SHE IS MINE! MY COMPANION!
I FOLLOWED YOU HERE FROM SWITZERLAND! I SUFFERED ENDLESS HARDSHIPS, COLD AND HUNGER!
HOW CAN YOU BREAK YOUR PROMISE TO ME?!
HOW DARE YOU?!
AWAY FROM HERE, UNHOLY MONSTER! NEVER AGAIN WILL I CREATE SOMETHING SO VILE AND HEINOUS AS YOU!
I WANTED TO GIVE YOU THE OPPORTUNITY TO AMEND YOUR SINS, FATHER! BUT YOU DENY ME WHAT NATURE HAS GRANTED TO ALL MEN AND ANIMALS!
YOU CONDEMN ME TO A LIFE OF SOLITUDE!

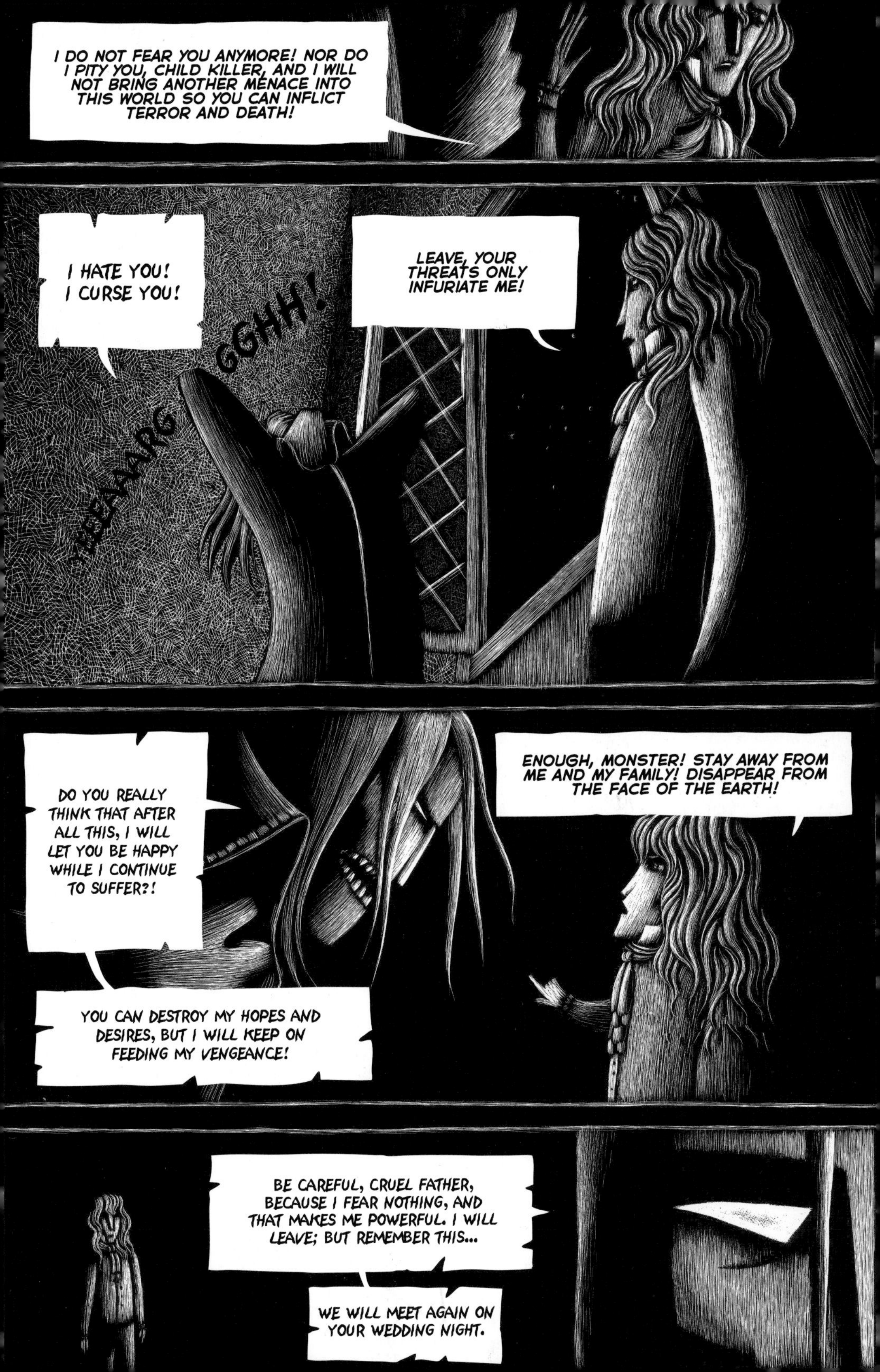
I DO NOT FEAR YOU ANYMORE! NOR DO I PITY YOU, CHILD KILLER, AND I WILL NOT BRING ANOTHER MENACE INTO THIS WORLD SO YOU CAN INFLICT TERROR AND DEATH!
I HATE YOU! I CURSE YOU!
YEEAAARG GGHH!
LEAVE, YOUR THREATS ONLY INFURIATE ME!
DO YOU REALLY THINK THAT AFTER ALL THIS, I WILL LET YOU BE HAPPY WHILE I CONTINUE TO SUFFER?!
YOU CAN DESTROY MY HOPES AND DESIRES, BUT I WILL KEEP ON FEEDING MY VENGEANCE!
ENOUGH, MONSTER! STAY AWAY FROM ME AND MY FAMILY! DISAPPEAR FROM THE FACE OF THE EARTH!
BE CAREFUL, CRUEL FATHER, BECAUSE I FEAR NOTHING, AND THAT MAKES ME POWERFUL. I WILL LEAVE; BUT REMEMBER THIS...
WE WILL MEET AGAIN ON YOUR WEDDING NIGHT.

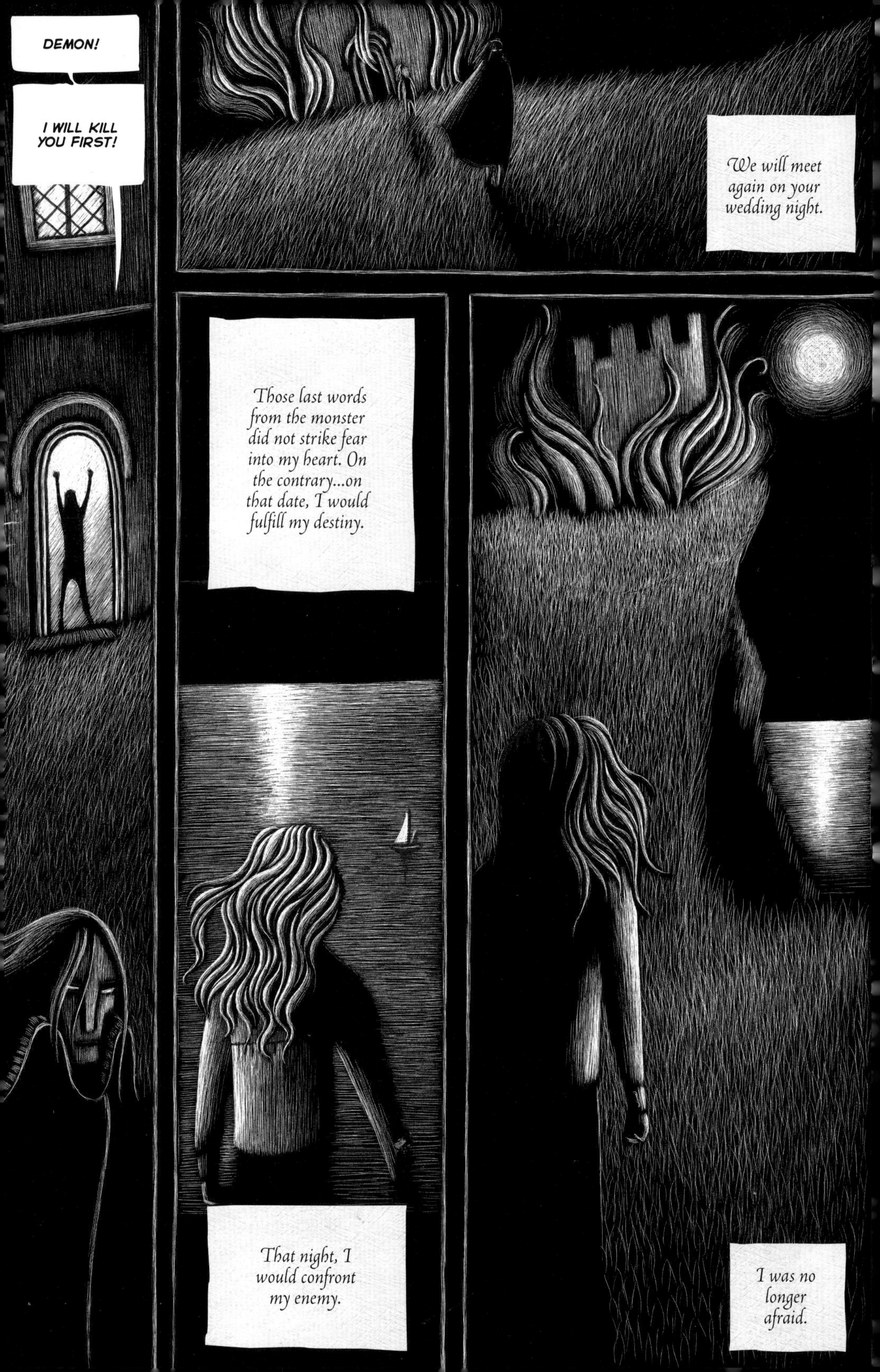
DEMON!
I WILL KILL YOU FIRST!
We will meet again on your wedding night.
Those last words from the monster did not strike fear into my heart. On the contrary...on that date, I would fulfill my destiny.
That night, I would confront my enemy.
I was no longer afraid.

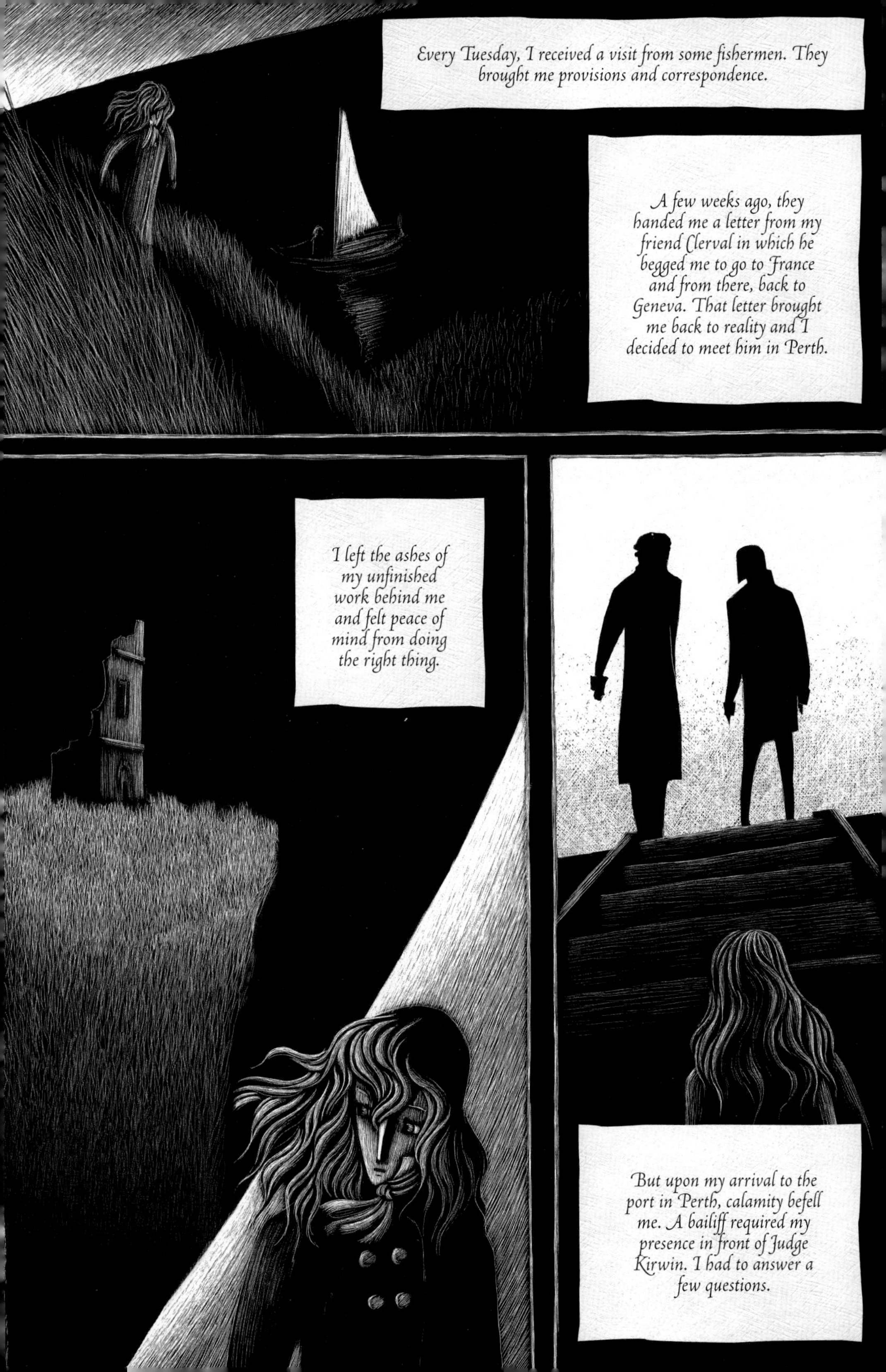
Every Tuesday, I received a visit from some fishermen. They brought me provisions and correspondence.
A few weeks ago, they handed me a letter from my friend Clerval in which he begged me to go to France and from there, back to Geneva. That letter brought me back to reality and I decided to meet him in Perth.
I left the ashes of my unfinished work behind me and felt peace of mind from doing the right thing.
But upon my arrival to the port in Perth, calamity befell me. A bailiff required my presence in front of Judge Kirwin. I had to answer a few questions.

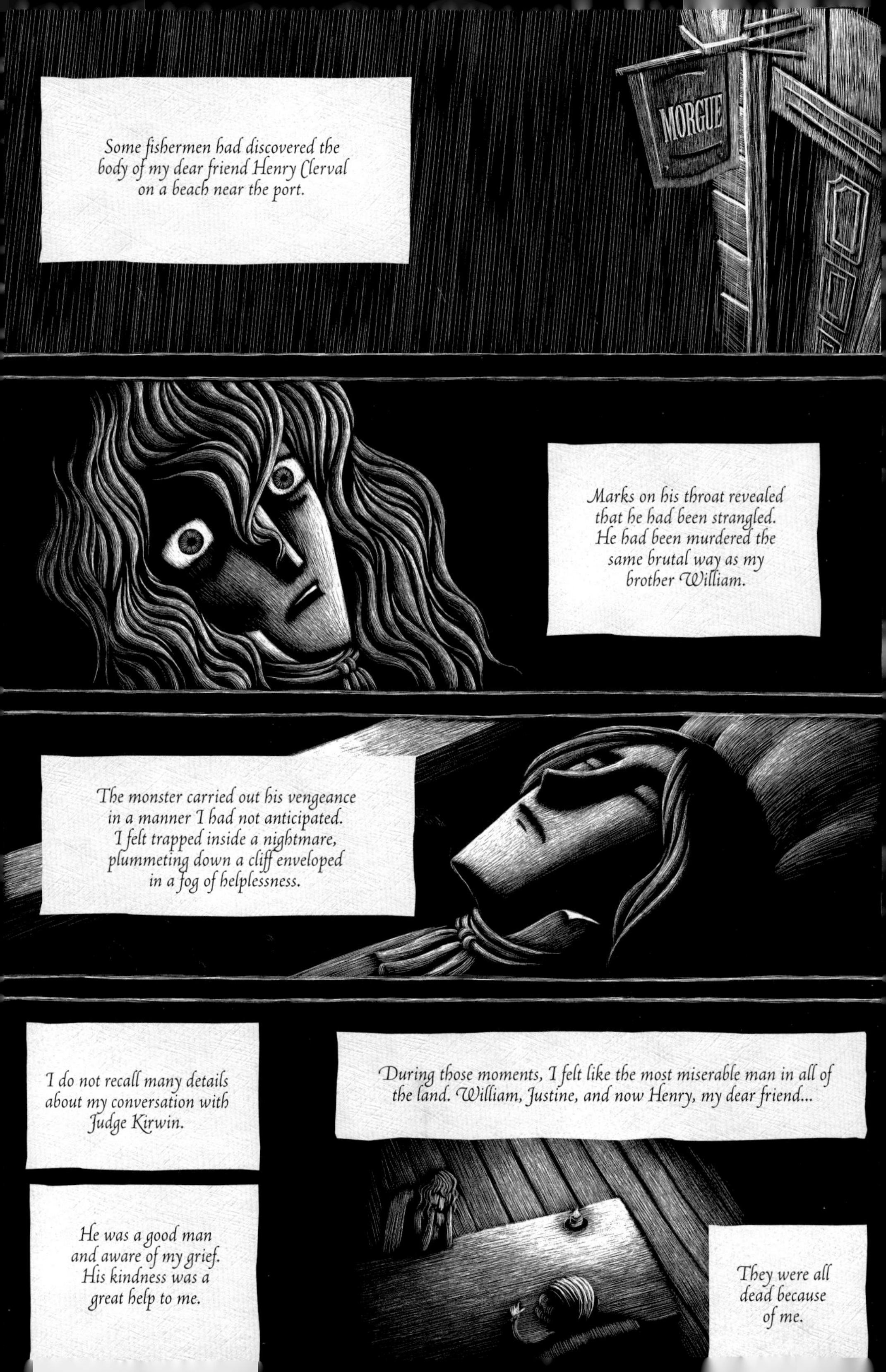
Some fishermen had discovered the body of my dear friend Henry Clerval on a beach near the port.
MORGUE
Marks on his throat revealed that he had been strangled. He had been murdered the same brutal way as my brother William.
The monster carried out his vengeance in a manner I had not anticipated. I felt trapped inside a nightmare, plummeting down a cliff enveloped in a fog of helplessness.
I do not recall many details about my conversation with Judge Kirwin.
He was a good man and aware of my grief. His kindness was a great help to me.
During those moments, I felt like the most miserable man in all of the land. William, Justine, and now Henry, my dear friend...
They were all dead because of me.

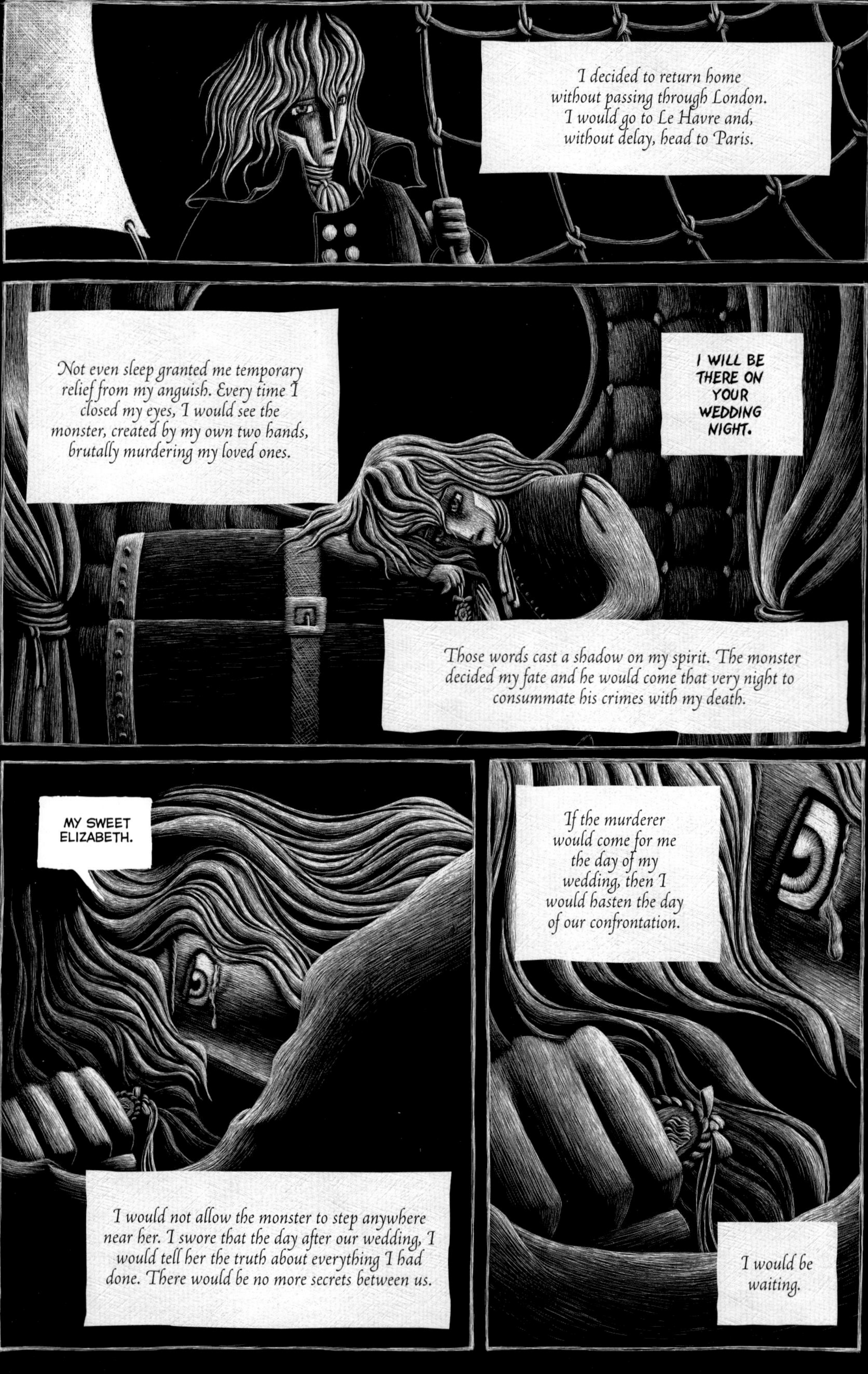
I decided to return home without passing through London. I would go to Le Havre and, without delay, head to Paris.
Not even sleep granted me temporary relief from my anguish. Every time I closed my eyes, I would see the monster, created by my own two hands, brutally murdering my loved ones.
I WILL BE THERE ON YOUR WEDDING NIGHT.
Those words cast a shadow on my spirit. The monster decided my fate and he would come that very night to consummate his crimes with my death.
MY SWEET ELIZABETH.
I would not allow the monster to step anywhere near her. I swore that the day after our wedding, I would tell her the truth about everything I had done. There would be no more secrets between us.
If the murderer would come for me the day of my wedding, then I would hasten the day of our confrontation.
I would be waiting.

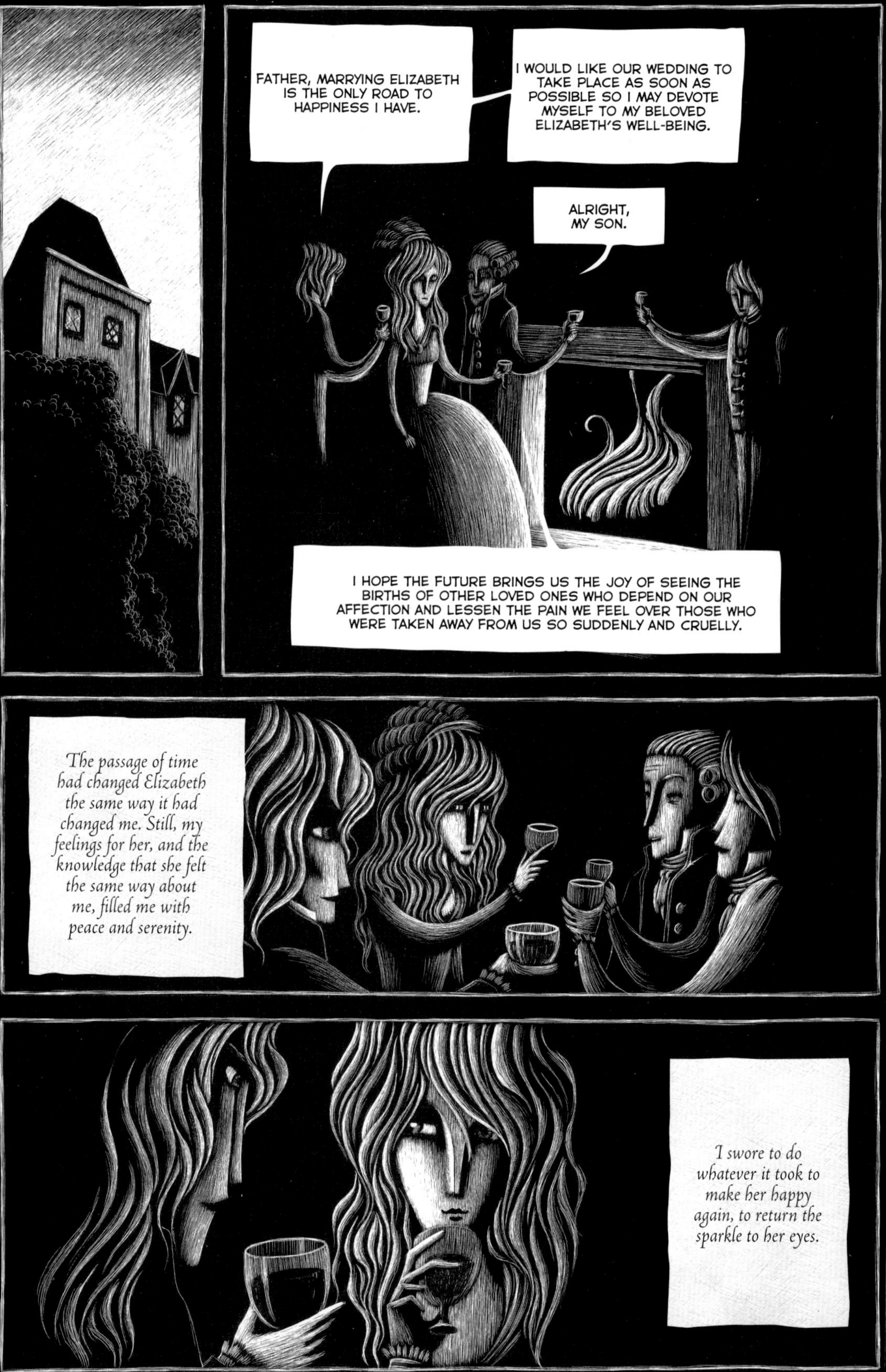
FATHER, MARRYING ELIZABETH IS THE ONLY ROAD TO HAPPINESS I HAVE.
I WOULD LIKE OUR WEDDING TO TAKE PLACE AS SOON AS POSSIBLE SO I MAY DEVOTE MYSELF TO MY BELOVED ELIZABETH'S WELL-BEING.
ALRIGHT, MY SON.
I HOPE THE FUTURE BRINGS US THE JOY OF SEEING THE BIRTHS OF OTHER LOVED ONES WHO DEPEND ON OUR AFFECTION AND LESSEN THE PAIN WE FEEL OVER THOSE WHO WERE TAKEN AWAY FROM US SO SUDDENLY AND CRUELLY.
The passage of time had changed Elizabeth the same way it had changed me. Still, my feelings for her, and the knowledge that she felt the same way about me, filled me with peace and serenity.
I swore to do whatever it took to make her happy again, to return the sparkle to her eyes.

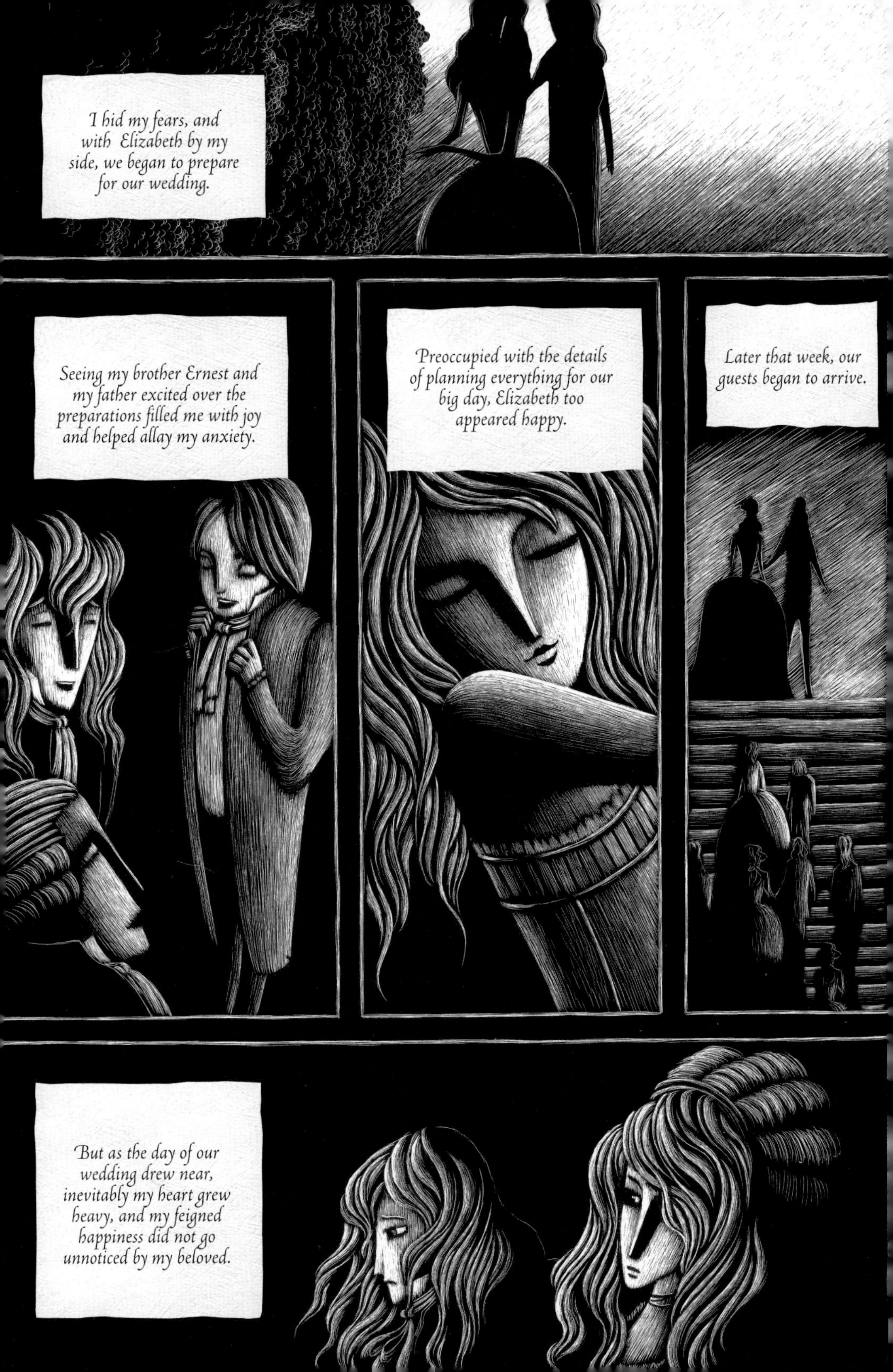
I hid my fears, and with Elizabeth by my side, we began to prepare for our wedding.
Seeing my brother Ernest and my father excited over the preparations filled me with joy and helped allay my anxiety.
Preoccupied with the details of planning everything for our big day, Elizabeth too appeared happy.
Later that week, our guests began to arrive.
But as the day of our wedding drew near, inevitably my heart grew heavy, and my feigned happiness did not go unnoticed by my beloved.

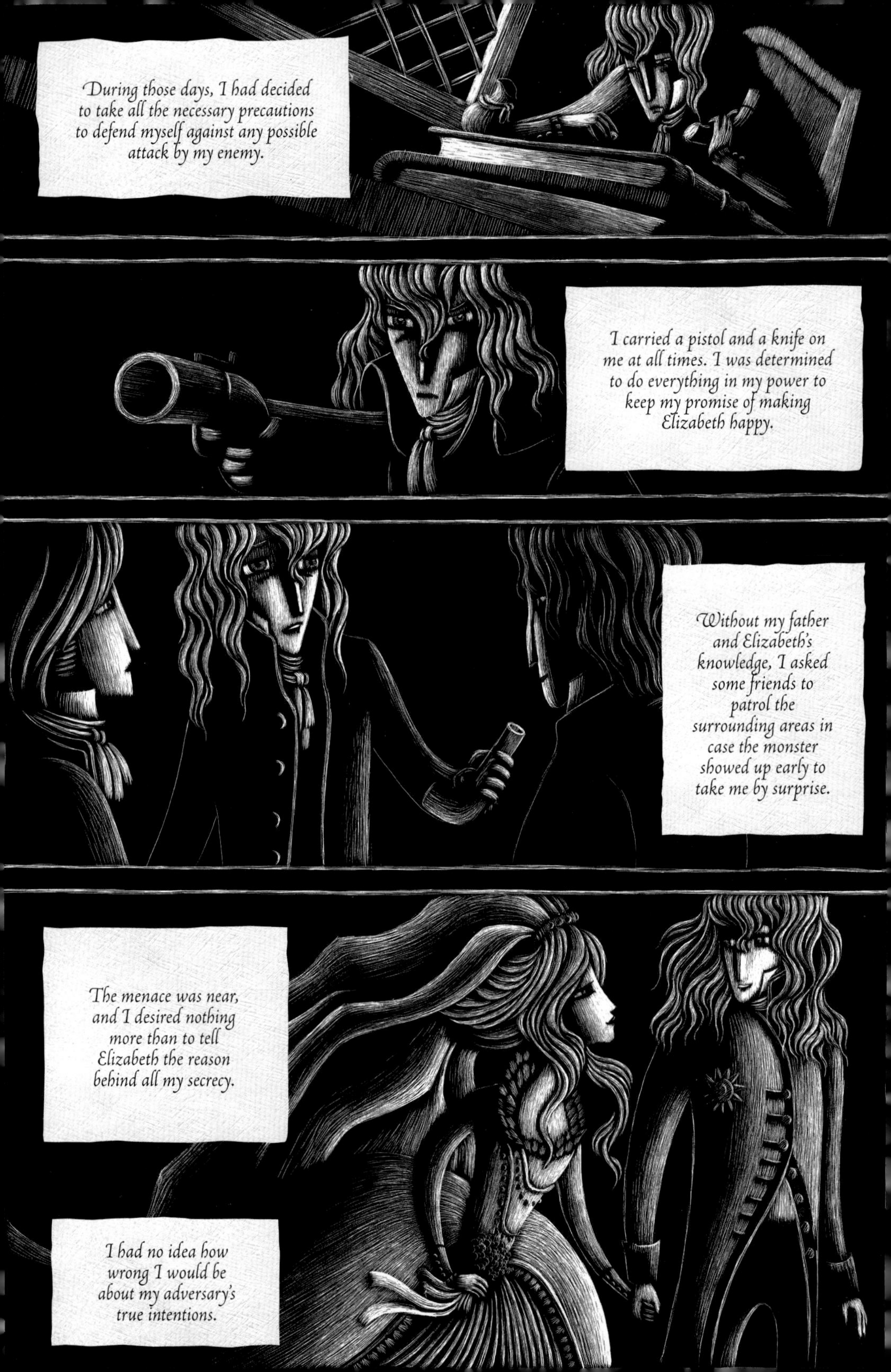
During those days, I had decided to take all the necessary precautions to defend myself against any possible attack by my enemy.
I carried a pistol and a knife on me at all times. I was determined to do everything in my power to keep my promise of making Elizabeth happy.
Without my father and Elizabeth's knowledge, I asked some friends to patrol the surrounding areas in case the monster showed up early to take me by surprise.
The menace was near, and I desired nothing more than to tell Elizabeth the reason behind all my secrecy.
I had no idea how wrong I would be about my adversary's true intentions.

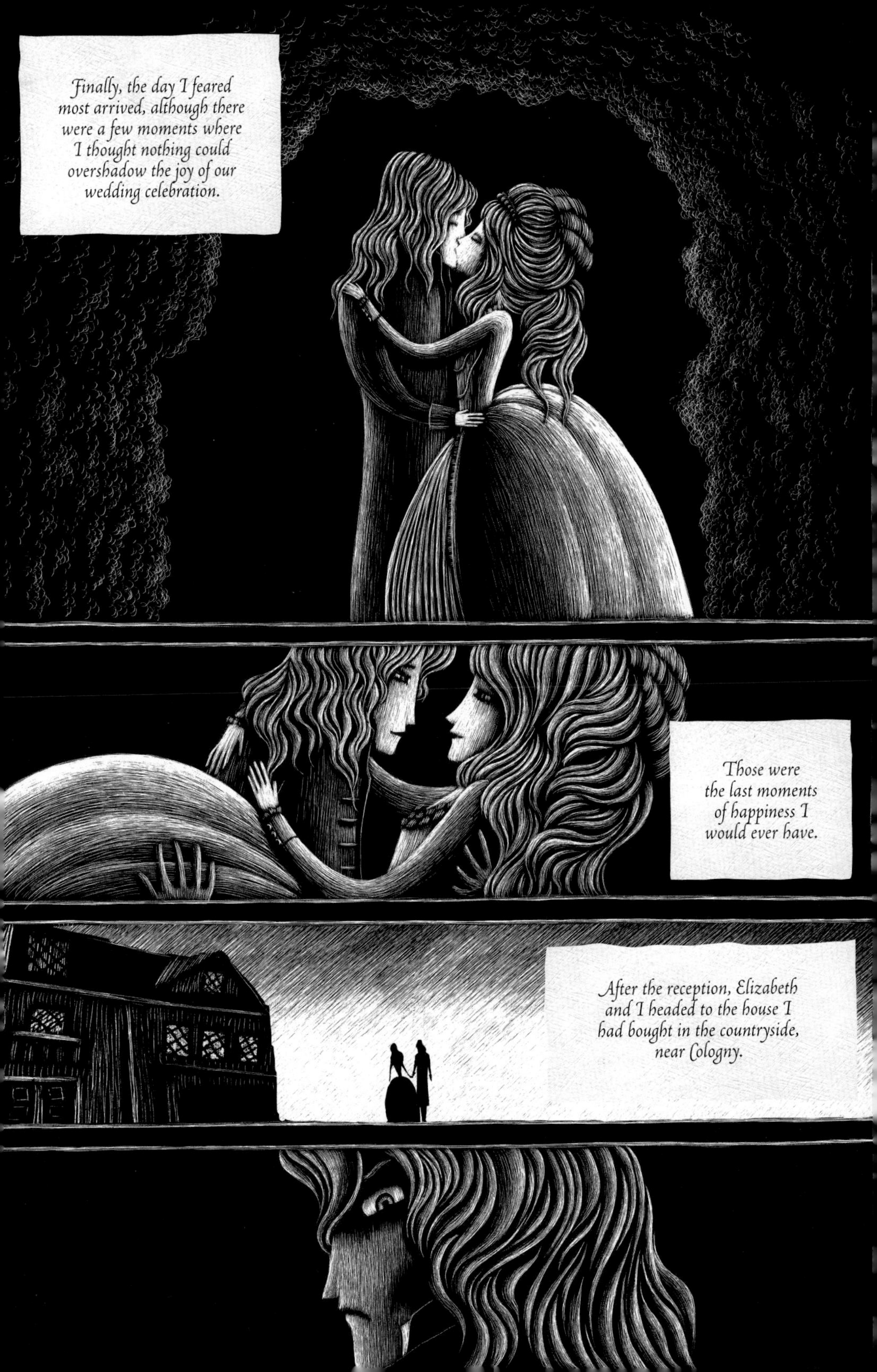
Finally, the day I feared most arrived, although there were a few moments where I thought nothing could overshadow the joy of our wedding celebration.
Those were the last moments of happiness I would ever have.
After the reception, Elizabeth and I headed to the house I had bought in the countryside, near Cologny.

WHAT IS THE MATTER, VICTOR? CAN YOU PLEASE TELL ME WHAT HAS BEEN TROUBLING YOU THESE LAST FEW DAYS?

DO NOT WORRY, MY LOVE, MY DEAR ELIZABETH.

Once she retired to our bedroom, I checked all the hallways. I checked every possible place my enemy could have hidden.

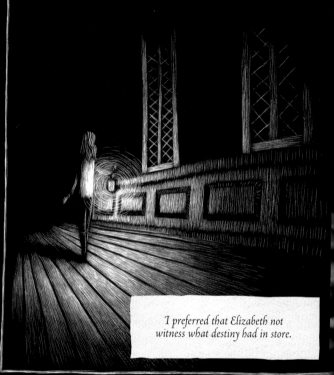

AFTER TONIGHT, EVERYTHING WILL BE ALRIGHT. PLEASE GO TO OUR BEDROOM AND REST; I WILL JOIN YOU SOON.

I preferred that Elizabeth not witness what destiny had in store.

Did the monster plan to wait until I fell asleep to attack me?

Finally, though still anxious, I returned to our bedroom.

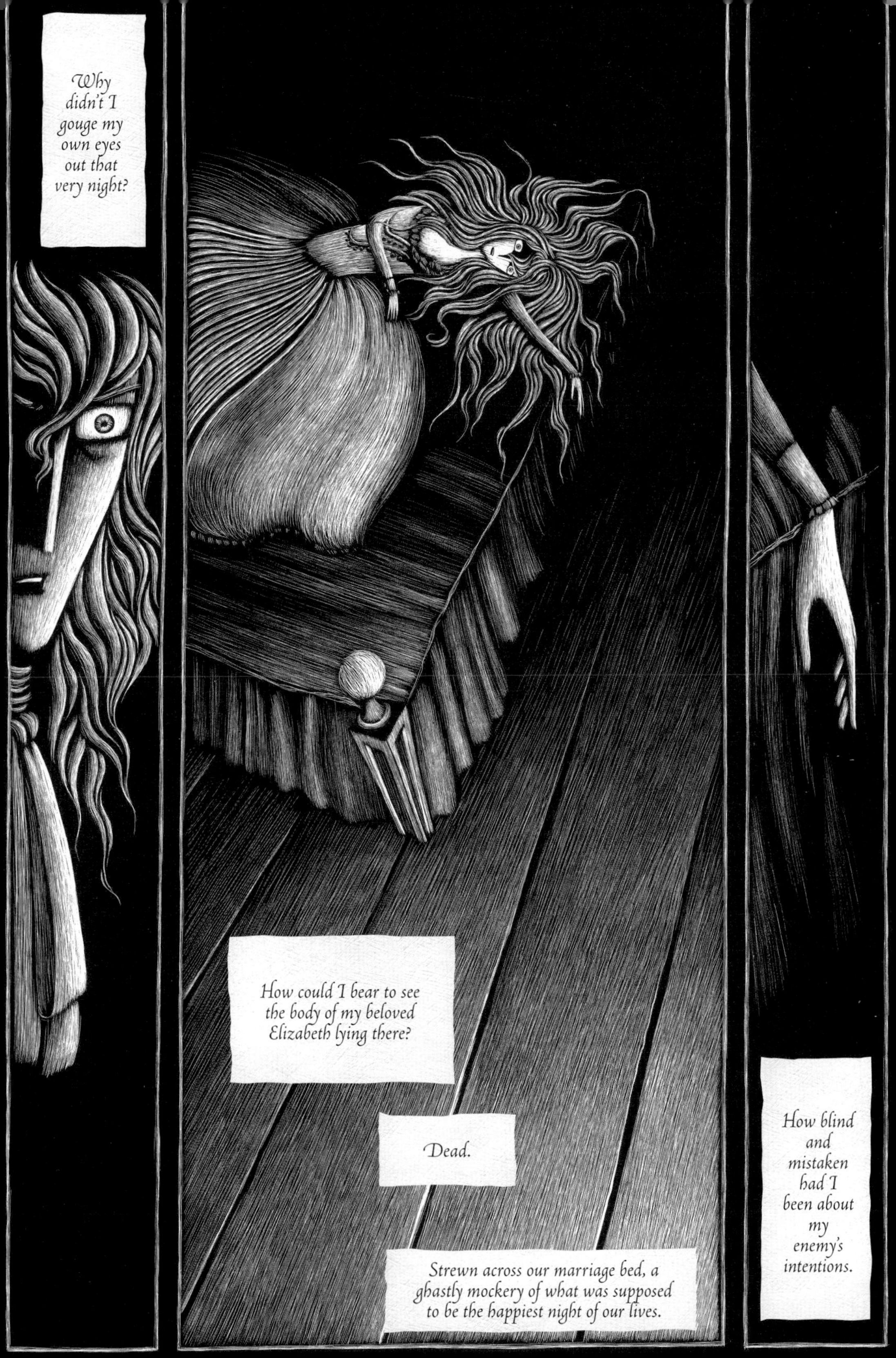
Why didn't I gouge my own eyes out that very night?
How could I bear to see the body of my beloved Elizabeth lying there?
Dead.
Strewn across our marriage bed, a ghastly mockery of what was supposed to be the happiest night of our lives.
How blind and mistaken had I been about my enemy's intentions.

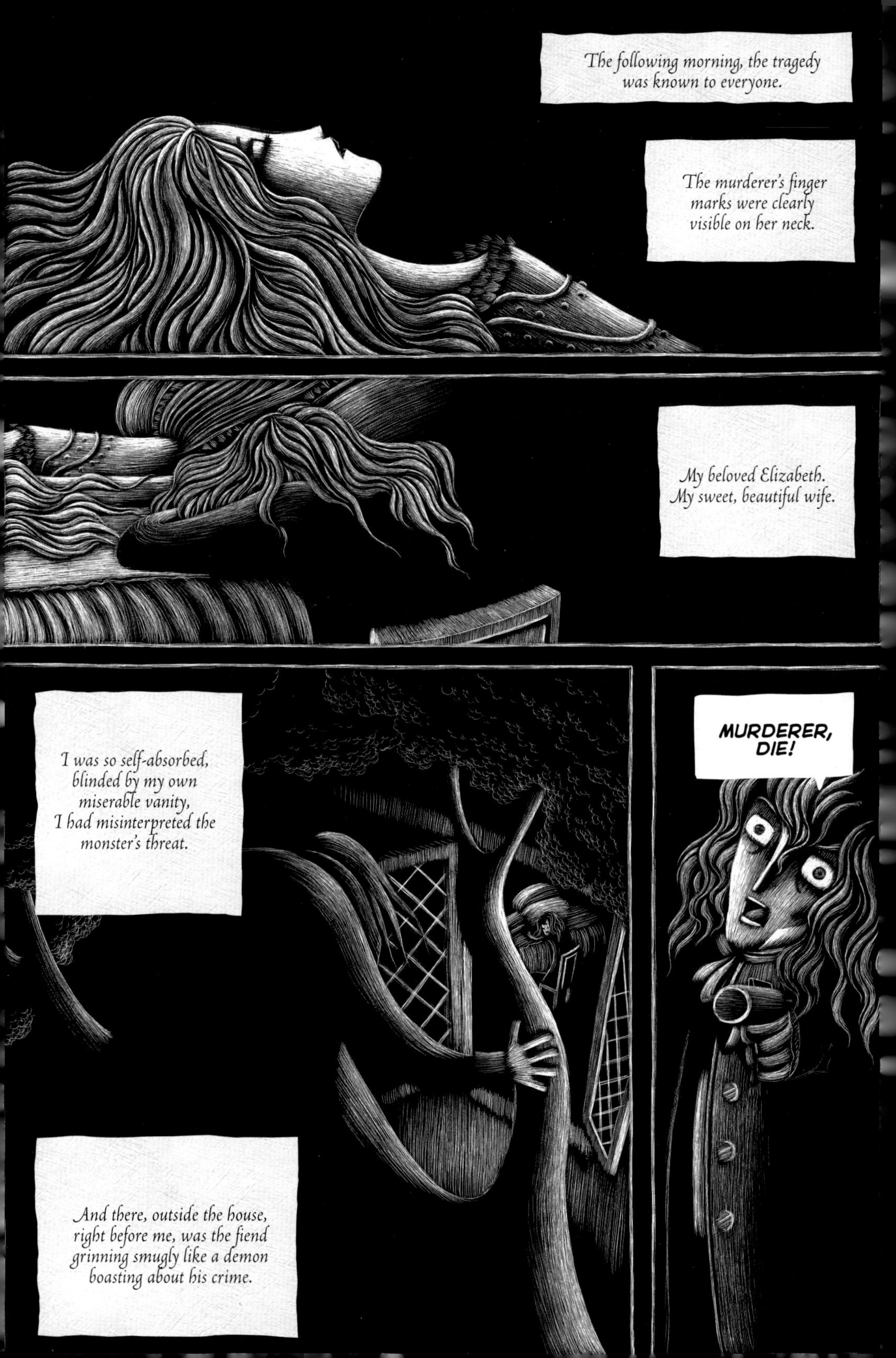
The following morning, the tragedy was known to everyone.
The murderer's finger marks were clearly visible on her neck.
My beloved Elizabeth. My sweet, beautiful wife.
I was so self-absorbed, blinded by my own miserable vanity, I had misinterpreted the monster's threat.
And there, outside the house, right before me, was the fiend grinning smugly like a demon boasting about his crime.
MURDERER, DIE!

The scoundrel laughed as he ran.

GET HIM!

DO NOT LET HIM ESCAPE!

HE KILLED ELIZABETH!

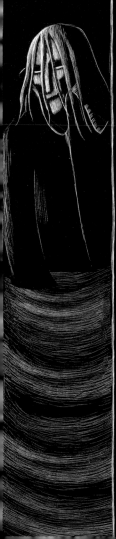

We separated into several hunting parties and searched around the lake. My blood boiled, and the desire to capture that fiend to make him pay for his crimes scorched my soul.

But again his superhuman abilities allowed him to make a fool of me.

Even some of those closest to me concluded that the intruder had been only a figment of my imagination.

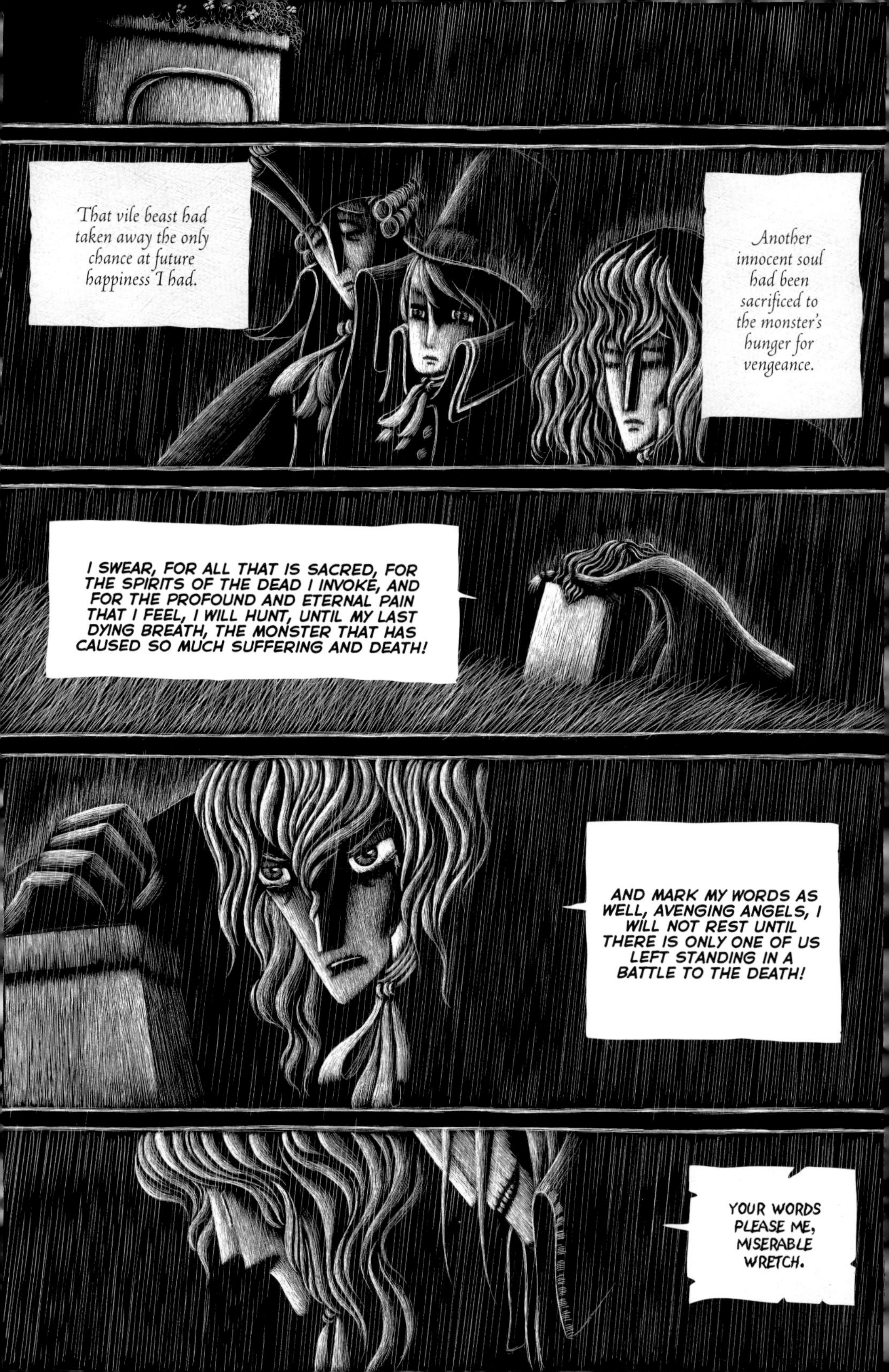
That vile beast had taken away the only chance at future happiness I had.
Another innocent soul had been sacrificed to the monster's hunger for vengeance.
I SWEAR, FOR ALL THAT IS SACRED, FOR THE SPIRITS OF THE DEAD I INVOKE, AND FOR THE PROFOUND AND ETERNAL PAIN THAT I FEEL, I WILL HUNT, UNTIL MY LAST DYING BREATH, THE MONSTER THAT HAS CAUSED SO MUCH SUFFERING AND DEATH!
AND MARK MY WORDS AS WELL, AVENGING ANGELS, I WILL NOT REST UNTIL THERE IS ONLY ONE OF US LEFT STANDING IN A BATTLE TO THE DEATH!
YOUR WORDS PLEASE ME, MISERABLE WRETCH.

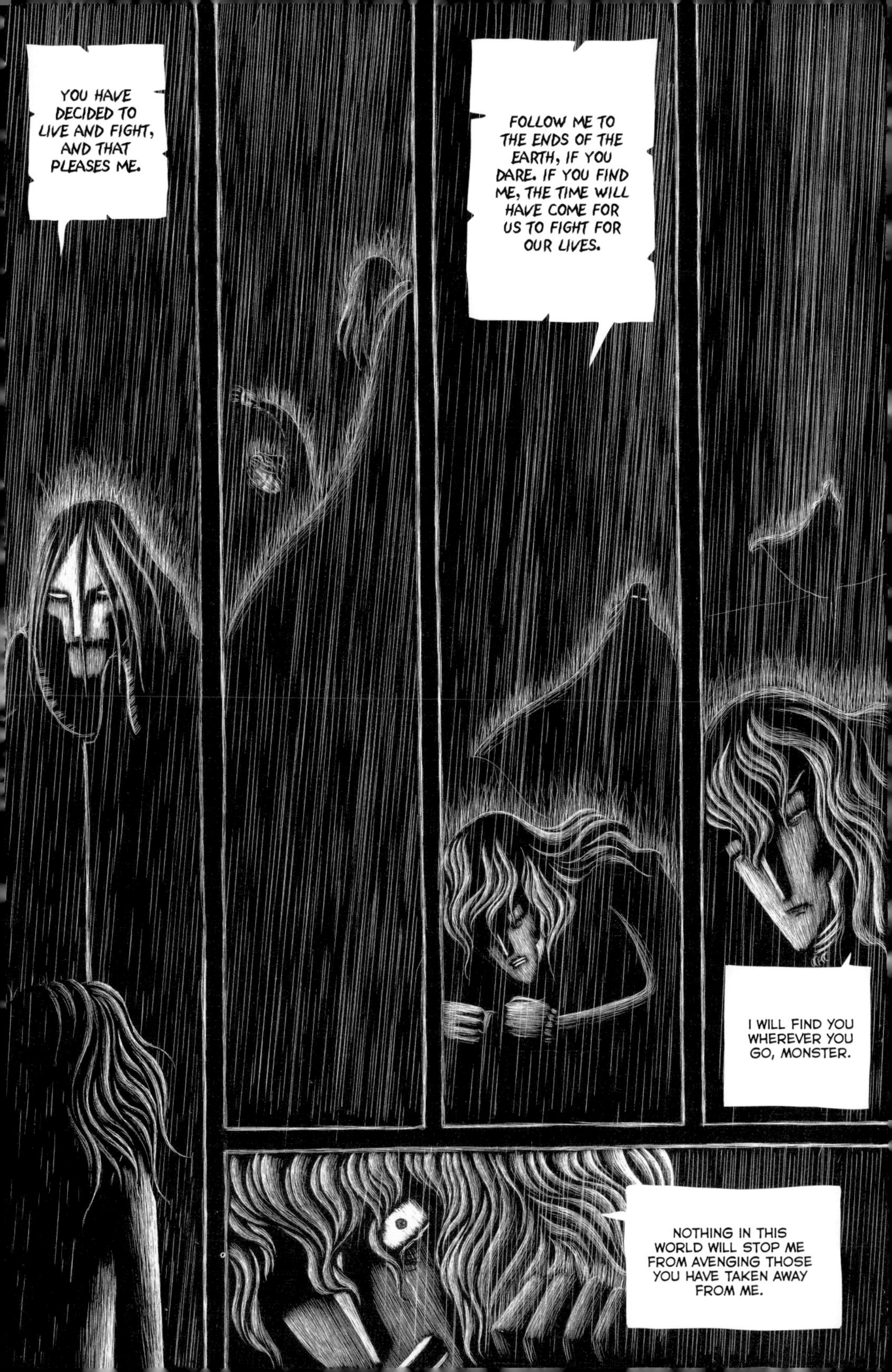
YOU HAVE DECIDED TO LIVE AND FIGHT, AND THAT PLEASES ME.
FOLLOW ME TO THE ENDS OF THE EARTH, IF YOU DARE. IF YOU FIND ME, THE TIME WILL HAVE COME FOR US TO FIGHT FOR OUR LIVES.
I WILL FIND YOU WHEREVER YOU GO, MONSTER.
NOTHING IN THIS WORLD WILL STOP ME FROM AVENGING THOSE YOU HAVE TAKEN AWAY FROM ME.

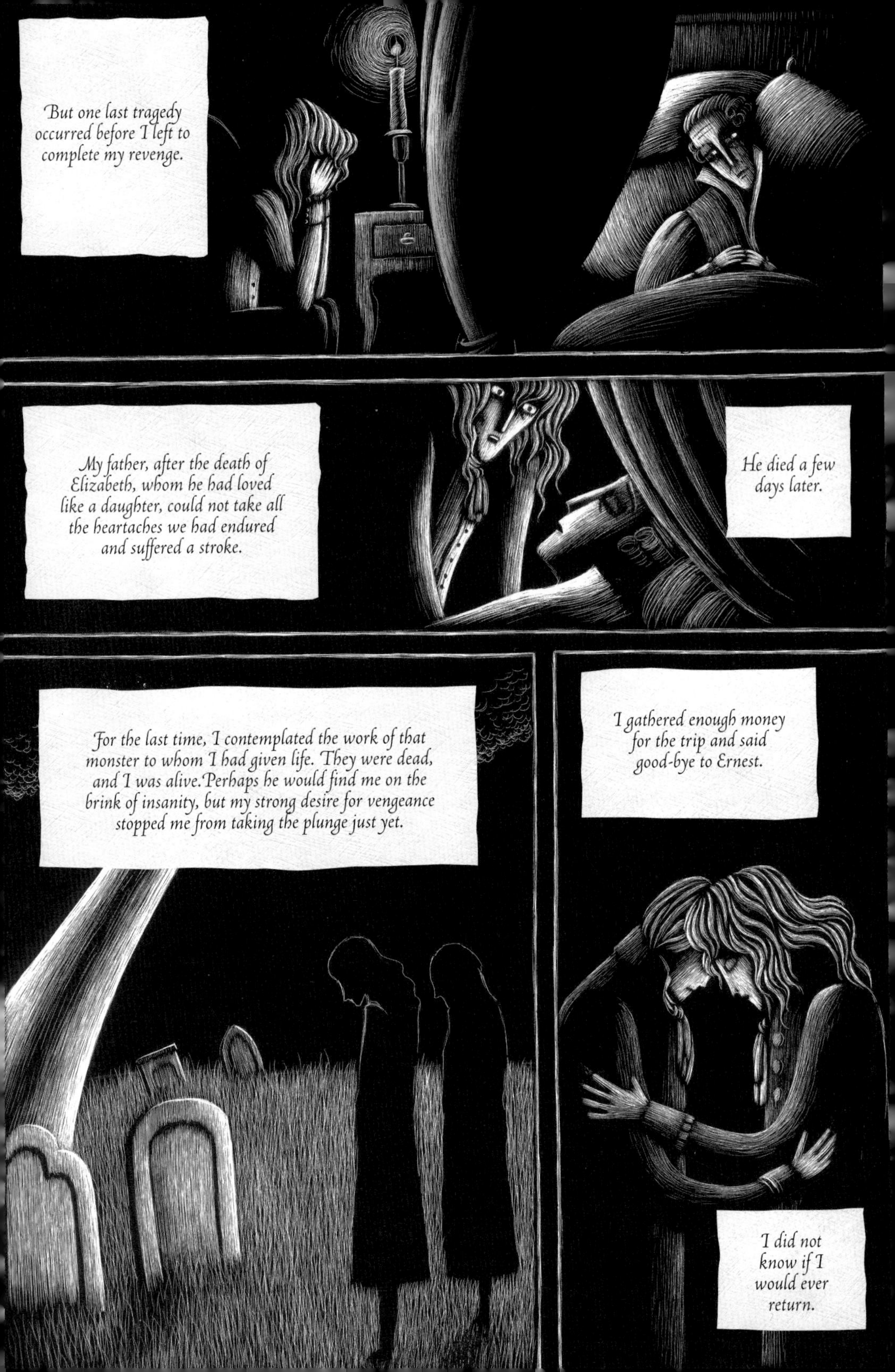
But one last tragedy occurred before I left to complete my revenge.
My father, after the death of Elizabeth, whom he had loved like a daughter, could not take all the heartaches we had endured and suffered a stroke.
He died a few days later.
For the last time, I contemplated the work of that monster to whom I had given life. They were dead, and I was alive. Perhaps he would find me on the brink of insanity, but my strong desire for vengeance stopped me from taking the plunge just yet.
I gathered enough money for the trip and said good-bye to Ernest.
I did not know if I would ever return.

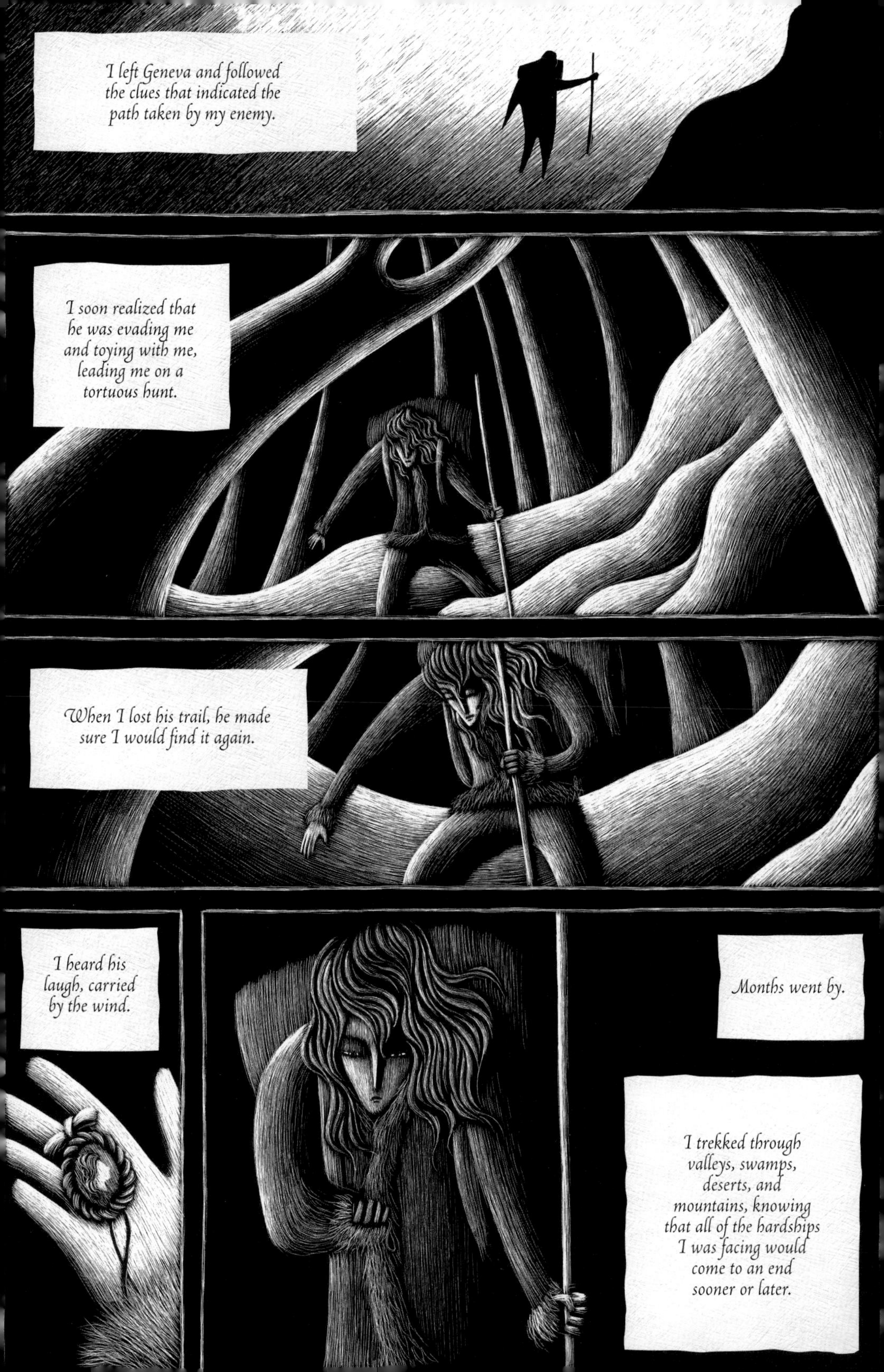
I left Geneva and followed the clues that indicated the path taken by my enemy.
I soon realized that he was evading me and toying with me, leading me on a tortuous hunt.
When I lost his trail, he made sure I would find it again.
I heard his laugh, carried by the wind.
Months went by.
I trekked through valleys, swamps, deserts, and mountains, knowing that all of the hardships I was facing would come to an end sooner or later.

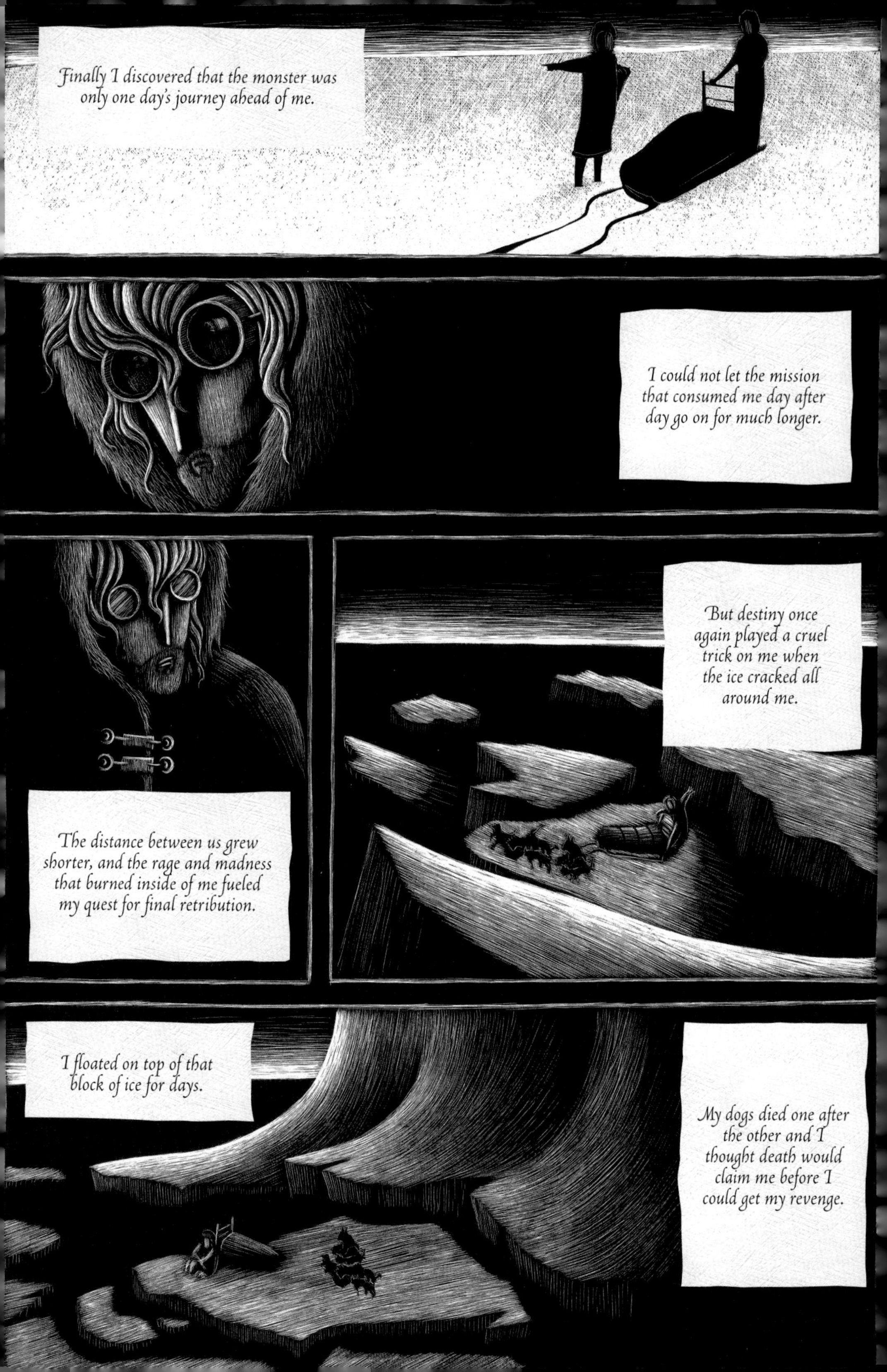
Finally I discovered that the monster was only one day's journey ahead of me.
I could not let the mission that consumed me day after day go on for much longer.
The distance between us grew shorter, and the rage and madness that burned inside of me fueled my quest for final retribution.
But destiny once again played a cruel trick on me when the ice cracked all around me.
I floated on top of that block of ice for days.
My dogs died one after the other and I thought death would claim me before I could get my revenge.

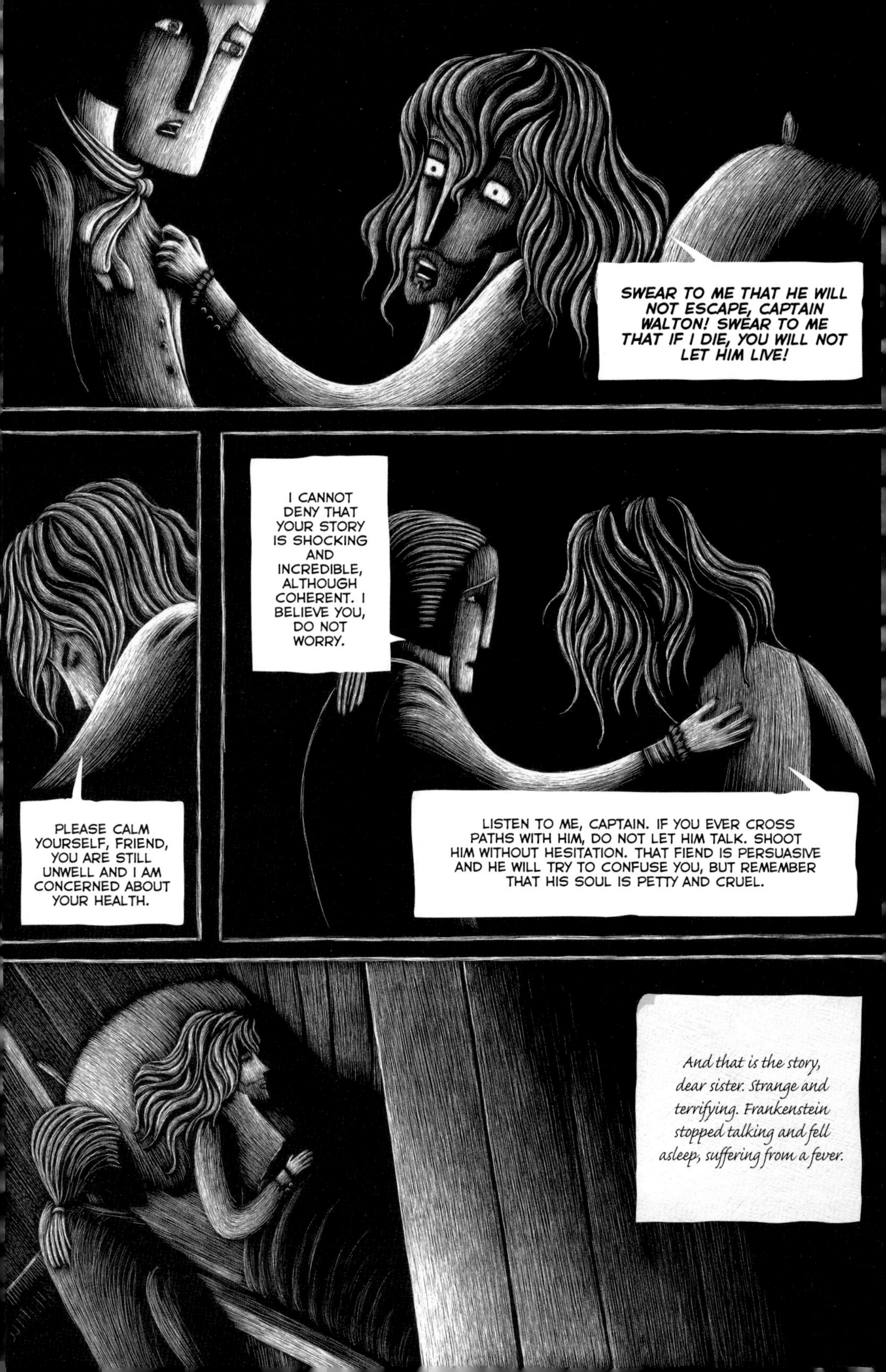
SWEAR TO ME THAT HE WILL NOT ESCAPE, CAPTAIN WALTON! SWEAR TO ME THAT IF I DIE, YOU WILL NOT LET HIM LIVE!
PLEASE CALM YOURSELF, FRIEND, YOU ARE STILL UNWELL AND I AM CONCERNED ABOUT YOUR HEALTH.
I CANNOT DENY THAT YOUR STORY IS SHOCKING AND INCREDIBLE, ALTHOUGH COHERENT. I BELIEVE YOU, DO NOT WORRY.
LISTEN TO ME, CAPTAIN. IF YOU EVER CROSS PATHS WITH HIM, DO NOT LET HIM TALK. SHOOT HIM WITHOUT HESITATION. THAT FIEND IS PERSUASIVE AND HE WILL TRY TO CONFUSE YOU, BUT REMEMBER THAT HIS SOUL IS PETTY AND CRUEL.
And that is the story, dear sister. Strange and terrifying. Frankenstein stopped talking and fell asleep, suffering from a fever.

I decided to record his story. He himself, with whatever strength he had left in him, helped me make the corrections; he saw my notes as his testament, as a tragic warning for posterity to heed.

Sometimes frustration and anguish took over, and he exploded into fits of rage.

Other times he fell into a long, feverish slumber, plagued by delirium and tears.

I pitied this noble man, tormented and ill, but at the same time, I admired him. Such an adverse and tragic destiny befell him.

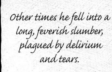

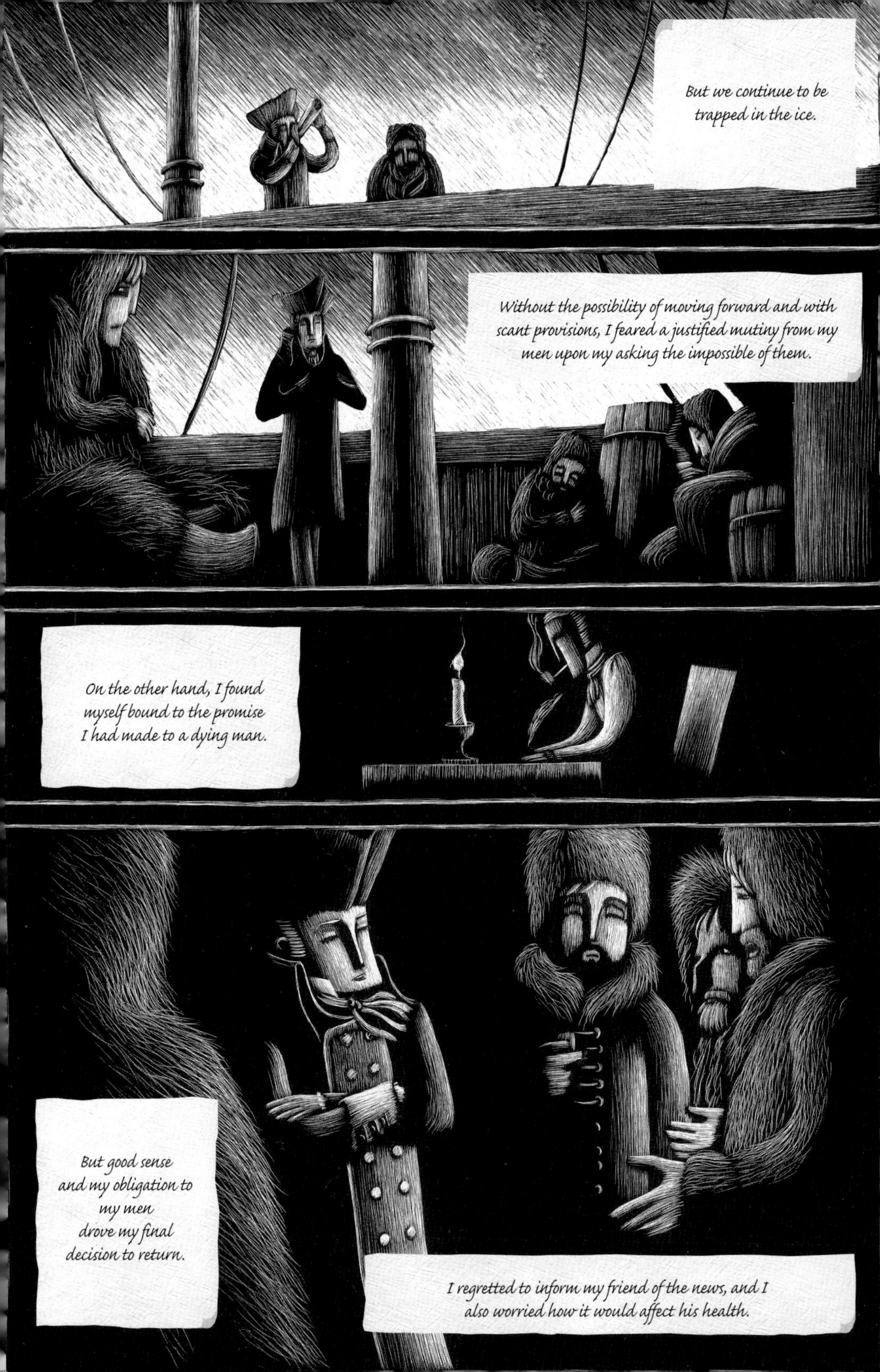
But we continue to be trapped in the ice.
Without the possibility of moving forward and with scant provisions, I feared a justified mutiny from my men upon my asking the impossible of them.
On the other hand, I found myself bound to the promise I had made to a dying man.
But good sense and my obligation to my men drove my final decision to return.
I regretted to inform my friend of the news, and I also worried how it would affect his health.

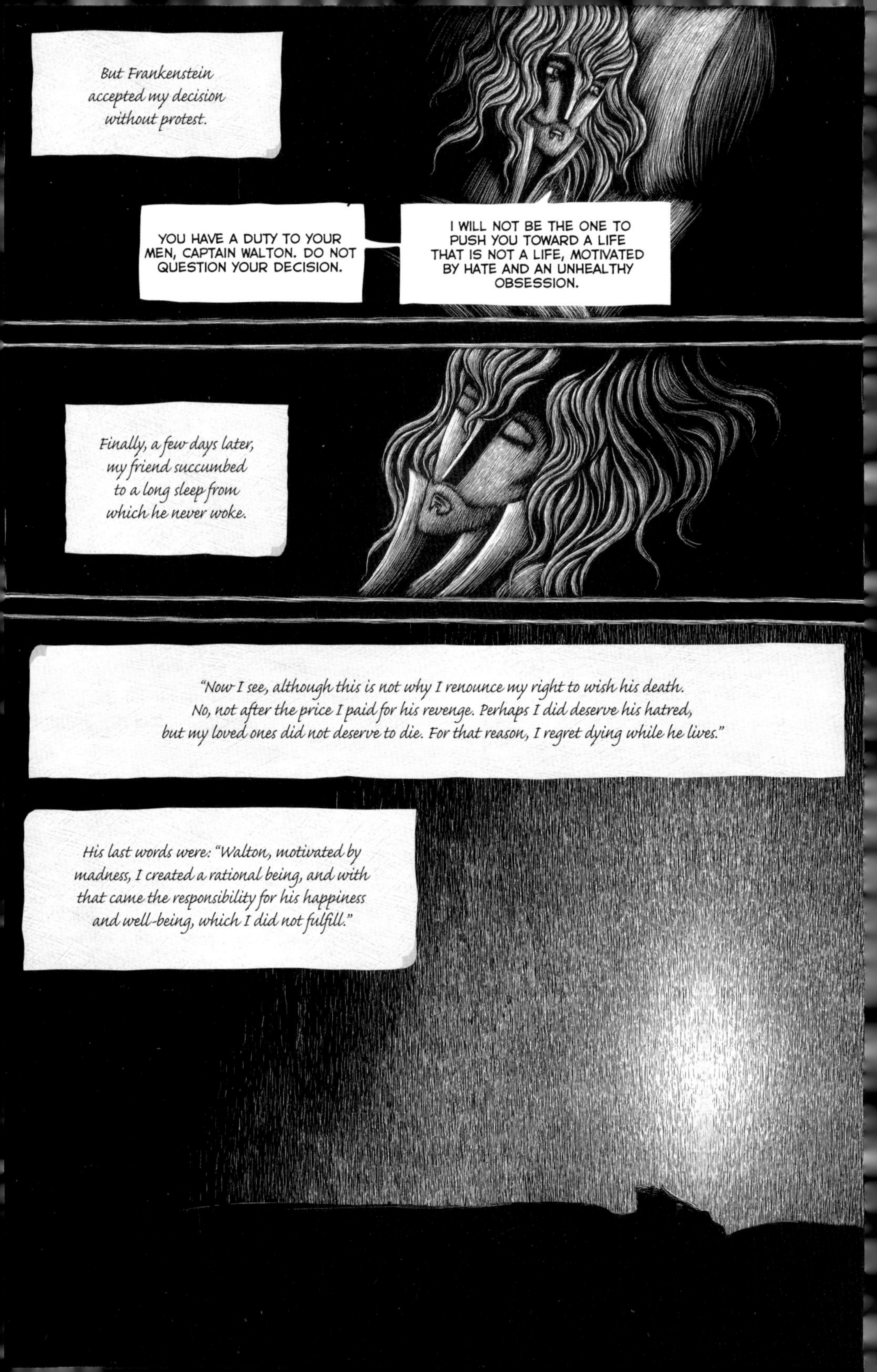
But Frankenstein accepted my decision without protest.
YOU HAVE A DUTY TO YOUR MEN, CAPTAIN WALTON. DO NOT QUESTION YOUR DECISION.
I WILL NOT BE THE ONE TO PUSH YOU TOWARD A LIFE THAT IS NOT A LIFE, MOTIVATED BY HATE AND AN UNHEALTHY OBSESSION.
Finally, a few days later, my friend succumbed to a long sleep from which he never woke.
"Now I see, although this is not why I renounce my right to wish his death. No, not after the price I paid for his revenge. Perhaps I did deserve his hatred, but my loved ones did not deserve to die. For that reason, I regret dying while he lives."
His last words were: "Walton, motivated by madness, I created a rational being, and with that came the responsibility for his happiness and well-being, which I did not fulfill."

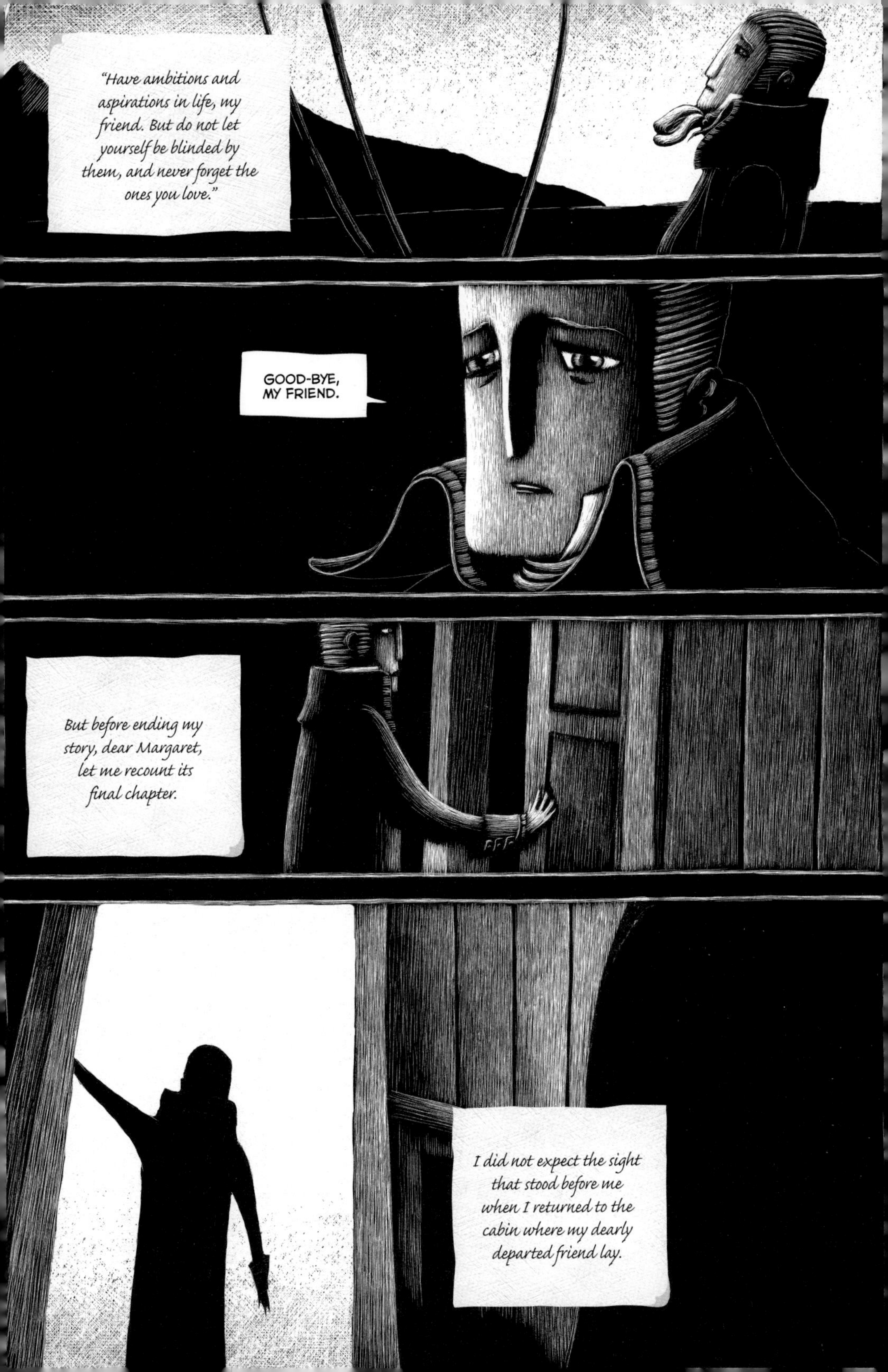
"Have ambitions and aspirations in life, my friend. But do not let yourself be blinded by them, and never forget the ones you love."
GOOD-BYE, MY FRIEND.
But before ending my story, dear Margaret, let me recount its final chapter.
I did not expect the sight that stood before me when I returned to the cabin where my dearly departed friend lay.

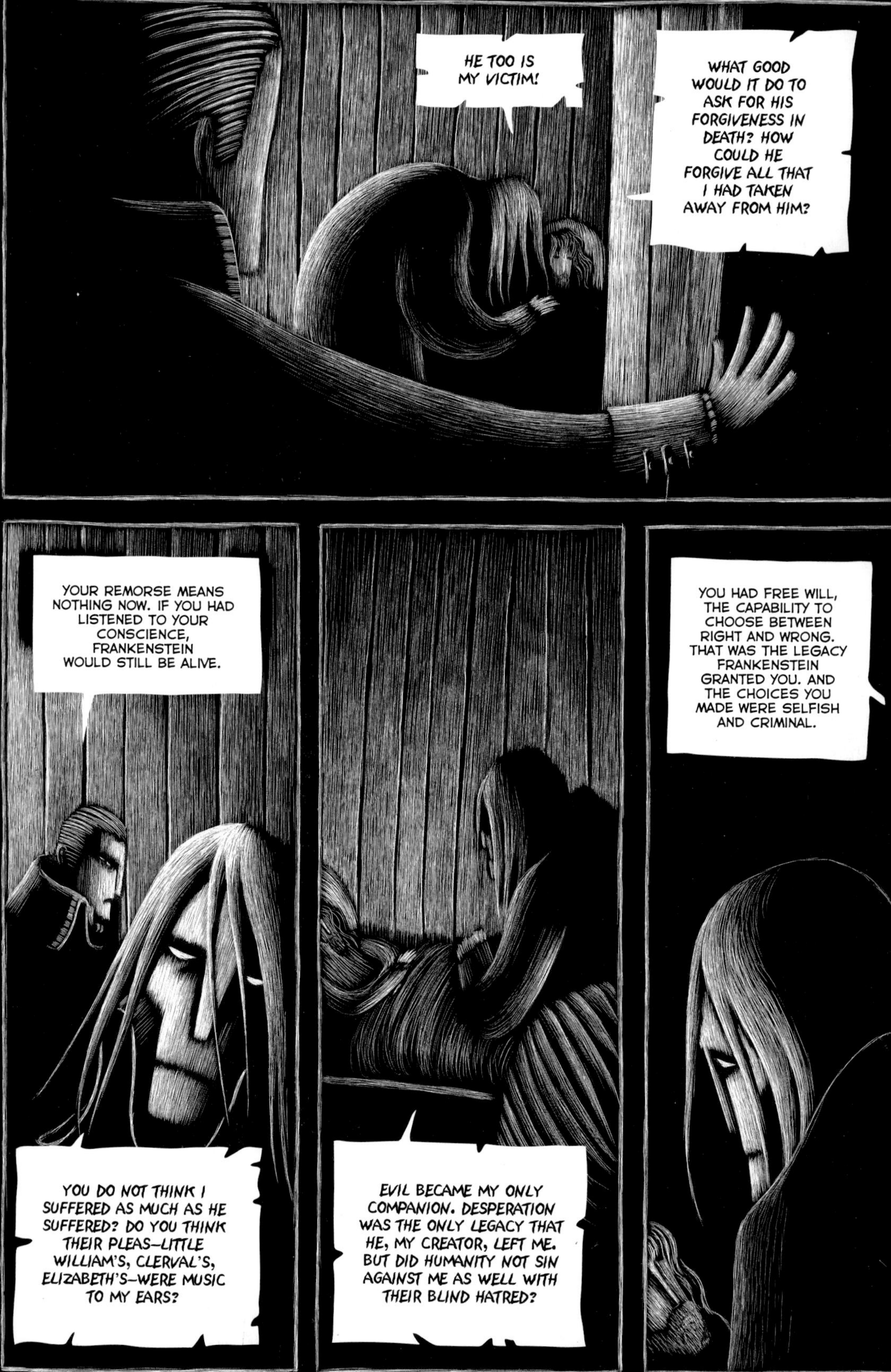
HE TOO IS MY VICTIM!
WHAT GOOD WOULD IT DO TO ASK FOR HIS FORGIVENESS IN DEATH? HOW COULD HE FORGIVE ALL THAT I HAD TAKEN AWAY FROM HIM?
YOUR REMORSE MEANS NOTHING NOW. IF YOU HAD LISTENED TO YOUR CONSCIENCE, FRANKENSTEIN WOULD STILL BE ALIVE.
YOU DO NOT THINK I SUFFERED AS MUCH AS HE SUFFERED? DO YOU THINK THEIR PLEAS—LITTLE WILLIAM'S, CLERVAL'S, ELIZABETH'S—WERE MUSIC TO MY EARS?
EVIL BECAME MY ONLY COMPANION. DESPERATION WAS THE ONLY LEGACY THAT HE, MY CREATOR, LEFT ME. BUT DID HUMANITY NOT SIN AGAINST ME AS WELL WITH THEIR BLIND HATRED?
YOU HAD FREE WILL, THE CAPABILITY TO CHOOSE BETWEEN RIGHT AND WRONG. THAT WAS THE LEGACY FRANKENSTEIN GRANTED YOU. AND THE CHOICES YOU MADE WERE SELFISH AND CRIMINAL.

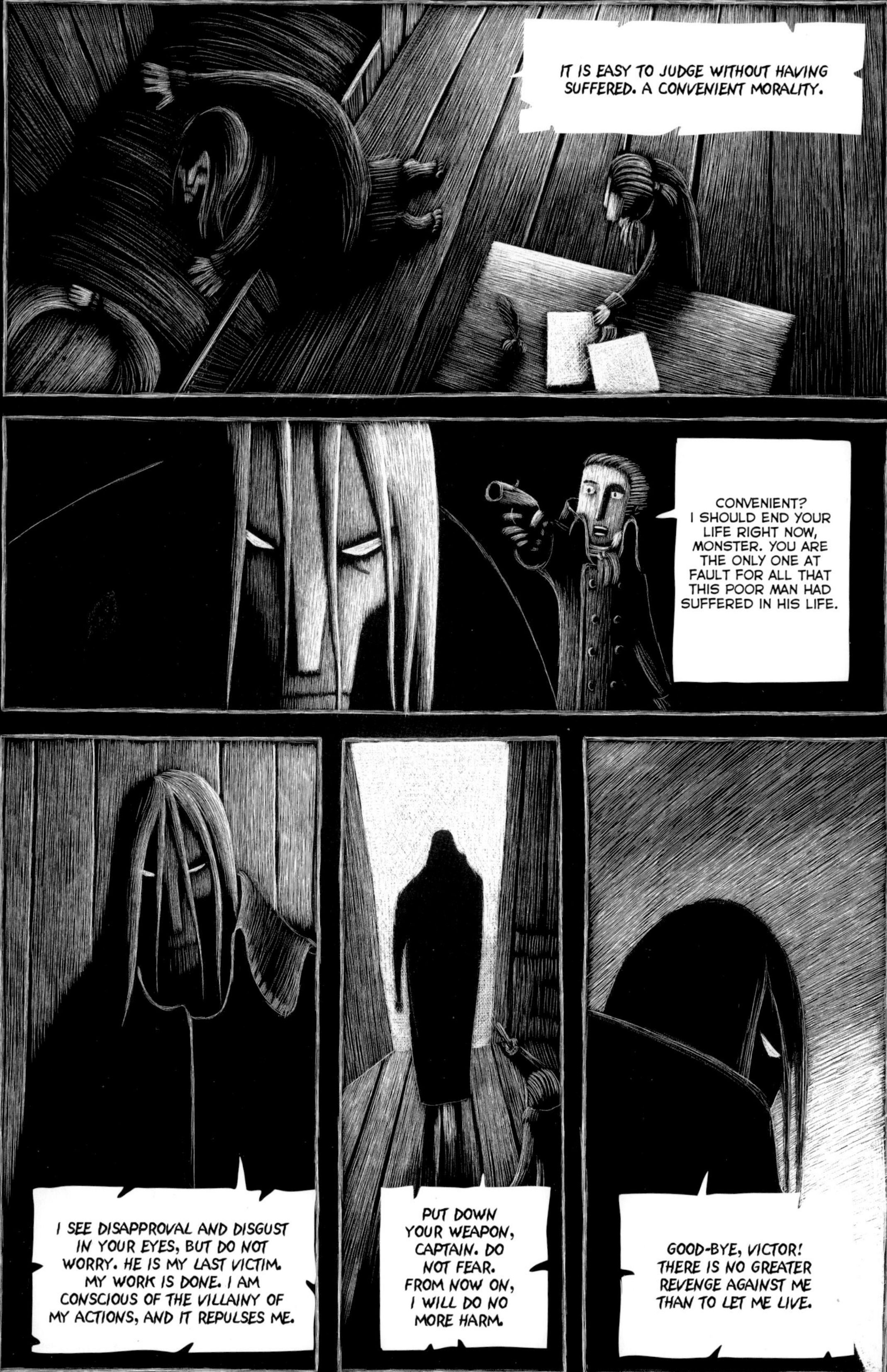
IT IS EASY TO JUDGE WITHOUT HAVING SUFFERED. A CONVENIENT MORALITY.
CONVENIENT? I SHOULD END YOUR LIFE RIGHT NOW, MONSTER. YOU ARE THE ONLY ONE AT FAULT FOR ALL THAT THIS POOR MAN HAD SUFFERED IN HIS LIFE.
I SEE DISAPPROVAL AND DISGUST IN YOUR EYES, BUT DO NOT WORRY. HE IS MY LAST VICTIM. MY WORK IS DONE. I AM CONSCIOUS OF THE VILLAINY OF MY ACTIONS, AND IT REPULSES ME.
PUT DOWN YOUR WEAPON, CAPTAIN. DO NOT FEAR. FROM NOW ON, I WILL DO NO MORE HARM.
GOOD-BYE, VICTOR! THERE IS NO GREATER REVENGE AGAINST ME THAN TO LET ME LIVE.

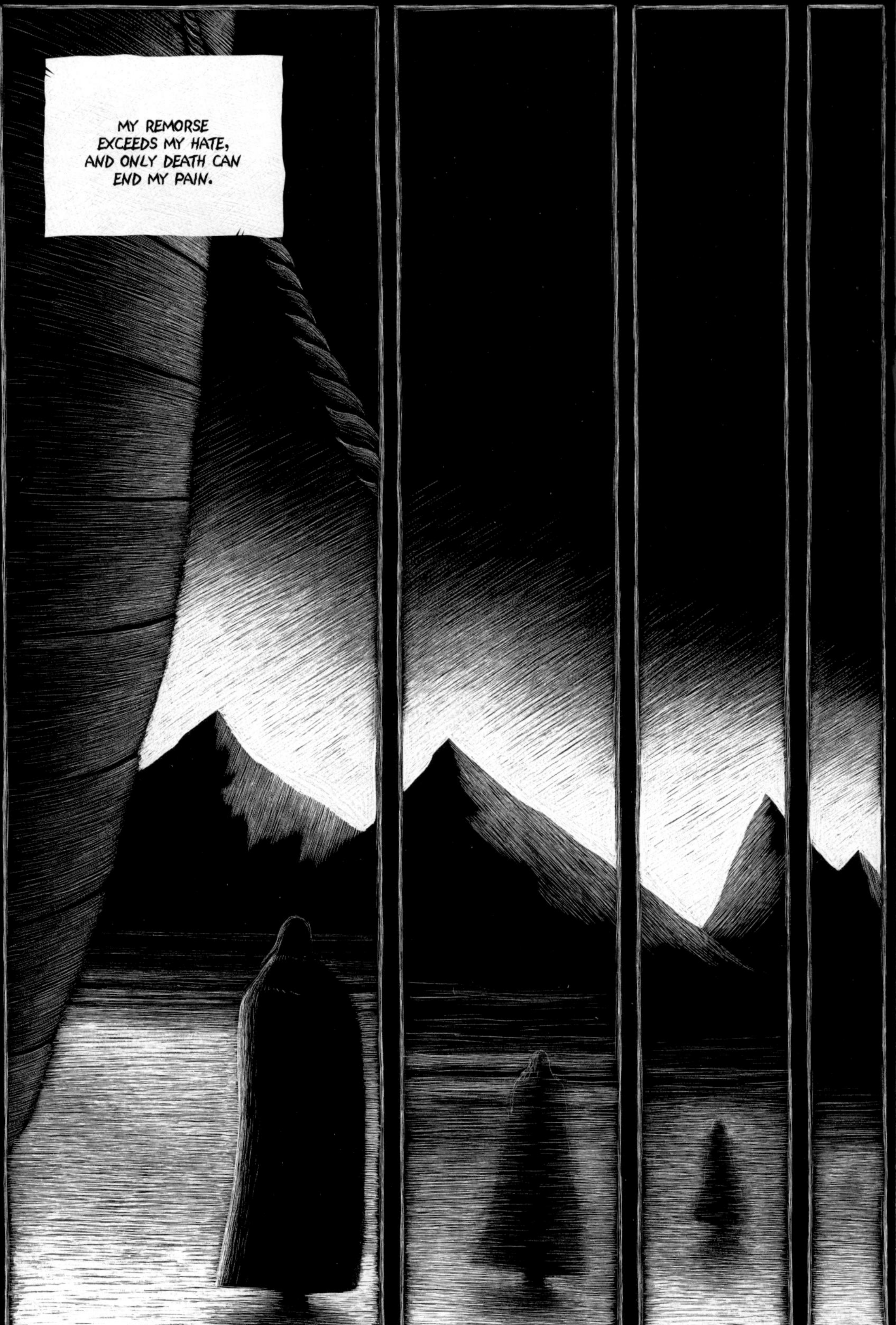
MY REMORSE EXCEEDS MY HATE, AND ONLY DEATH CAN END MY PAIN.

FURTHER READING

BOOKS

Francis, Pauline (adaptation). *Frankenstein.* New York: Skyview Books, 2010.

Shelley, Mary. *Frankenstein.* Hollywood, Fla.: Simon & Brown, 2011.

Wells, Catherine. *Strange Creatures: The Story of Mary Shelley.* Greensboro, N.C.: Morgan Reynolds Publishing, 2009.

INTERNET ADDRESSES

My Hideous Progeny: Mary Shelley's Frankenstein
http://www.maryshelley.nl/

Mary Wollstonecraft Shelley
http://people.brandeis.edu/~teuber/shelleybio.html

The Literary Gothic: Mary Shelley
http://www.litgothic.com/Authors/mshelley.html